Ali Blood spent years as a crime reporter in London. He covered murders, terrorist attacks, robberies and riots for various newspapers.

His next career move was into television news as a producer before setting up his own TV production company. He's always had a passion for crime fiction and is now a full-time author living in Hampshire – where he pours blood, sweat and tears into his writing! *The Prisoner's Wife* is his debut novel.

THE PRISONER'S WIFE

ALI BLOOD

avon.

Published by AVON
A division of HarperCollins*Publishers*
1 London Bridge Street
London SE1 9GF

www.harpercollins.co.uk

HarperCollins*Publishers*
Macken House, 39/40 Mayor Street Upper
Dublin 1
D01 C9W8
Ireland

www.harpercollins.co.uk

A Paperback Original 2023

1

First published in Great Britain by HarperCollins*Publishers* 2023

Copyright © Ali Blood 2023

Ali Blood asserts the moral right to be identified as the author of this work.

A catalogue copy of this book is available from the British Library.

ISBN: 978-0-00-852716-7

Typeset in Minion Pro by Palimpsest Book Production Limited, Falkirk, Stirlingshire
Printed and bound in Great Britain by CPI Group (UK) Ltd, Croydon CR0 4YY

*This book is dedicated to little Isaac Proctor,
the latest addition to our ever-growing family.
Wishing him a long and happy life.*

PROLOGUE

When the dream ends, I suddenly become aware of myself. I'm lying in the pitch black, but the pain in my head tells me that I'm awake. And yet I don't know where I am.

As I try to move, I discover that I'm crouched in a ball in a cold, confined space. The vibrating floor beneath me and the growl of an engine register suddenly. It's a car. I'm trapped in the boot of a car.

A gut-churning wave of terror overwhelms me, and I instinctively start to cry out and bang my clenched fists against the boot lid.

But it doesn't achieve anything. The car keeps moving and nobody responds.

I gulp in air, trying to fill my lungs, as I attempt to understand what's going on.

Questions scream inside my head. How did I get here? Where am I going? Who is doing this to me?

Then a memory swims to the surface and it chills my blood. And, in that moment, I know for certain that I won't survive the night.

CHAPTER ONE

The call I've been waiting for comes through at two on Tuesday afternoon.

'The jury has reached a verdict, Emma,' my husband's lawyer tells me. 'Court will reconvene at three, so I suggest you get here as quickly as you can.'

'Already? How long were they out?' I ask him.

'Only three hours,' he replies.

My heart skips a beat. I know from the many crime dramas I watch on TV that that's not a good sign.

Our flat on London's South Bank is only a short cab ride from the Old Bailey, so I manage to arrive well before the proceedings get under way.

My husband's mother and his brother are waiting for me in the packed public gallery of Court Number Two. They slide apart as I approach – a pointed move – and I take the hint, sitting on the bench between them and placing my handbag on the floor.

'We need to brace ourselves,' Ruby Driscoll says, her voice thin and shaky. 'I've got a bad feeling about this. We need to be strong for my son.'

When the trial started a week ago, Ruby was upbeat because Tommy's expensive legal team had assured her that they would get him off. But as the prosecution presented the case against him, her outlook slowly began to sour.

I, on the other hand, felt simply numb as my husband of eighteen months pleaded not guilty to constructive possession of a firearm, namely a Glock 17 revolver. It was found in the glove compartment of his car by police who stopped him following a tip-off. I kept my expression neutral as Tommy insisted that he'd been stitched up, that the gun had been planted and didn't belong to him. He declared to the court that his prints were on it because, just before he was stopped, he'd reached into the compartment for a cigar and found the weapon. The police hadn't believed him, of course, hence the trial – or if they did, they didn't care. They'd been wanting to pin something on him for a very long time but until now had failed to gather enough evidence.

I didn't even flinch when the prosecution told the jury that Tommy's involvement in organised crime was common knowledge and that he had only managed to evade justice through a combination of bribes, threats and intimidation. Or as they reeled out statements from two anonymous witnesses who claimed they used to work for him. But the more I heard, the harder it became to stop myself crying.

Liam Driscoll pats me on the knee and I'm pulled out of my reverie. I'm glad I'm wearing trousers. The last thing I want is to feel his fingers on my flesh. He leans closer to whisper in my ear. His breath smells of his last cigarette, and I fight the urge to visibly recoil.

'I want you to know that if he goes down, you'll be looked after,' he says. 'You'll want for nothing, Ems.'

I brace myself for the worst; it must be bad if Liam is making such promises. And his remark provides me with little comfort. I've never got on with the guy and I've always sensed that he resents me being part of the family. He's rarely struck up a conversation and has made a few snide remarks about me having a lot of free time on my hands.

At twenty-nine, he's the same age as I am, and five years younger than his brother. And the two of them couldn't be more different. Liam is short, plump and lacking in social skills. Tommy, on the other hand, is tall, slim and a complete charmer. He won me over the moment he started speaking to me that night two years ago in the restaurant where I was working.

'Tommy is more concerned about you than he is about himself,' Liam continues. 'You know that, don't you, Ems?'

I nod without looking at him. Instead, my eyes are fixed on the courtroom as things start to happen. Members of the jury are filing back in, their heads down, faces impassive. The legal teams are taking up position, and I see that the journos in the press box are ready and waiting to record the verdict. Whatever the outcome, it'll be fodder for the tabloids.

And then Tommy makes an entrance, and my heart jumps. He looks straight at the gallery and smiles when he spots me. As I smile back, I can sense lots of other pairs of eyes on me. My mouth dries up and I feel my cheeks burning red, as a flush spreads up from my neck. I hold my breath and chew on my bottom lip, trying as hard as I can not to let emotion overwhelm me.

Tommy averts his gaze as he steps into the dock. I can't help thinking how smart he looks in his favourite pinstripe suit, white shirt and red tie. His thick brown hair is neatly combed back from his high forehead, and despite the circumstances, he hasn't lost his swagger. But I can see the stress in his pale, handsome face.

He stands with his hands behind his back and looks at me again. This time, he doesn't smile, but he does mouth the words, 'I love you.'

Before I can respond, I'm distracted by the loud instruction to 'all rise' as the judge enters the room and makes his way to the elevated bench.

When we're all seated again, I look back at Tommy, but now his eyes are closed and I wonder if he's saying a silent prayer.

'Oh, my poor boy,' Ruby laments. 'This shouldn't be happening. It's a travesty. A fucking travesty.'

I turn to her and realise that she suddenly looks much older than her sixty-seven years. Her face is gaunt and colourless, and her hands are balled into fists on her lap. There's no love lost between my mother-in-law and me – I've never been good enough for her golden boy – but in that moment, I can't help feeling a twinge of sympathy for her.

I open my mouth to reply, but the clerk stands and a hush falls across the room. My heart is beating furiously as he asks the jury foreman to stand.

'Have you reached a verdict on which ten or more of you agree?' the clerk says.

'We have,' the foreman replies, and then proceeds to hand over a document to the bailiff, who passes it to the judge.

After silently scanning it, the judge hands it to the clerk, who says to the foreman, 'On the charge of constructive possession of a firearm, do you find the defendant guilty or not guilty?'

There's a short pause, then: 'Guilty, your honour.'

I hear Ruby suck in a loud breath and Liam drops his face into his hands. The air locks in my chest and blood surges through my veins.

There's a ripple of excitement in the court. A few gasps.

Ruby starts to sob and Liam swears out loud. I continue to stare at my husband. He's shaking his head and clenching his jaw. That wasn't what he expected. He was convinced he'd be cleared, that the jury would believe his story about being framed.

He glances at me and his lips move again, but this time I can't read them. I'm finding it difficult to focus and even to breathe. My body is shaking and my heart is pumping out of control.

But I still hear the judge tell the court that he's going to pass sentence.

'I don't think I can bear to listen to this,' Ruby says, but makes no move to get up.

When I glance sidelong at her, I see that her face is red and distorted and her eyes are brimming with tears.

'Stay strong, Ruby,' I try to placate her. 'It might not be so bad.'

But it is. The judge seems to take pleasure in telling Tommy that he's being sentenced to a minimum of five years in prison.

Chaos descends, and I'm aware of Ruby breaking down in tears and Liam yelling an obscenity at the judge, but I ignore them and focus on my husband.

I can see the pain tugging at his features. He's obviously trying to process what's happening, but even from this distance, I can tell that he's struggling to hold in that legendary temper of his.

And then he looks at me again, and, for the final time, I lock eyes with the man I loved, married and swore to stand by for better or worse. And, knowing that I'm now free from his clutches for five years, I find it terribly hard not to let him see me smile.

CHAPTER TWO

The outcome of the trial has left me numb with shock. I desperately want to be by myself in order to take it all in and contemplate my new future. But that's not going to be possible, so I will just have to hold it together as best I can.

At least, Ruby makes it easier for me to fade into the background as we exit the courtroom. She's an emotional wreck, sobbing and shaking, as her youngest son leads her out of the public gallery, an arm around her shoulders. I follow behind with my eyes cast down while clutching my handbag tight against my chest as if a shield.

Members of Tommy's legal team are waiting for us in the corridor. To my dismay, I'm the focus of their attention, the distraught wife of the man who is now on his way back to prison, where he'll reside for five years.

'I'm so very sorry, Mrs Driscoll,' his lawyer tells me. 'We'll appeal, of course, and do whatever we can to get the conviction overturned.'

His name's Kevin Mosley and, try as I might, I can't bring myself to like him. He seems too full of himself, and I'm sure he looks down his nose at me. He's been on my husband's payroll for years and has helped him to cover up his dirty dealings and keep the law at bay.

I want to tell him that I don't want them to lodge an appeal, but I remain silent because I know they'll have to go through the motions. That's okay so long as they don't succeed. Today, a judge and jury have freed me from a relationship that I feared I'd be trapped in for life. It'll be tragic if that result is reversed.

Over almost two years, Tommy has broken my spirit and turned me into someone I never wanted to be. Now I finally have a chance to regain my self-respect and independence. I can once again look forward to the future.

During the four months he's been in custody awaiting trial, I've tried not to build my hopes up. He was so sure he'd be found not guilty and that he would soon be back with me. So, for better or worse, I forced myself to play the part of the loyal wife. During visits and phone calls, I told him what he wanted to hear. Knowing he could be free again soon, I had no choice but to play it safe and assume that my own freedom would be short-lived. I even told him that I was praying for him, and I have no doubt that he believed me. Where I'm concerned, he only sees what he wants to see. It's how it's always been and I hate that he's seemingly blind to the fact that he turned me against him.

'There's a media circus out on the street,' Mosley says as we all move towards the exit.

It doesn't surprise me because the case has attracted a lot of attention, but it's the last thing any of us wants.

Liam responds by telling us that he's arranged for a car to be waiting. It'll take us to his mother's house in Dulwich, where we'll have the privacy to discuss what has happened and the implications.

I don't want to go, but I know I have to. The time isn't right for me to begin to distance myself from this family. It's too soon. But I certainly don't intend to hang around.

Men in suits surround us as we leave the building, and they provide a barrier between us and the press as we make our way along the street towards the car.

Whenever I see this sort of thing on the news, it looks so intense and uncomfortable, with all the shouting and clamouring. And now I know for myself what a dreadful experience it is. My breath is coming in heaves and gasps and I feel my face overheating.

'What's your reaction to the verdict and sentence, Mrs Driscoll?' one of the reporters shouts out.

I don't respond, just keep on walking with my head down. It's already been agreed that after we've gone, Mosley will give a brief statement for the cameras. I don't know what he's going to say and I don't care. I just want to get away from it all, away from the flashbulbs and judgemental looks, and away from the stark brightness of this cold November afternoon.

My gaze falls on a familiar face standing next to a shiny black Range Rover parked at the kerb. He's smiling at me, more than one gold tooth flashing in the sunlight. Jack Fraser, my husband's best friend and closest colleague, the one person Tommy trusts as much as me.

Fraser is the archetypal villain – bald, tough-looking and extremely dangerous. But for once I'm glad to see him because I know he'll keep the media vultures away from us. They're still following us as we approach the car, pointing their cameras and screeching their questions.

I know that if Liam wasn't shielding his mother, he'd be screaming at them to fuck off. He's got a short fuse and a fiery temper, something that I realised a while ago is a family trait.

When we reach the car, Liam takes the front passenger seat and Fraser guides Ruby and me into the back. He then closes the doors before hurrying around to the front and getting behind the wheel.

As the car pulls away from the kerb, Liam sticks two fingers up at the hacks who are lining the pavement.

'I'd like to run the bastards over,' he fumes. 'They're all fucking shitbags.'

Fraser puts his foot down and soon the Old Bailey is behind us and we're consumed by London's heavy traffic.

Ruby's still sobbing. Tommy is her favourite son, after all, and the one she's most proud of. He's done much more for her than her younger son has.

She wipes her eyes with a hanky before turning to me.

'You'll need to go and see him as soon as you can, Emma,' she says. 'There'll be things he'll want to tell you that he was hoping he wouldn't have to.'

I'm sure she's right, but I stay silent. Our eyes lock for only a couple of seconds before she turns away from me and stares out of the window.

It makes me wonder if her behaviour towards me will now change. She no longer has to pretend that she likes me. I've always known that she doesn't. That became clear early on. And she never seemed to care that he treated me so badly. It's as though she thought it was the price I had to pay for being part of the Driscoll family and enjoying the lifestyle that their ill-gotten gains afforded them.

'Are you all right, Emma?' Fraser asks without taking his eyes off the road.

Coming from him, the question doesn't surprise me. During the two years I've known Fraser, he's often asked how I am and has given me the impression that he's been concerned at times about my well-being. But I've held back from sharing my true feelings with him because of his intense loyalty to Tommy.

'Not really,' I tell him. 'I still can't believe what's happened. It's crazy.'

He doesn't ask a follow-up question and I'm glad. I don't want to talk because I need to gather my thoughts before we arrive at Ruby's place. It's going to be even more intense there and the pressure will be on to keep up the loving and distraught wife act.

I try not to panic, but I can already feel the muscles knotting in my stomach, the pulse beating high up in my throat.

Thankfully I've managed to have very little contact with Ruby since Tommy's arrest. She did orchestrate a couple of meetings where she made it clear that she expected me to stand by him whatever the outcome. And I don't know how she'll act with me now that Tommy will spend the next five years behind bars.

But I do know that I can't afford to let my guard down. If they find out what is really going on in my head, they might take the view that without Tommy here to control me, I might pose a threat to the Firm.

And then I wouldn't put it past them to make me disappear.

CHAPTER THREE

I stare out of the window at the parts of South London that I know the Driscoll family regard as part of their fiefdom. We drive past the club that acts as a front for their money laundering, where the men managing the doors probably do more for my husband than just that. On the Driscoll payroll, you could be selling drugs, counterfeiting money and passports, or taking care of anything, or anyone, that Tommy viewed as a problem that needed fixing.

I sigh then, thinking back to the day I found out that I'd married a true monster. I had no idea he was a seasoned criminal until three months before he was arrested. When we met, I believed what he told me – that he was a successful businessman who managed various companies and a large property portfolio.

In the beginning, I trusted him implicitly; he made me feel so happy and special. By our third date, I was sure that I was in love with him – it was like starring in a romantic movie. When he proposed, I thought I'd found my happy ending.

But the dream didn't last and I found myself in a situation from which there appeared to be no escape.

Now, after so many months of suffering, I'm glad Tommy will be languishing in a prison cell for five years. I'll finally be able to make new friends, go where I want to go, and say and do things that won't get me into trouble. My heart leaps as I realise that I can finally be my own person again. And that's something I've longed for since I first saw the man behind the mask. All I have to do now is struggle through the next few hours and days.

Ruby's detached house backs onto Dulwich Park and is far too big for her, with its four bedrooms, large rear garden and two flights of stairs. I know how much the place means to her; she often proudly recounts tales of it like they're notable moments of history: the day Tommy was born in the front room, the garden where Liam famously lost his first tooth, the bedroom where Roy, Ruby's late husband and the boys' father, died a few years ago.

At the front, there's an electric gate and a short driveway. As Fraser brings the car to a stop, Liam turns in his seat and looks at me, his expression mournful.

'Tommy was prepared for what's happened even though he didn't expect it,' he says. 'I need to pass onto you what he told me, Ems. It won't take long. Jack will take you home after.'

I'm hoping this will be my last visit because the place makes me uncomfortable. I don't like being here. Tommy has always known this, even though it didn't stop him from forcing me to come at least once a week with him. Ruby has never made me feel welcome. She rarely spoke to me and, when she did, the tone of her voice was distinctly unfriendly.

As we exit the vehicle, I'm careful to maintain the long face and stooped posture. But deep down I'm desperate to go home, where I can finally relax and fully digest what has happened.

Liam opens the front door and waves us in, Ruby first, then me and Fraser. In the hallway, I stop to take off my coat and see myself in the full-length mirror on the wall. I'm not a pretty sight. I was in such a hurry to leave the flat that I didn't bother to refresh my make-up. And rather than spend time sorting out my hair, I dragged it into a tight ponytail. As a result, my puffy eyes, pale complexion and dry lips are fully exposed.

Tommy would never have let me go out with him looking like this. He would have made some disparaging remark about how I needed to make more of an effort with my appearance so that I wouldn't embarrass him. And I'm pretty sure he'd disapprove of the grey sweater and tight black trousers I've got on. He's always urged me to wear bright colours, that they suited me best. But now it doesn't matter what he thinks. I'm my own person again.

'Do you want coffee, tea or a cold drink, Emma?'

It's Fraser, polite as always. He's standing beside me,

reaching for my coat so that he can hang it up. Ruby has popped upstairs and Liam's using the loo.

'I'll have a tea please,' I say. 'White, no sugar.'

'Are you sure you don't want something stronger? A glass of wine maybe.'

'No, tea is fine, thanks.'

Fraser nods as he takes my coat. 'You can go straight through to the dining room if you like. I'll bring the drinks in.'

Fraser has always behaved like the perfect gentleman where I'm concerned, and I've really appreciated it. Unlike the rest of Tommy's circle, he's courteous and thoughtful, and he doesn't lace his language with expletives. But that doesn't mean he's a soft touch; far from it, he's the only man I've ever seen yell at them when he felt they were treating him like a servant rather than a key player in their organisation.

The air suddenly feels heavy around me as I head for the dining room. This is the last place I want to be right now, but I need to hear what Liam has to say. I haven't a clue what my husband has told him, but I suspect it has to do with the running of the gang's various operations.

I've always been kept outside the loop when it comes to business. Early on, curiosity compelled me to ask questions, but I'm aware now why Tommy was always so eager to change the subject. He wanted me to think that everything he did was above board and that it was too complicated for me to understand. But of course it's not a difficult thing to understand that my husband and his family are a bunch of callous criminals.

The house is dated and depressing, with dark grey walls, dull brown carpets and well-worn furniture. Ruby has turned down Tommy's offers to pay for a makeover because she says too many memories are attached to the fixtures and fittings.

I can understand that since my own mother, who is also a widow, lives in a flat that looks exactly like it did twenty years ago.

This place has far more photographs, though. They're everywhere, and they give the impression that the Driscolls are like any other ordinary South London family.

Except they're not. They never have been.

When I finally learned the truth about what my husband really did for a living, the whole sordid family history came out. How his grandfather was a career criminal who extorted money from local market traders. His son, Roy, followed in his father's footsteps and Ruby was at pains to tell me how proud she was of her husband, who worked his socks off to provide for his family before he died aged sixty-three after a boozy binge brought on a seizure that caused him to have a fatal heart attack.

From that moment on, Tommy and Liam were expected to take up the reins of the criminal empire that had been established. From what I've heard, they jumped at the chance and, over the years, they transformed the business into an operation that was far more discreet and lucrative.

They're both looking at me now from the dozens of framed photographs that adorn the walls of the dining room, and it makes me feel sick. Their mother worships them, and it's as though she's tried to capture on camera every significant moment of their lives. She took quite a few photos during the past year and I remember being made to pose for some of them alongside Tommy. But none of those are on display and I assume it's because she doesn't want to see my face every time she comes in here.

It's a large room with a glass table, six chairs and a cabinet on which are displayed a selection of photos showing Ruby and Roy together. He was a handsome guy when they married all those years ago, with thick black hair and prominent features. But by the time he died, he was raw-boned and bald.

Ruby, on the other hand, has aged well and has kept most of the wrinkles at bay with regular doses of Botox.

Silently, I place my bag on one of the chairs and stand there looking out over the rear garden with its lush lawn and flower beds, experiencing a brief moment of calm as I watch the sun hovering in a clear blue sky.

But within seconds my mind drifts back to the court-room and Tommy's face when the jury foreman returned the guilty verdict. I wish I could find it in me to feel sorry for him, but I can't. Not after everything he's put me through.

I'm still reflecting on what's happened when I hear voices behind me. I turn just as Ruby and Liam walk into the room, and when they spot me, they stop speaking to each other.

'Are you all right, Ems?' Liam asks as he pulls out a chair from under the table for his mother.

I nod and draw in a long, ragged breath.

Liam forces a smile onto his face and gestures for me to sit down.

'I'll be as quick as I can,' he tells me. 'As soon as Jack is here with the drinks, we'll get started.'

I'm not sure how Liam feels about taking over the business. Until now, he's lived in his brother's shadow. It was Tommy who called the shots and shouldered all the responsibility. Liam just did what he was told – collecting money, doing his brother's bidding, throwing his considerable weight around and ensuring that supply lines were not disrupted. It was up to Tommy to do the deals, plan ahead and engage with the corrupt coppers in the Met.

Liam lives by himself in Streatham and spends most of his free time gambling, drinking and cavorting with prostitutes. Tommy has frequently complained about his behaviour, but Liam has always insisted that it has never impacted on his performance as the Firm's number two.

But as he sits down opposite me now, I'm willing to bet that he's worried shitless about not having Tommy around to do the real work.

The first thing he does is to take a folded hanky from the breast pocket of his jacket and hold it out for his mum, who is clearly struggling with her emotions. She takes it from him and dabs at her eyes and then the corners of her mouth.

The three of us sit in uncomfortable silence. I'm tempted to say something, but I don't because Ruby seems to be lost in the past as she stares forlornly at the photos.

Fraser appears with the tray of hot drinks and places it on the table. After he's put the mugs of tea and coffee in front of us, he sits down, and this is Liam's cue to start speaking.

'I'll begin by stating the fucking obvious,' he says. 'This is a sad day for our family. Tommy should be here with us, not locked up in a cell. And I swear I won't rest until I've punished the bastard who fitted him up.'

He throws a glance my way and I feel a jolt of alarm. But his eyes give nothing away. I hold his gaze even as my stomach twists with grim apprehension.

'First of all, let's be clear about one thing,' he continues, turning from me to Fraser and then to his mum. 'Tommy is still the main man and remains in charge. While he's away, I'll be acting as head of the Firm and Jack will be my second in command. All our operations will continue as normal.'

He pauses and reaches into his jacket pocket. He takes out a white envelope and places it on the table in front of him.

Then he turns back to me and says, 'Tommy wants you to know that you'll receive a regular income, Ems. And, of course, you'll remain in the flat. I've told him that we'll look out for you and that's reassured him. All he asks from you in return is your loyalty. But that goes without saying, of course. You are his wife.'

He pauses again, and I'm sure he's expecting me to

respond with reassurances that Tommy needn't worry. When I stay silent, he shakes his head.

'Nothing to say, Ems?' he asks, his voice now stretched with tension. 'Forgotten those vows you took? What happened to the for better or worse?'

I open my mouth to speak, but he raises a hand to stop me and it causes a rush of heat to burn in my chest.

'Don't bother, Ems. We all realised a while ago that you don't like being part of this family.' He smiles. 'But that's too bad, because Tommy loves you more than anything in the world and he's not prepared to let you go.'

His words slice through me like a razor blade and hot bile burns in my throat.

'What's that supposed to mean?' I manage to utter.

He pushes the envelope across the table towards me. 'I'll let Tommy tell you for himself.'

A tremor of anxiety floods through my veins. I can't for the life of me imagine why Tommy would write something down on paper that he wouldn't have told me face to face or over the phone. I've a bad feeling about it and my hands shake as I pick up the envelope and open it. Inside is a single sheet of paper with a typewritten note on one side.

I feel the bottom drop out of my stomach as I read the words, and every muscle and sinew in my body freezes.

Emma, my darling. If you are reading this, then the worst has happened and I've had to go away for a while. But I know you'll be a good wife and wait for me. On our wedding day, you vowed to obey me, and so I've drawn up this list for the sake of our marriage.

- *You must remain loyal to me and not apply for a divorce*
- *You must not go out after 9 p.m. unless in emergencies or on a pre-authorised visit*
- *You must not go to any nightclubs or parties*
- *You must not get a job – there's no need to anyway*
- *You must stay living in the flat*
- *You must not leave the country for any reason*
- *You must do what my mum and brother tell you to do*
- *You must send my brother copies of your bank statement each month*

'As you can see, these are rules that your husband expects you to abide by while he's serving his sentence,' Liam says.

His words crash through me and I feel a flash of rage, but I stamp on it, push it down.

They all stare at me, and I fight a powerful urge to scream and lash out because I know it's what they expect me to do and I don't want to give them the satisfaction of seeing me suffer.

'Surely, he's not serious?' I say eventually, as evenly as I can. 'He can't expect me to agree to this?'

Liam shrugs. 'If you don't, you'll have to face the consequences. . . both you and your family. He's not willing to let you go without a fight.'

I turn to Ruby, imploringly, hoping desperately that despite our differences she will understand that I'm a woman in my own right, not a piece of Tommy's property to be locked away in one of his safes. But instead, she narrows her eyes at me and says, 'If you really believe that my son will let you just walk away and start a new life without him, then you're an even bigger fool than I first thought.'

CHAPTER FOUR

I'm back in the flat, but I'm in no mood to celebrate. My eyes feel swollen and scratchy and discomfort stirs in the pit of my stomach. Any hope I had of escaping this nightmare has been dashed. I've been placed in an impossible position by my brute of a husband.

I should have known that he would not let me go, that he would seek to control me even from his cell. He obviously doesn't think it will be that difficult since his brother and mother are around to do his bidding.

After I'd read the note, Liam told me that Tommy had every right to draw up a list of rules for me to follow. 'It's your duty as his wife to be there for him,' he said. 'And I'm sure you can see why it's important that you are – for your sake, as well as his.'

That was when I decided I had to get out of there. I didn't want them to see me cry, and losing my temper would have served no purpose.

Liam instructed Fraser to take me home, but I said no and rushed out of the house. I got an Uber to pick me up and managed not to collapse in a flood of tears until I had closed my front door behind me.

My eyes are dry now and I feel calmer having had a hot tea. But every time I look at Tommy's note, which Liam insisted I bring home with me, I feel flames of anger begin to rise once again.

If only I could afford not to take it seriously. If only I could tell him to go to hell. But my husband is a law unto himself. He's powerful, ruthless and extremely dangerous. He's forgotten what it's like not to get his own way, or to have someone refuse to obey his orders.

I'm a treasured possession that he's not prepared to let go of under any circumstance. It doesn't matter what I want or think; it's all about him. He lords over his family just like he does his criminal empire, with a merciless tyranny. And he's determined not to allow his incarceration to change anything.

Around and around my thoughts go in a loop. I don't doubt that there are women who would comply with the type of rules he's drawn up for me, out of loyalty or out of fear. But I don't want to be one of them. Even if I still loved my husband, I can't imagine dangling on the end of his chain for five years, maybe even longer if he misbehaves inside. And then being stuck with him for the rest of my life after his release.

I'm still trying to process what it all means when the landline rings. I don't answer it, fearing it could be Tommy.

But it reminds me that I switched my mobile off before I walked into the Old Bailey and I still haven't turned it back on.

When I do, I'm not surprised to see a bunch of missed calls and text messages. What surprises me is that none of them is from my husband. Most are from Amanda, my elder sister, who's been trying to reach me since the end of the trial. The texts grow increasingly concerned as they go on. Guilt prompts me to call her straight away.

'Why the hell haven't you been answering your phone?' Amanda shouts when she picks up. 'Mum and me have been desperate to talk to you since we heard the news.'

'Is Mum with you now?'

'Yes, and she's worried sick. Are you all right?'

'I'm okay. Just thankful that the jury didn't believe his story that someone planted the gun.'

'Well, we don't believe it either, as you know. And it won't surprise you to hear that Mum and me aren't at all sorry that he's staying in prison. He wasn't good for you, Ems. He was a wrong 'un.' She sighs. 'But now you've been given a chance to be shot of him and start over. Tommy Driscoll is out of your life and out of ours. You should be thankful.'

Amanda lives in Kennington with her financial adviser husband and two daughters, aged eight and ten. We've always been close, which is why I confided in her about Tommy's controlling behaviour and then about how he really made his money. I've lost count of the number of times she told me to leave him. And she never did understand why I couldn't.

I feel the urge to come clean about the latest development, but I resist. If I told her about the letter, I would have to tell her about Liam's threat to both me and the family if I refuse to go along with it. Amanda would freak out, she would want to call the police, but I know that would be a mistake. It'd be impossible to prove that a threat had been made and just as impossible to stop Tommy from seeking retribution. The Driscoll Firm has the means and the money to make us all suffer, and I would never forgive myself if something bad happened to any of my loved ones.

'So where are you now?' Amanda asks.

'Back at the flat. I went to Ruby's house after the case ended. Sorry, but I forgot to switch my phone back on.'

'Do you want me to come over?'

'Not today. I need to spend some time by myself, getting my head around what's happened.'

'Are you sure?' she says. 'Mum doesn't think you should be alone. And I think we should be out celebrating.'

'I'm really not up to it. And you can tell Mum not to worry. I'm going to be fine.'

'You can tell her yourself. She's trying to grab the phone from me.'

Before I can say anything else, my mum's voice is on the line, telling me that she saw me on the news as I left the Old Bailey. Her voice cracks with emotion as she tells me how relieved she is that Tommy was found guilty.

'I won't be shedding any tears, Emma. And you shouldn't either. Tommy Driscoll is where he belongs. Now you can divorce him and marry someone who'll treat you right,' she says. 'And don't keep blaming yourself for being taken in by him. He's a good actor and had everyone fooled, including me.'

I recall the day I introduced her to Tommy. He won her over with his charm and she loved it when he told her that her name, Christine, was one of his favourites. She liked him even more when he forked out a small fortune for our wedding and promised to make me the happiest woman alive.

When I eventually broke it to her that I was no longer happy being married to him, she didn't want to believe me. It was only after I described in detail his abusive and controlling behaviour that she finally accepted he was not the man she thought he was. At the time I couldn't tell her about what he really did for a living because I didn't know.

Mum would keep me on the phone for ages if I let her. But I'm desperate for some alone time, so I cut the conversation short by pretending there's someone at the door.

After hanging up, I walk listlessly from room to room wondering if I really am destined to remain here for years to come. It would become a prison rather than a home. And how ironic that I'd be confined just like Tommy even though he's the one given the sentence.

Tommy had paid several millions for this flat and when I first saw it, I was completely bowled over. It sits on London's South Bank, with three bedrooms, a large balcony and a spectacular view over the Thames. It even has a room that Tommy turned into a studio for me.

When he learned that I'd always loved painting, he encouraged me to do it full time. I thanked him effusively and with unrestrained emotion. It was such a thoughtful thing to do and it made me so happy. Sadly, it took a while for me to realise that it was a ploy on his part to stop me from going out to work, somewhere that was outside of these four walls and his control.

I no longer enjoy painting, but I continue to do it just to fill the time. Yet it's the last thing on my mind as I return to the living room.

I check the time and see it's after seven already, so I decide to go to bed and try to put this day behind me. But just then my phone rings. I pick it up off the coffee table and see the call is from an unknown number. I let it ring because I suspect it's Tommy. By now, he'll be back in Wandsworth Prison with access to the hidden mobile he uses.

The ringing eventually stops, but seconds later, my phone pings with a message.

Don't fucking ignore me, Ems. I know you must be in a right state, but we need to talk. I'll call again later if I can. Make sure you answer.

I go into the kitchen to dig out a couple of sleeping pills and wash them down with a glass of cold water. Then I sit on the sofa and close my eyes. Before long, my thoughts stop veering off in all directions and settle on that one fateful day when Tommy Driscoll first came into my life, and changed it forever.

CHAPTER FIVE

Two years ago

It's eight o'clock on Saturday evening and the restaurant is already busy. It always is at weekends. The Silhouette has been a popular venue for years in London's West End, but I've only been waitressing here for five months.

I don't enjoy the work, but my options are limited. Unlike my sister, I didn't go to university and left school with just three GCSEs. Against the advice of my parents, I chose not to follow a particular career path because I didn't want to. Back then, it was all about having the freedom to enjoy my life. I wanted to concentrate on having fun, on travelling the world, on not allowing myself to be restricted by the demands of a profession that might or might not make me happy.

During those early years, it suited me perfectly. I did bar work in a couple of Mediterranean resorts and had a few flings that didn't work out before I came back to England. Since then, I've had more boyfriends, but love has eluded me.

At the same time, I've flitted from one job to another in the hospitality sector, and I continued to enjoy myself even as the debts piled up. A year ago, I was forced to move out of my rented flat in Bermondsey and in with my mum. And that's where I reside now. I have my own room and I'm more than happy.

This job at The Silhouette pays quite well and I intend to stick with it for the foreseeable future. The restaurant has a reputation for being posh and expensive, and it attracts well-heeled diners. For the most part, they tip well, which means the staff get to share a pretty substantial pot at the end of each week.

I'm one of three waitresses and two waiters working tonight. I've been assigned four tables and only one of them is still empty. It's been reserved for a party of two in the name of Mr Tommy Driscoll, and they were due to be here half an hour ago.

The other tables are keeping me busy enough, though. Two couples and a group of five women celebrating one of their birthdays. They're all tucking into sumptuous steaks and tasty fish dishes while guzzling down expensive wines.

The late arrivals turn out to be two smartly dressed men I've never seen before. Mr Driscoll, who introduces himself to Ted, the maître d', is tall, slim and handsome in a tailored blue suit. His companion is taller still but less attractive, with a bald head and hard facial features.

Mr Driscoll apologises to me for being late and as I hand him the food and drinks menus, I can't help but notice the way he runs his eyes over my body, as though he likes what he sees. And, to my surprise, I feel flattered rather than uncomfortable.

'My name is Emma,' I say, smiling. 'I'll be your waitress for the evening. May I get you drinks while you decide what you'd like to eat?'

Mr Driscoll smiles back at me and his face lights up. 'We've heard some good things about this restaurant, Emma, which is why Jack and I have come here to celebrate the successful completion of a rather lucrative business deal. I think we'll kick off the evening with a bottle of champers. What would you recommend?' I find his voice highly attractive. It's low, but clear, and there's a faint Cockney twang to it.

I lean forward, take the drinks menu from him and point to the list of champagnes. 'The one at the top is our most popular,' I tell him. 'But it also happens to be the most expensive.'

Without even looking at the price, he says, 'That'll do perfectly then. Have you had a taste of it yourself?'

I can't help but giggle. 'I'm afraid not, but I've been told that it's delicious.'

'Then bring an extra glass so that you can sample it,' he says instantly. 'My treat.'

I pause, debating the best way to respond. 'That's very kind of you, Mr Driscoll, but I don't think my boss will approve.' I nod towards Ted, who is showing another couple to their table.

'Then don't tell him,' he replies with a sexy growl. 'It'll be our secret. And please call me Tommy.'

I can feel the blood enter my cheeks as I turn and head for the kitchen. I'm used to male diners being flirtatious and usually it doesn't provoke a reaction, but this is different. This guy has piqued my interest and he happens to be hellishly attractive.

When I return to the table with the champagne, along with three glasses, I suddenly feel self-conscious as Tommy looks up and smiles at me.

'I hope you don't mind me saying this, but you're very pretty,' he tells me.

I catch my breath and feel my jaw drop. 'Thank you. . . Tommy,' I say after a moment. 'It's kind of you to say so.'

My answer seems to please him and he reaches for the champagne bottle, beating me to it. His companion, Jack, leans forward and picks up his glass.

'Allow me to do the honours,' Tommy says. 'Your boss appears to have left the room so you can join us in a quick toast to our new business venture.'

As he hands me a glass, I look over my shoulder to make sure he's right about Ted. And he is.

They both clink their glasses against mine and I take a sip of the most expensive champers I've ever tasted.

'It's delicious,' I say, and mean it. 'It certainly beats Prosecco.'

I down one more mouthful before replacing the glass on the tray.

'Thank you so much for that, Mr Driscoll. I mean Tommy.' I reach for my notepad. 'Now are you ready for me to take your orders?'

The rest of the evening flies by and throughout it I'm aware of Tommy Driscoll watching me. Several times we make eye contact and beam at each other.

When I serve them their steak dinners, he formally introduces me to his companion, Jack, and describes him as his business colleague. And by the time I collect their plates, he asks me where I live in London and if I'm in a relationship. I answer him truthfully, even though I don't have time to be drawn into a conversation because I'm run off my feet.

One of the other waitresses becomes aware of the attention he's paying me and says, 'I think that fella really fancies you, Ems. I bloody wish he'd look at me like that.'

I laugh. 'He's gorgeous, isn't he?'

It's ages since I've been out with anyone, let alone in any kind of relationship, so I feel somewhat nervous because I'm already attracted to this man even though I know nothing about him.

They finish the bottle of champagne and order more drinks. Tommy opts for a neat whisky on the rocks and Jack chooses brandy with no ice. After they've downed them, Tommy asks for the bill and I feel my heart pound.

'That was a great meal,' he tells me. 'The steaks were delicious and the service impeccable. Thank you.'

I feel myself blush and a sense of panic stirs inside me. What if that's as far as he's going to take it? What if he leaves here and I never see him again?

And that's when I realise that I'm already smitten.

He pays the bill, adding a more than generous tip, and then both men get to their feet, causing my heart to drop.

'Before I go, can I ask if it would be possible for me to see you again, Emma?' Tommy says. 'I'd really like to take you out and get to know you better.'

The relief surges through me like a gust of warm wind and a moment later I'm giving him my phone number.

CHAPTER SIX

The present

I lay on the sofa, my eyes drifting shut, still absorbed in the memory. I'll never forget how pleased I was when Tommy rang me the very next morning and invited me out to lunch.

He offered to pick me up from home, but I didn't want him to see the dingy block of flats I was living in with my mum, so I said I'd be happy to meet him at whichever pub or restaurant he had in mind.

'That's the thing,' he said. 'I haven't decided yet. But I'm sure I will have by the time I get to you.'

I reluctantly gave him the name of the estate in Deptford, South London, and he said he knew it well.

'It's not that far from where I was brought up,' he told me and I wondered if it was true or he was just being nice.

I waited downstairs and he arrived in the back seat of a sleek silver Mercedes that was chauffeur-driven by Jack.

I remember thinking that this couldn't be happening to me, that I was out of my depth and that I'd need to make the most of this first date because it would most likely be the last.

But I couldn't have been more wrong.

Tommy took me to the plush Hilton Hotel on Park Lane, a place I'd never visited before, and he treated me like a princess. He was so kind, gentle and considerate, and he struck me as the perfect gentleman. He asked me lots of questions about myself and I couldn't help but feel embarrassed when I explained that I lived with my mum because I couldn't afford a place of my own. But I detected not a shred of judgement in his eyes or his voice and that came as such a relief.

His responses to my questions were illuminating. I learned that Jack Fraser, who made himself scarce during the lunch, worked for Tommy as a personal assistant and minder.

'People in my line of work require a degree of protection,' he pointed out. 'In this day and age, it's better to be safe than sorry. Successful businessmen are often the potential targets of disgruntled rivals, professional scammers and jealous individuals.'

He went on to tell me that he ran several businesses, including an investment management company and a money transfer firm. Plus, he managed a significant retail and residential property portfolio, including several nightclubs and bars. I was impressed even though I didn't really understand a word of it.

And, of course, I had no idea then that it was all bollocks.

I also learned during the lunch that he lived in a flat overlooking the Thames in Central London and that he'd been married and divorced. But he didn't reveal the gory details surrounding the disappearance of his ex-wife. That would come later.

The meal ended all too soon and Tommy used his phone to summon Jack, who drove us back to Deptford.

'I'd love to spend the rest of the day with you, Emma, but I have some important business to attend to,' Tommy said when they dropped me off on the estate.

'No problem,' I told him, hoping it wasn't just an excuse to cut short our time together. 'I've had a lovely time. Thanks so much.'

'It was my pleasure. I'll call you later today and we can arrange our next date if that's okay with you.'

'Of course it is. I'd like that.'

He kissed me on the cheek then and it was electrifying.

'I've got a good feeling about this, Emma,' he said. 'And I'm beginning to think that fate brought us together for a reason.'

It was all so very romantic and I convinced myself that it was the start of something really special. But I could not have been more wrong.

As I wait now for the sleeping pills to take effect, I reflect on how quickly romance blossomed between Tommy and me. I succumbed to his easy charm and allowed him to beguile me, to spoil me, to consume me. The chemistry between us was like nothing I had ever experienced with my previous boyfriends. From the start, the energy was explosive, the sex incredible. The two of us became our own world.

Tommy lavished gifts and money on me during those first few weeks and I told him more than once that he didn't have to, that I was with him for who he was and not for what he had. He took me to pubs, clubs and restaurants all across London, and I was surprised at how many people he knew. They were mostly men who were always so respectful to him. What I failed to notice at the time was that some of them seemed nervous in his company, as though they were wary or even scared of him.

He made a point of never talking about his businesses to me or in front of me.

'If you get me started, I tend to ramble on and it'll bore you to tears,' he'd say and I'd believe him.

Soon, he introduced me to his mother and his brother. Ruby was polite enough, but she didn't smile much and I couldn't tell whether she liked me. I remember worrying that his brother Liam came across as cold until Tommy explained that he was like that with everyone.

We were just a month into our relationship, and I still hadn't introduced him to my own mum and sister, when he told me that he loved me. It made me so happy because I had already fallen in love with him.

Two months later, he asked me to move in with him and it was a no-brainer. I'd realised by then that he was the man I wanted to spend the rest of my life with. So naturally I said yes and it proved to be the biggest mistake of my life.

The memories fade and are replaced by a deluge of regrets. I really want to bring this day to an end, but suddenly my thoughts are too loud, screaming in my head, and I feel wide awake again.

In need of a distraction, I switch on the TV, using the remote to flip through the channels until I get to a news one. I don't have to wait long before they run a report on Tommy's trial. As I see myself leaving the court through the screen, it occurs to me how pathetic I look, like someone who has done something terribly wrong and is afraid to face the cameras.

'Driscoll's wife declined to be interviewed after he was convicted and sentenced. She left the Old Bailey alongside his mother and brother,' the reporter says in voice-over. 'However, the lead defence lawyer, Mr Kevin Mosley, did make a brief statement.'

Mosley is shown standing on the pavement facing a large group of journalists and photographers. 'Today's outcome has come as a shock to me and the rest of the defence team,' he declares. 'Our client continues to maintain his innocence. Someone placed that revolver in the glove compartment of Mr Driscoll's car, and we are not convinced that the Metropolitan Police have tried hard enough to find out who they were. We will therefore be lodging an appeal against both conviction and sentence. Meanwhile, Mr Driscoll's family wants it to be known that they are standing by him during this difficult time.'

A photo of Tommy flashes across the screen and the reporter explains how the gun was found when he was stopped by police while driving along a street in Vauxhall near to where his office is located.

'It was alleged in court that Mr Driscoll has for some years been involved in organised crime in the capital while posing as a respected businessman,' the reporter continues. 'This is something he vehemently denies. He has no previous criminal convictions.'

I can't help but smile at this because I know Tommy's spotless record had nothing to do with his innocence and everything to do with his ability to stay one step ahead of the law, the endemic corruption within the Met, and the help of bent coppers on the Firm's payroll.

As soon as the report ends, I turn off the TV. The pills are going to my head now and hopefully I'll soon be spark out. In the meantime, I feel as though I'm once again trapped in a gilded cage. There might not be any bars on the windows of the flat, but it still feels as much a prison as my husband's cell. And I need to find a way to escape.

My mobile continues to buzz and I can't help but take a look. Amanda wants to know how I am, so I text her back saying I'm having a bath and then an early night and I'll call her tomorrow.

Then Tommy rings me twice, presumably from his cell. I don't answer, which prompts another threatening message.

I'll only put up with this for so long, Ems. Stay in the flat and be ready to talk to me tomorrow morning. If I call and there's no fucking answer I won't be happy.

43

I'm hoping that if I can manage a good night's sleep, I'll be able to get my thoughts together and be ready to confront him by then. I just have to be careful not to give him a reason to suspect that I'm hiding something from him. But it won't be easy because I definitely am.

And if he finds out what it is, my situation will become a whole lot worse.

CHAPTER SEVEN

I wake up at 7 a.m. on Wednesday with a splitting headache and a parched throat. Thankfully, the sleeping pills worked and I didn't lie awake all night wondering what I'm going to say to my husband when I speak to him today.

I'm dreading it, but I know I can't continue to ignore his calls. I need to hear what he has to say and then try to make him see sense and abandon his 'rules'.

His attempt to take his coercive control of me to a whole new level is outrageous. But I know he won't view it that way. He'll expect me to submit to his demands because I'm his wife, and because when it comes to our marriage, he's always been the one in the driving seat.

During the early days, I was so blinded by love that I didn't realise what he was doing. It was subtle and insidious. The way he reacted to something I said by slowly shaking his head and tutting. The way he looked at me through critical eyes if I disappointed him. The way he slowly chipped away at my self-confidence and without me realising that it was happening.

Now that he's in prison, I no longer have to walk around my own home on eggshells all the time. I can gradually become more like my old self, the younger carefree Emma, and less like a trophy wife who has no mind of her own. Or can I? Will his abhorrent rules mean that very little will change?

In a healthy relationship, there's meant to be equality and compromise, but there isn't in ours. Like a lot of powerful men, Tommy Driscoll has a sense of entitlement and a grandiose view of himself. In other words, he thinks he's the dog's bollocks.

As I get out of bed and pad into the bathroom, I can already hear his voice in my head telling me how much he loves me and how he would never hurt me. But he only said those things during the initial heady days of our relationship, when Tommy's true self had yet to surface. They're now a cruel reminder of the dream that faded like the light in my life.

The hot shower jerks me back to the present and I stay under it for almost five minutes, letting the water blast my face and body.

I take my time getting dressed. All the while, my anxiety grows, making it hard for me to focus on the tasks at hand. I know full well that it's going to be impossible to persuade Tommy to let me go. He's made up his mind to keep me on a leash so that I won't stray. I should have been prepared for this because since he's been remanded in custody there have been enough clues. He's tried to make me feel guilty about doing anything other than sitting with him in the prison visiting hall. Even there, he would keep reminding me about our marriage vows, how we're supposed to confront challenges together and overcome them together. He's even told me more than once that I'll still need to have his cloak of protection around me for years to come because being his wife means that his enemies are my enemies.

I'm in the kitchen making coffee when the sound of the doorbell startles me. The concierge hasn't called up to tell me I have a visitor, so it has to be either Liam or Fraser. They've both been given permission by Tommy to bypass security and enter at will. I've been told that Liam doesn't have a front door key, but I strongly suspect that he does.

It turns out to be the two of them, and I don't try to disguise my displeasure.

'What are you doing here?' I demand. 'You're lucky I'm not still in bed.'

'Well, that's where I'd be if you had bothered to answer Tommy's calls,' Liam snaps. 'He's told me to come over and make sure you don't ignore him when he rings this morning.'

I shake my head. 'I don't frigging believe it.'

'Yes, you do, Emma. You know what my brother is like. And you shouldn't kid yourself that things will be any different just because he's banged up.'

Liam doesn't wait to be invited in. He steps over the threshold and barges past me as though I'm not there. At least Fraser has the good grace to ask if it's okay for him to follow his boss into the flat – although we both know it's a formality.

Less than a minute later, they're both sitting on stools at the breakfast bar as though they own the place and resignedly I'm serving them coffee.

'Tommy will be calling between eight and quarter past,' Liam tells me as he takes a sip. 'Once you've spoken to him, we'll fuck off. There are a lot of things that need sorting after what happened yesterday.'

It's only ten minutes to eight and their presence heightens the tension inside me.

'There's no need for you to be here,' I try again. 'I didn't want to talk to him last night because I was too upset—'

Liam thrusts his jaw in my direction. 'But I'm guessing you're not as upset as your poor husband, who now has to spend five fucking years behind bars for something he didn't do. It's a nightmare for him and it'll be even worse if he can't count on you for support.'

'But he's expecting too much of me.' I swallow. 'It's not right that he still wants to control every aspect of my life.'

Liam twists his mouth sideways and squints at me. 'You seem to think you have a choice, Ems, but you don't. You made your bed when you married Tommy and so I suggest you make it easy on yourself by playing the part of the loyal wife, even if you don't want to. That way you won't piss my brother off and he won't have to take steps to keep you in line.'

Just then my phone rings. It's resting on the breakfast bar and when I hesitate, Liam picks it up and answers it.

'Hi there, bruv,' he says breezily. 'You okay? Good. Yeah, we're at the flat and so is Emma. And she's keen to talk to you.'

He hands me the phone and I feel a cold rush of blood through my veins.

Liam then signals for Fraser to follow him into the living room so that I can have a private conversation with my husband.

I have to clear my throat before speaking and even then the words splutter out of my mouth. 'I'm so sorry I didn't answer your calls yesterday, Tommy,' I tell him hurriedly. 'I was in shock. And I wouldn't have known what to say to you.'

'That's no fucking excuse,' he responds, his voice loud and sharp. 'I felt like shit and I needed you to help me through the worst day of my life.'

His words sit cold inside me and I have to swallow down the rock in my throat before responding.

'I can only apologise, Tommy. I can't even imagine how terrible you must feel.'

'Well, don't let it happen again. I won't get through this without your support. And you need to understand that it's not my fault that we're in this situation. I was set up. And we've got no choice but to find a way to survive it. The appeals are unlikely to work in my favour and that means we need to prepare ourselves.'

His words make me shiver and I decide to take the opportunity to make my position clear.

'I realise that, Tommy,' I say. 'It's just not what I expected would happen. I can't see—'

'Stop there, Emma. I want you to listen to what I have to say because I haven't got long before I have to leave the cell.' He pauses and I hear him draw a breath. 'I didn't expect this either. But I had to plan for it because I'm aware that it's going to be hard for you to cope without me. That's why I drew up the list of rules. You probably think I'm taking liberties, but I have to do all I can to hold us together, otherwise there's a good chance you won't hang in there and there's no way I am going to let that happen.'

Another long pause and I sense that he wants me to react. But I don't because my heart is in my mouth and it feels like cold fingers are stroking my spine.

'You'll just have to accept that what I'm doing is for your own good,' he continues. 'Just be patient and take it one day at a time. When I'm eventually released, we'll still be young enough to pick up where we left off and start a family. And, believe me, my life won't be worth living if I don't have that to look forward to. That's why the rules are in place. It's the best way forward for both of us. And don't think for a minute that in time I'll change my mind. I won't. Liam and my mum will be my eyes and ears. If you ignore any of the rules, or make the mistake of going to the police, they'll inform me and something bad will happen.'

He pauses again and the hairs on my neck start to prickle in dread at what he might say next.

'Look, Emma, I'm confident that you won't betray me because you're my wife and I know that deep down you still love me just as much as I love you.' He's softened his tone now and lowered his voice, but it's still menacing. 'Right now, your head is fucked up and you're having all kinds of crazy thoughts. But I want you to know that I forgive you for that because I can understand how hard this is for you.'

So many questions have built up inside my head, but I can't ask them straight off because my heart is pounding in my throat.

When I finally find the courage to respond, before I've even finished a word, Tommy interrupts to say that he's got to go, an officer is banging on his cell door.

'I'll call again later,' he says. 'But just remember that I love you with all my heart, even though I don't always show it. And don't forget that marriage is a contract, and there will be repercussions for you if you break it.'

The line goes dead and I feel a crushing sense of despair as I place the phone back on top of the breakfast bar.

For a while I don't move, I just stand there as my thoughts swirl around in feverish circles.

'That was bloody quick,' Liam says as he comes back to the kitchen and I have to assume that he was out in the hall the whole time listening to what turned out to be a one-sided conversation.

'He had to cut it short,' I respond.

'But did he have enough time to put you in the picture?'

'He told me what he expects of me.'

Liam nods. 'That's good. He wanted to get it off his chest.' He reaches into his jacket pocket. 'He also wanted me to leave this with you.'

He hands me a photograph, one that I haven't seen before. It shows my sister and her two daughters walking out of their house in Kennington.

'It was taken yesterday,' Liam says slowly. 'Tommy thought it would be a good idea to remind you that it won't be hard for us to punish your loved ones if you decide to turn your back on him.'

CHAPTER EIGHT

After Liam and Fraser leave, I go out onto the balcony on autopilot. It's a clear, bright morning and the sun is high in the sky. Even though I'm only wearing a thin cotton sweater, I'm oblivious to the chill in the air. My heart is still drumming in my chest and I'm suppressing the urge to scream.

I now know where I stand and it's not a good place. My husband doesn't make idle threats, ever, and I know what he and his brother are capable of. The photo of Amanda and my nieces leaving their home was meant to scare me and it's done the trick.

Tommy would not think twice about harming them if it served a purpose. All he would have to do is instruct Liam to sort it. His brother would then make a call and something shocking would happen. And there would be no evidence to link either of them to the crime.

Before I found out that Tommy wasn't the upstanding businessman he pretended to be, I never paid much attention to all the stories in the papers about organised crime. So I didn't realise the extent of the atrocities committed by London's gangs, even those that specialise in so-called sophisticated operations, such as money laundering, cybercrime and smuggling. But now I know just how ruthless and morally bereft are those who prosper in the underworld. And I'm aware that Tommy won't hesitate to do whatever it takes to keep me shackled to him.

But I can't let that happen, though right now I'm not sure how I can stop it.

At this stage, going to the police is not a viable option. They wouldn't be able to protect me or my family from a firm as well connected and resourced as the Driscolls.

The extent of my predicament is terrifying and it makes me feel helpless and ashamed. A wave of emotion wells up inside me and tears quickly follow. I rush back inside, dry my eyes, and pour myself a fresh cup of tea. I sit on the sofa to drink it while I try to think of a way to safely break free from my husband. But if there is a way, I'm not seeing it, and the longer I force myself to concentrate, the harder it becomes to make sense of anything.

When I moved in with Tommy just three months after we met everything seemed to make perfect sense. I was totally in love with him and we seemed so right together. I was on cloud nine, so when my sister and best friend Sadie warned me not to get too used to it, I had just assumed they were jealous.

Those first few months when we started living together were the best. When Tommy found out I had debts amounting to several thousand pounds, he insisted on paying them off for me without hesitation. And he introduced me to a lavish lifestyle that included a weekend in Rome for my birthday, a new wardrobe of designer clothes, plus lots of jewellery. He even managed to persuade me to give up my job.

'You don't need to work as long as you're with me, Ems,' he told me. 'Concentrate on your painting and enjoy life. If you're not doing some crappy job from nine to five, we can spend more time together. I'll transfer a regular sum into your bank account each month and pay all the bills. Call it early retirement.'

He told me he had plenty of money and that it came from the salary he paid himself and the profits he took from stocks and shares he owned.

He was always ready with an easy answer to the questions I asked him. He explained that he didn't have a presence on social media because he didn't want to leave himself exposed to scammers and trolls. And he said I was the first serious relationship he'd had since he divorced his wife.

I'll always remember how shocked I was when he got around to telling me about his marriage and how it ended. And then what happened to his ex-wife after they had divorced.

'She was murdered,' he suddenly said one night while we were lying in bed after making love.

At first, I thought it was a tasteless joke, but then he continued.

'Her name was Pauline and she was a model.' His voice was solemn. 'We met at a New Year's Eve bash five years ago. We couldn't get enough of each other at the start and it was just three months before we rushed into getting married.'

He was living in a small detached house in Herne Hill back then and for six months they lived there together and all was well.

'But then she started complaining about not having enough freedom,' he said, and I could tell that he was finding it difficult to talk about her. 'A different side of her character gradually emerged, one that I didn't like. She became moody and argumentative.'

He explained that as her modelling career took off, she spent more time away on photo shoots for magazines, and eventually it aroused his suspicion.

'I then discovered she'd been having an affair with a photographer she'd been working with,' he revealed. 'She told me she was sorry and that she'd fallen in love with him. It broke my heart.'

They split up then and she moved in with the other guy. Four months later, Tommy divorced her. But a month after that she suddenly disappeared in suspicious circumstances.

The police launched an investigation and the photographer was arrested after her blood was found in their flat and in the boot of his car. Even though her body has never been found, the evidence against him convinced a jury to find him guilty of murder.

'He was given a life sentence,' Tommy told me that night. 'But he won't get to serve his time, because soon after his conviction he was beaten to death in prison. And he went to his grave without telling anyone where he had hidden Pauline's body.'

Even now, I can remember vividly that conversation with Tommy and how he struggled to hold in his emotions.

The next day, I felt compelled to read about the case online. There were photographs of the photographer, a man named Greg Caplan, along with pictures of Pauline Wilder. She was a stunning blonde with a warm smile. Tommy got only a brief mention in the news stories and was described as the businessman the victim was married to when she began her affair with the man who would go on to kill her.

It's weird how the memories keep coming, ballooning in my mind. It's as though I've suddenly started reliving parts of my life all over again. Perhaps it has something to do with the process of coming to terms with the way things are now. I'm unconsciously seeking answers to the many questions that continue to haunt me.

How the hell did I get here? How could I have been so naive? What clues did I miss along the way? Why didn't I somehow find the strength to stand up for myself?

It feels as though the room is closing in on me. I decide to call my sister in the hope that just hearing her voice will ease the anxiety that is threatening to overwhelm me. But as I cross the room to get my phone, my eyes are drawn to the framed wedding photo on the shelving unit next to our small collection of books. I stop and stare and feel something lodge in my chest.

The nuptials took place six months after we met. It didn't matter to me that it was so quick because Tommy Driscoll had well and truly captured my heart. In the photo, we both look so happy and content, me in my hugely expensive dress and him in his smart Hugo Boss suit.

My mind suddenly transports me back to that day when he slipped the ring on my finger and made me believe that we would have a wonderful future together as man and wife.

CHAPTER NINE

Eighteen months ago

The venue is a plush hotel near Sevenoaks in Kent. Tommy chose it because one of his pals is a director there. But that was okay with me since the location is stunning and it has its own small lake that will be perfect for the photos.

Everything was organised in a rush as it's taking place just five weeks after he had flamboyantly gone down on one knee in a restaurant to propose.

No expense has been spared and once again I can't believe how lucky I am. It's like I'm living the dream.

Most of the sixty-odd guests are from Tommy's side and include a significant number of men who he introduced as friends and business associates. He handled the invitations and when I went through the list with him, he said that most of them work for companies and organisations that he has dealings with. Some are people he has known since childhood.

They're all so polite and respectful and my friend Sadie sidles up to me at one point in the evening and whispers, 'Blimey, Emma. Your fella has an impressive bunch of mates. But, to be honest, some of them come across as a bit scary.'

Funnily enough, I'd been thinking the same. More than a few of them are rough-edged and look more like boxers than businessmen. But their presence makes me feel safe and protected, just as Tommy did by taking charge of things and looking out for me.

It helps that my mum reckons that some of them remind her of my father. Dad was tall and tough with broad shoulders and a broken nose. He worked as a warehouse manager in London and rarely took a day off. It's such a shame he can't be here today.

The wedding is going down a treat with everyone. We have a live group ready to get going and plenty of food and drink. Champagne flowed during the reception and the meal was to die for. Now it's time for the speeches and toasts.

Tommy starts by thanking everyone for coming and for making our day so special. And he makes a point of praising both our mothers and expressing regret that our fathers aren't here to help us celebrate the marriage.

'I want you all to know that I feel like the luckiest man alive today,' he goes on to say. 'Emma is the best thing that's ever happened to me and I promise to take good care of her. It really was a case of love at first sight when I walked into that restaurant where she used to work as a waitress. And it wasn't just her film-star looks. She drew me in right away with her warm smile and bubbly personality. I was delighted she said yes when I asked her out. And then yes again when I asked her to marry me. The future now holds so much promise for both of us. Therefore, allow me to propose a toast to my lovely wife.'

By now, there are tears in my eyes and my heart is punching my ribs. I can't believe I've been so blessed.

Liam, as best man, then stands up to make his speech. Unsurprisingly, he pokes fun at the groom, and reveals something I hadn't been aware of – that Tommy has never learned how to swim! It raises a laugh, as does the remark that he once kept count of the number of times his brother looked at himself in the mirror over the course of a single day.

'It was no less than six fucking times,' he says, not caring that the expletive might offend some in the audience. 'Even I couldn't believe it, and I know how much he loves himself.'

Tommy takes it in good faith and hits back with a few one-liners of his own. But for the most part, Liam's speech is serious and sincere. He praises his brother and says a few nice things about me.

After the meal, as I mingle with the guests, Pauline's name crops up unexpectedly during a conversation with the wife of one of Tommy's friends.

The woman, who appears to be slightly drunk, says to me, 'I'm so glad you've come into Tommy's life. He needs to settle down. I just hope that, unlike Pauline, you can accept him for what he is.'

Her words provoke a twinge of unease and in response, I say, 'What's that supposed to mean?'

She shrugs. 'Well, Pauline knew when she married him that he likes to be in control of everything and that he has a jealous streak. She thought she could change him and when she couldn't, she decided to fuck him over. And look where that got her.'

Before I can ask her to explain herself, she turns away from me and hurries off to talk to someone else, leaving me wondering what the hell she meant.

A little later, while I'm dancing with Tommy, I point her out to him and tell him what she said.

He laughs. 'That's Gloria Penn. You should just ignore her. She's known for slagging people off and spouting complete rubbish. She and I have never really got on. And it doesn't help that her own marriage is on the rocks.'

When the dance ends, Tommy pulls me even closer to him and tells me yet again how much he loves me.

'Now that we're married, I want us to start trying for kids straight away, Ems,' he says. 'We're not getting any younger and I want at least two, maybe even three.'

It's the first time the subject of children has come up and I'm not sure how to respond so I don't. The truth is, I'm in no hurry to start a family. I want us to spend time together as a couple before we go down that road. I decide it's probably best not to tell him that yet, at least not on our wedding day.

The party runs into the early hours and it's such a joyous occasion, even better than I'd hoped it would be. But, sadly, it ends on a sour note once Tommy and I retire to our suite, and he relays something that he overheard Sadie tell her partner Phil.

'She told him that she doesn't reckon our marriage will last,' he says and his eyes ignite with anger. 'She said I'm not your type because I'm too flash and that you're only interested in the size of my wallet anyway.'

I'm so shocked that I get him to repeat it.

'I don't believe it,' I tell him. 'Sadie wouldn't say something like that.'

'But she did,' he insists, and the words rasp in his throat. 'I was standing right behind her and it took all my will-power not to give her a mouthful.'

It really hurts, and it's all I can think about that night. Even as Tommy and I consummate our marriage, in my mind I can still see his eyes flashing with an anger I'd never seen before.

CHAPTER TEN

The present

As I continue to stare at our wedding photo, I move on to thinking about when I confronted Sadie. Tommy and I were two days into our honeymoon at a plush hotel on the Isle of Capri, and the issue of what Sadie had said at the wedding resurfaced after she sent me a text message saying that she hoped I was having a good time.

'The two-faced cow,' Tommy snarled. 'You should tell the bitch that you know what she thinks of the pair of us. If she was my friend, I wouldn't want anything more to do with her.'

I'd never seen him that angry before, but I did understand where he was coming from. We had both tried to push her remarks to one side and the blasted text had shoved them right back in our faces.

'Has she ever slagged me off to you?' he went on.

I shook my head. 'Never. I thought she liked you and was happy for me.'

'Well, I reckon she's a jealous bitch and a nasty piece of work.'

He held my gaze, daring me to contradict him. But I didn't, because I'd come to believe that he was probably right. Maybe she was jealous of my good fortune, or maybe she had turned against me now that I couldn't meet her as often as I used to prior to being with Tommy.

'You ought to call her,' he prompted me. 'And tell her that I heard what she said. If you don't, then it'll play on your mind forever. And make it clear that you're finished with her.'

His words had their desired effect. By then, I was so worked up that I grabbed my phone and jabbed in her number.

When Sadie answered, she seemed surprised and pleased to hear from me, but when I told her why I was calling, she was mortified. She denied telling Phil that I was only interested in Tommy's wallet and that she thought he was too flash for me. But I could tell from her voice, and the way she stumbled over her words, that she was lying.

'If I'd known how you felt, I wouldn't have invited you to the wedding,' I shouted. 'Tommy means the world to me and I love him for who he is, not what he's got. I'm so disappointed in you, Sadie.'

'Please don't let him turn you against me, Emma,' she pleaded. 'You're my friend and always will be.'

'Well, I don't want a friend who slags me off behind my back,' I replied abruptly and then hung up while tears streamed down my face.

I turned to Tommy, who'd been listening to my side of the conversation.

'It's the right thing to do, Ems,' he said, taking me in his arms. 'You can't stay friends with someone who is clearly jealous of you and wants our marriage to fail.'

An hour later, I'm still in the flat. I've had two short phone conversations with my sister and my mum, but they failed to lift my spirits. I agreed to meet Amanda for lunch at a restaurant close to Borough Market near her workplace, although, to be honest, I'm not looking forward to it. I know she's going to bang on about how it's time for me to press on with a divorce. I can't tell her why it isn't as straightforward as that, of course.

I've got the television on and I'm sipping my third cup of tea of the morning. The trial is no longer on the TV news bulletins, but it's all over the internet and in the papers. I've seen pictures of myself and Tommy with headlines such as: *Alleged London mobster sentenced to five years* and *Tommy Driscoll found guilty by Old Bailey jury.*

A story on the online *Metro* news feed quotes a police source saying that the Driscoll syndicate controls a hefty proportion of London's crime trade:

'Much of what we now know about the criminal operation was only revealed during the trial. Police officers explained how Driscoll himself had been under investigation for years

and had been questioned a number of times in connection with various offences. According to the National Crime Agency, their powerhouse is south of the river, but their reach extends across the capital and they're involved in drugs, money laundering, cybercrime and extortion. The gang has been linked to numerous killings but until now the major players have appeared untouchable. Tommy Driscoll had always maintained a low profile and presented himself as a respectable businessman. He has a younger brother, Liam, who has denied any involvement and rejected claims that he will take over the running of the operation.'

Tommy hasn't phoned back yet and I'm on tenterhooks waiting for the call. I try to focus yet again on what I can do to escape from him, but thinking about the wedding earlier has caused a raft of other memories to surface.

I recall our very first serious disagreement. It happened only a week after we returned from our honeymoon. I noticed that a string of men I'd never heard of were suddenly eager to be my friend on Facebook, while others wanted to follow me on Twitter. I showed Tommy and he wasn't happy. He'd already made it clear that he didn't want me to plaster his name and face all over social media, which was why, much to my regret, I hadn't been able to boast about any of the things we did together or the places we'd been to.

He urged me to stop using social media altogether because his enemies in the business world could use it to collect information about him. But I told him that I didn't want to lose contact with my friends and that I thought he was worrying unnecessarily anyway.

'Trust me, Ems, it's asking for trouble,' he said. 'Now that you're with me, it's dangerous to put anything about our personal lives out there. That's why I don't do that stuff myself. It's too risky.'

To keep him sweet, I agreed to post fewer updates and pictures but insisted on keeping the accounts open. And that's what I did for a couple of weeks. But that still wasn't enough for my husband and he continued urging me to stop using all social media platforms.

In the end, he wore me down. I felt it was too early in the marriage to have a major bust-up over something that I could live without. I told myself that a good relationship is all about compromise, and that I had to accept that Tommy's primary objective was to keep us both safe.

It wasn't until much later that I realised that the whole episode was in fact less about keeping me safe and more about controlling what I did and who I engaged with.

Tommy phones just as I'm about to leave the flat to meet up with Amanda. For a moment, I contemplate not answering but then realise almost straight away that it'd be a very bad idea. So I sit down and take the call.

He sounds less tense this time and I'm relieved, but it still feels as though I'm talking to a stranger rather than my husband.

'Did you have a good night's sleep?' he asks me abruptly.

After our tense conversation this morning, this casual direction catches me by surprise. 'Not really,' I tell him. 'How about you?'

'I was awake most of the night thinking about us.' He sighs. 'It's bad enough trying to get used to the idea that I'm going to be stuck in here for years and that I still don't know who did this to me. But I've got the added worry that you don't seem as keen as I am to hold our marriage together. It's killing me, Ems, and that's why I'm having to get tough with you. Right now you don't know your own mind, so it's up to me, as per usual, to sort out what's best for both of us.'

I can barely believe my ears. 'But you shouldn't use threats against me and my family, Tommy. It's not right. I'm not your enemy. I'm your wife.'

'Then please act like it and there won't be a problem.' His voice has taken on a hard edge now. 'I don't want to hurt anyone, Ems, but if you give me no choice, I will. That's who I am.'

I swallow. 'But things have changed, Tommy. You won't be around for years and yet you expect me to put my life on hold, even though things haven't been right between us for a while now.'

'All couples go through rough patches and that's all this is. If I hadn't been arrested, I'm sure that things would have got back to normal by now and we'd be moving forward with our lives.'

It's hard for me to believe that he doesn't realise how bad things had got for me, how depressed and unhappy I already was prior to his arrest. But I suppose it's possible because I had always been too scared to draw his attention to it. And he'd always been so preoccupied with his business and with portraying himself as the master of his universe to notice me anyway. He had never taken the time to attend to my emotional needs or even to acknowledge that his controlling behaviour was putting a distance between us.

'It's no good having this kind of conversation over the bloody phone,' he says sharply. 'I need to see you so that we can talk face to face. Have you arranged a visit?'

'Not yet, there's been no time,' I lie. The truth is I haven't bothered to arrange one.

'Well, make the time. You know the routine and you know that strings have been pulled so your visit can get fast-tracked. If there's a problem or delay, just call my lawyer.'

'I'll get onto it.'

'And in the meantime, don't lose sight of the fact that we vowed to spend the rest of our lives together. There's no fucking way I'm going to let you abandon me.'

Before he can continue, I hang up, unable to bear it any longer. I know he won't be happy, but I don't care. I switch off my mobile and the landline.

The urge to vent my anger and frustration is so strong that I jump up and hurl my empty coffee mug across the room, where it makes a dent in the wall as it shatters.

But that's still not enough. I find myself rushing over to the shelving unit, where I grab the wedding photo frame and use it to sweep the books and ornaments off the shelves, sending them crashing to the floor as well.

I'm shaking all over and can barely breathe as I let the frame slip from my hand. Then, for good measure, I stamp on it to break the glass.

And that's when I spot an unfamiliar black object lying next to it. It's the size and shape of a small ice cube and it appears to have fallen out from inside one of the books I'd pushed onto the floor. There's a wire attached to it which extends behind the shelving unit, presumably to a power point.

It doesn't take me long to realise that it is a mini surveillance camera, the kind that can be bought on the internet. And that my bastard of a husband has been spying on me.

CHAPTER ELEVEN

It's not at all obvious that Amanda and I are sisters. She's four years older and looks nothing like me. She has short natural blonde hair, a much fuller figure and our mum's soft features. She also dresses far more conservatively than I do. Today, for instance, she's wearing a smart grey suit and white blouse, whereas I'm sporting tight blue jeans and a bright yellow V-necked sweater.

She's already at a table in the restaurant when I arrive. Before I can sit down, she gets up and wraps her arms around me.

'My God, I've been so worried about you,' she says, hugging me tightly, and it's as though she hasn't seen me in months when in fact it's only been a couple of weeks.

'There's no need to worry,' I tell her when we're both seated. 'I'm doing okay. I'm just glad the trial is over.'

'We all are, Emma. But I gather the bastard intends to appeal?'

'That's right. He doubts it'll be successful though.'

'When did you speak to him?'

'This morning. He called me.'

Amanda raises her brow. 'And did you tell him that you want a divorce?'

I feel my chest contract as I search for the right words.

'No, I didn't,' I say. 'And I'm not sure I will just yet. I need to think it through.'

Her face curls into a frown. 'Are you out of your mind? This is the opportunity you've been waiting for.'

I break eye contact with her and gnaw at my lower lip. I want to tell her the truth, that it's not that I don't want to end my marriage to Tommy, it's out of fear of what harm will come to my loved ones – including my nieces, her daughters – if I do. But I can't let her know the truth for all our sakes.

'I've decided to bide my time,' I finally say. 'There's no need for me to rush things. I have a lot to sort out.'

'Jesus, Emma! This is crazy. What possesses you to want to hold on for a second longer? In fact, if the man had an ounce of decency, he would be urging you to divorce him so you can have a life.'

I feel a deep sense of shame for lying to my sister, but I know it's the right thing to do, at least until I've come up with an alternative plan.

The waiter arrives at our table just as Amanda is about to continue her tirade. I'm glad because it gives me a few moments to collect my thoughts.

Amanda suggests we share a pizza and asks me what I want to drink.

'Just a lemonade for me,' I say.

'Are you sure you wouldn't like a glass of wine? That's what I'm having.'

'I told you I'm steering clear of alcohol, at least for a while. It got to the stage where I struggled to get through the day without drowning my sorrows in drink. It won't hurt to have a break.'

When we're alone again, she leans across the table and her eyes bore into mine.

'I really don't understand you, Emma,' she says seriously. 'You told us you were no longer happy being with him, that he didn't treat you right. And that's obviously why you drank so much. So why the hesitation now? Is it because he's got such a hold over you that you don't feel you can break away. For heaven's sake he's going to be in prison for years.'

I shake my head. 'It's not that. There's so much to think about. And it seems so callous to tell him I'm finished with him just after he's been told he faces five years behind bars.' I will the anxiety out of my voice as I speak, even though I can still feel it deep in my stomach.

'It'd be different if you still loved him, Emma,' Amanda says firmly. 'But you've led me to believe that you don't. And that's understandable given that he's a control freak and a bully, and that's on top of being a bloody gangster. You have to find the strength to walk away now.'

'But he's still my husband and our marriage hasn't been a total disaster. We've had good times as well as bad, and he's done a lot for me,' I argue and have to force the words out.

She snorts derisively. 'So, is that the reason you're pulling back? You don't want to give up the luxury flat and expensive lifestyle? Has he told you that you can carry on living like lady muck as long as you don't leave him?'

She's torn into me like this before and I've always let it wash over me. But now her words really sting and I'm sorely tempted to get up and walk out. I don't though, because at the end of the day she's my big sister and this is merely her way of getting me to do the right thing. As far as she's concerned, the door to a better life has finally opened up for me and if I don't walk through it, she's the one who needs to push me.

I succeed in holding back the tears even though I can feel the pressure building behind my eyes. 'It really isn't like that,' I tell her. 'Right now, I'm all messed up and can't think straight. I just need time. But you've got to understand that this so-called "luxury" lifestyle and the expensive flat mean nothing to me. I'd rather just be happy and I wouldn't care how much money I had or where I lived.'

After a pause, Amanda's expression softens and she reaches across the table to take my hand. 'I just want what's best for you, Emma,' she says. 'And the thought of you being tied to that man even when he's locked up chills me to the bone.'

There's so much I want to tell her, but I can't. I daren't. To share my burden with my sister would be a terrible mistake. It's for me alone to sort out, even if right now I can't see how this is possible without provoking a devastating response from my husband.

'Here come the drinks,' Amanda says as she gently squeezes my hand. 'Let's tone down this conversation for now and toast the fact that at least you're one step towards freedom and a much better life.'

I manage to smile and it helps to keep the tears at bay. At least for now.

CHAPTER TWELVE

We parted company after what for me turned into a long, awkward hour. My sister dropped the aggressive tone after the drinks had arrived and then did her best to comfort and reassure me by employing a range of seemingly banal platitudes. And I let her think that she had made me feel a little better. But in truth her words just reminded me of my predicament.

Before heading back to work, Amanda hugged me. 'I'm here for you, sis. Don't you forget that. And never forget what we used to say to each other as kids – it's us against the world.'

Now, as I wander through Borough Market, it occurs to me that my phone is still switched off and I decide to leave it that way for the time being. I need some time to think without being interrupted.

I can't face the prospect of going straight home and so, when I exit the market, I head for the Old Thameside Inn, a charming pub that overlooks the river. The place is all exposed brickwork and flagstone floors and a favourite with tourists, but thankfully it's relatively empty when I arrive. I order a lemonade at the bar and take it out onto the terrace.

It's still chilly even with the sun high in the sky, but I'm warm enough wrapped up in my overcoat and scarf.

I have a table to myself and I hope that sitting here for a while will ease the knot in my stomach and help me to relax. But soon my mind is drifting back over the past eighteen months as I recall how well it started despite the tensions surrounding our wedding day. I was deeply in love and able to enjoy the trappings of Tommy's success.

Those early days when everything was so perfect are precious memories still, a time when I was full of hope. After a while, my life as Mrs Emma Driscoll pretty much fell into a routine: shopping, yoga classes, painting, evenings out, lunches at Ruby's house, and a lot of waiting at home for Tommy to get back from wherever he'd been. I had no debts, no more pressure to work unsocial hours in odd jobs, no more worries about making ends meet. Everything was new, exciting and easy. I revelled in the way people looked at us when we were out together. It was as though they considered us to be the perfect couple, and that was exactly how it felt back then. We were always laughing, kissing and enjoying each other's company. Tommy would splash the cash and he had made it clear that he liked showing me off. I even got used to having Jack Fraser around for much of the time, even though I remained blissfully unaware as to what his role really entailed.

Tommy encouraged me to spend lots of time in my makeshift studio and I did my best to impress him with my drawings and paintings. He seemed full of admiration for them and told me that once I had built up a sizable collection, he would arrange for me to exhibit and then sell them.

But it never happened because I eventually got bored of spending so much time by myself and stopped painting as often. I reached a point where I longed to do something more with my time in the company of others while Tommy was out.

But when one day I casually told him I was thinking of getting a part-time job and asked if he had any vacancies within any of his companies that might suit me, his reaction shocked me.

'Are you fucking serious?' he snapped. 'You've got it made, Emma. Most women would give their right arm to be in your position and not have to go to work.'

'But sometimes I get bored when I'm here alone, Tommy,' I responded, almost apologetically because although I'd seen glimpses of my husband's anger, it had never been fully directed at me before. 'And I feel the need to engage with more people and make myself more useful. Why is that a bad thing?'

'Because it proves to me that you're so bloody ungrateful for what I've done for you,' he replied acidly. 'I've made it possible for you to do something you enjoy rather than pissing away your time waiting at tables or sitting behind a desk in an office. I thought it would make you happy.'

'It did. It does. But I—'

'No buts, Emma. If you don't appreciate how lucky you are then there's no point discussing it. And if you do get a job, then you will have to help pay the fucking bills.'

On this note, he stormed off, leaving me speechless and on the verge of tears.

For days afterwards, he continued to drop these spiteful comments, and in the end, it worked. I felt so guilty that I completely dropped the idea of going back to work and instead resumed my old routine of painting, shopping and acting like Tommy's version of a dutiful wife.

But the issue did mark the start of a change in our relationship because it helped convince me that I needed to find other, smaller ways to become independent and assertive. I started making a conscious effort to stop just going along with everything he said and did and to express myself more forcefully. I began by telling him that if I wanted to invite my friends to the flat, then I should be able to without it creating a fuss. And I insisted that it should be me and not him who chose what I wore when we went out at night. But in response, he became more controlling, more possessive, and far more aggressive. Rather than being cut some slack my life became even more constrained.

The truth slowly dawned on me that he'd been under-mining my confidence from the very start in subtle yet insidious ways. I'd been so caught up in the way my life had suddenly taken off that I'd either ignored or completely failed to notice the signs. I recalled the incident on our honeymoon when I was piling up my plate at the all-inclusive buffet.

'I don't think you should stuff your face with all that crap,' he'd snarled at me. 'You have to think of me as well as yourself from now on. The last thing I want is a fat pig as a wife.'

I ignored it then because I didn't think for a minute that he was being serious. But now I know he was.

On another occasion, he insisted on knowing my mobile phone password so that he could use it in the event of an emergency. I complied because I naively assumed it to be a thoughtful gesture rather than the blatant invasion of my privacy that it really was.

Over time, I began to view elements of his behaviour in a different light: the way he appeared to analyse everything I did – always negatively; the way he tried to isolate me from others by making it difficult for me to go out without him; the way he chose to ignore or dismiss my opinions; and how he often complained about the length of time I spent on the phone talking to my sister and mother.

It took me far too long to see how his easy charm had turned to scheming manipulation and how completely he had managed to pull the wool over my eyes in those early days of our courtship about who he really was.

*   *   *

As I return to the present, I'm annoyed with myself for taking yet another unsettling trip down memory lane. And I know that if I don't stop now, it'll lead me back to those awful ten months that I had to endure before Tommy's arrest. That was when things truly got much worse for me, when Tommy's behaviour became even more threatening and obsessive and I realised how hopeless my situation had become.

'Enough is enough,' I say aloud to myself as I decide to finish my drink and head home.

But that's when I hear a voice behind me. I snap my head towards it and the sight of the tall, imposing figure towering over me causes my heart to jump.

'Hello, Mrs Driscoll,' says the man who had arrested my husband and got him sent down. 'How are you today?'

And there was me thinking that this day could not get any worse.

CHAPTER THIRTEEN

Detective Chief Inspector Dave Brannigan is a leading member of the Scotland Yard team that combats organised crime. He's in his fifties with cropped, iron-grey hair, heavy smoker's lines around his mouth and a nose that is too small for his face.

When he gave evidence at Tommy's trial, he told the jury that my husband was one of the most powerful gangsters in London and it was therefore no surprise that he carried a weapon in his car.

'There's no need to be alarmed,' he says. 'I just want a quick word, I promise it won't take long.'

I swallow, then take a deep breath. 'How did you know I was here?'

'I drove to your flat earlier and was about to get out when I saw you leaving the building,' he replies. 'So I followed you. I didn't want to spoil your lunch with your sister, so I waited across the road until you finished. I was going to approach you when you got home, but you decided to make a pit stop, so here I am. It's worked out well actually because I doubt that we'll be spotted here by any of your husband's minions.'

I'm surprised that Brannigan feels so confident about that last point. Surely it must have occurred to him that Tommy might be having me followed.

'What do you want?' I demand. 'I'd hoped I had seen the last of you at court yesterday.'

His grin widens as he sits down opposite me. 'When we last spoke, we didn't know how your husband's trial would turn out. But now we know that he won't be released for five years. It'll be longer if we can secure evidence that links him to organised crime. And that's where you come in. I'm hoping that you might be persuaded to reveal some of the secrets you've been keeping.'

'What are you on about?' I respond after looking around to make sure we're not being watched.

He makes me wait while he unzips his blue parka and takes a pack of cigarettes from his inside pocket. He lights one up and after blowing smoke at the sky, he finally speaks. 'We interviewed you several times, Emma, and you insisted that you knew nothing about your husband's business affairs. You told us you had no idea where he kept his cash or who he had dealings with. But I've never believed you, and neither did my boss. We reckon you were keeping schtum because you were scared – that's understandable. But now there's no need to be. He's nicely tucked up in prison and we'll make sure that he and his family never know that you've talked to us.'

I sit up straight as I try to appear calm and in control. A small voice inside me urges me to open up to him, to tell him what little I know about Tommy's affairs and to ask him to help me out of the mess I'm in. But another, much louder voice warns me not to be so reckless. And that's the one I listen to.

'I had nothing to say to you then and I have nothing to say to you now, Detective Brannigan,' I tell him. 'I didn't know my husband was a criminal until *you* told me. I have no idea where he hid any money that he didn't declare through his legitimate businesses. He did not involve me in anything he got up to. At least one of your officers told me that men like my husband rarely confide in their wives for obvious reasons.'

He audibly sighs. 'It's probably no surprise to you that I knew you'd say that, Emma. I told my boss as much, but he insisted I touch base to let you know that we haven't lost interest in you yet. And we know from experience that women who find themselves in your situation often fall on desperately hard times, or their husbands make their lives a misery. Many of them look to us for help, but in some cases, they leave it too late. I know of at least one woman who took her own life because things became so intolerable. . . and I wouldn't like that to happen to you.'

As I return his stare, I'm sure I can see a trace of compassion in his dark, narrow eyes.

'What makes you think it will?' I ask him.

He shrugs. 'Because Tommy Driscoll will refuse to accept that he can't still have things all his own way. The loss of control will tie him in knots and make him paranoid, jealous and resentful. He'll take it out mainly on you and his brother, who we all know has assumed control of the Driscoll syndicate.'

I hold his stare, just to show I'm not intimidated by him, even though I secretly am.

'I don't need your help now and I won't need it in the future,' I say. 'And there's nothing I can tell you that you don't already know.'

'Oh, I doubt that very much, Emma. You were with the man for two years. You must have been privy to what was going on. And if you're worried about what he might do in the unlikely event that he hears you've spoken to us, then we will of course provide protection for you and your family. And I can assure you—'

'Stop there,' I blurt out. 'I've heard enough.' By now, my heart is pumping so hard in my chest that it hurts.

I grab my bag, leave my drink and stand up. He does too.

'If you follow me again, I'll report you for harassment,' I say. 'Just leave me alone. My life is shit already and I don't want you to make it a thousand times worse. So, stay the fuck away from me.'

Before he says anything else, I step out from behind the table and walk briskly away without looking back.

CHAPTER FOURTEEN

By the time I get home, I am emotionally drained. For the first fifteen minutes, I pace the floor in the living room, trying to run from my thoughts.

My mobile is still switched off and so is the landline. I don't want to talk to Tommy or anyone else for that matter.

The encounter with Detective Brannigan has given me something else to worry about. I didn't expect to hear from him again after the trial ended, but I should have known that the police would press on with their bid to break up the Driscoll syndicate and seize its assets. It's something they were working on long before Tommy was arrested. And the pressure it put him under was the reason he later gave for why his behaviour towards me had changed. But I knew that was just a pathetic attempt to justify his actions.

The truth is, my husband was, and is, a fully fledged narcissist. He has a huge sense of entitlement and an uncompromising attitude to life. He's self-centred, selfish and demanding, and he lacks empathy. It took me a long time to realise that I was an object to be controlled and manipulated, someone who could feed his ego and make him feel good about himself.

I got to know the real Tommy during those ten months leading up to his arrest. That was when it became abundantly clear to me that he did not regard our marriage as a partnership of equals.

During that period, he gradually ramped up his coercive behaviour towards me. He became even more demanding and less tolerant. He didn't like me to do things without him; he was forever criticising my choice of clothes; he tried to make me feel guilty for not wanting to visit his mother every week; he insisted on handling every aspect of our finances; and he got angry whenever I had a period because he desperately wanted me to fall pregnant.

He became increasingly obnoxious and antagonistic towards me, but the first time I really felt threatened was after he found out that I lied to him about why I was late returning from a yoga class one evening.

I didn't expect him to be there when I got home and so I instantly panicked, knowing the truth would anger Tommy. I made up a story on the spot, a small lie that I went for a coffee after yoga with my sister. I could tell he was a little drunk. He was slurring and there was an empty glass on the table next to a bottle of Scotch.

I left him in the living room and went to have a shower. When I came out of the en suite, a towel around me, he was sitting on the bed and holding up my mobile.

'You just had a message from your old friend Sadie,' he said, and then proceeded to read it aloud to me in a deliberately crude girly way. *I'm so pleased we bumped into each other this evening, Ems. I really enjoyed our drink, and I'm glad you now know why I stopped calling you. Please stay in touch, and let's meet up again. There's no need for Tommy to know if you don't want him to.'*

I fought to keep my voice steady as I tried to explain why I chose not to tell the truth. 'It was all so unexpected,' I said. 'She was in a taxi when she spotted me. She stopped the cab and came rushing over. She pleaded with me to let her explain why she had stopped talking to me, hadn't reached out to me in so long. So, I let her buy me a drink. What she told me came as a shock; I thought it best not to say anything to you until I've got my mind around it.'

The fact is not only was I struggling to believe what she'd said. I also didn't want to believe it.

'What did she say to you?' he asked, his voice cold.

I didn't want to have to tell him, but at the same time I was eager to see how he'd respond.

'She admitted that she did slag us both off at the wedding,' I said. 'And she said she was desperate to apologise, which is why she initially kept ringing me. But she claimed she stopped because you went to her flat and threatened to hurt her if she didn't stay out of my life.'

'The bitch was trying to turn you against me, for fuck's sake,' he bellowed. 'And I wasn't prepared to stand for it.'

'It's true then?' I gasped.

'Of course it fucking is. But that's not the issue here. The issue is that you told me an outright lie and that makes me wonder how many more lies you've told me.' He stood up then and dropped my phone onto the floor. Then stamped on it.

'You bastard!' I yelled. 'You had no right to read my messages or to threaten my friend. I'm your wife, not one of your lackeys.'

He stepped towards me, his posture threatening, his face fuming.

'I'm not the one who's in the wrong here, Emma. You are. You've let me down big time and you deserve a good fucking hiding.'

'For God's sake, Tommy, calm down,' I urged, alarmed by his reaction and the menace in his voice. 'You don't mean that. It's the drink talking.'

He shook his head. 'I'm not drunk. I'm angry and I have every right to be. You talked about me to that bitch behind my back and then lied about it.'

'But it wasn't like that. Honest.'

He shook his head. 'Bollocks. You're treating me like one of the pussy blokes you used to go out with. And that's a mistake.'

'I can't listen to this any more, Tommy,' I said. 'You're upsetting me.'

'Well, that serves you right for upsetting me,' he shouted.

And with that, I stormed past him and headed for the walk-in wardrobe to get dressed. After I closed the door behind me, I feared he would throw it open and come charging in. But he didn't, and when I emerged ten minutes later after having a good cry, he wasn't in the room or in the flat.

He didn't return until the following morning when he gave me a big bunch of flowers and told me that he was sorry he lost his temper.

I was taken aback. The flowers, the apology, the contrition etched into his features. Hope swelled in my chest that what had happened was just a blip, something that wouldn't be repeated.

'But please don't do it again, Emma,' he said. 'I'm your husband and you shouldn't keep things from me.'

'But you overreacted, Tommy, and it really scared me.'

'Well, I've apologised, but you only have yourself to blame.'

I just stood there, lost for words, as he took a mobile phone from his pocket and handed it to me.

'This is to replace the one I stamped on,' he said. 'Make sure you delete that bitch's number from your contacts. I won't be happy if you stay in touch with her.'

What I should have done then was walk out on him, but I couldn't bring myself to do it, for various reasons, including the fact that I still believed I loved him and that things would get better over time.

But not long after this episode I started to wonder if our marriage was destined to go the same way as Tommy and Pauline's. He'd said to me himself that Pauline had complained about not having enough freedom, and Gloria Penn had warned me at our wedding about Tommy's controlling behaviour with Pauline and how she thought she would be able to change him.

It still strikes me as strange even now that Pauline left Tommy for another man, Greg Caplan, who then allegedly murdered her before he himself was murdered in prison. Ever since I read those stories online about the killings and the court case, the whole thing had played on my mind. And the more thought I gave to it, the more suspicious I became.

What if the jury got it wrong and Caplan wasn't Pauline's killer? After all, her body has never been found. Was it therefore conceivable that it was Tommy who carried out the murder or got one of his enforcers to do it on his behalf in revenge for what she did to him? Knowing Tommy as well as I do now, I certainly believe it's something he'd be capable of.

And if it was him who did it, then did he also arrange for Caplan to be killed in prison by a fellow inmate with links to the Driscoll Firm?

I realise suddenly I've done it again. I've allowed my mind to take me to places I don't want to go. It does this all too frequently these days, and the only way to resist the pull of the past is to keep myself busy.

Fortunately, there are things I need to do, starting with searching the flat for more hidden cameras.

It takes longer than I anticipated because I realise belatedly that there are so many places that my husband, or one of his gang members, could have placed them. I check the plants, the lights, the various ornaments, the pictures on the walls, every nook and cranny. By the time I'm finished, I notice that it's almost dark outside as the afternoon turns to early evening. I don't find any more devices, but I can't be sure I haven't missed one. Or even that someone hasn't been watching me carry out the search.

My body is tight with tension and I'm feeling nauseous. I need to keep myself occupied so I decide to check my phone. Tommy called my mobile twice soon after I hung up on him. He also left two voicemails.

'You need to get a fucking grip, Emma. There's only so much of this shit I'll take. Remember that.'

And then: 'Wives should be there for their husbands. So pick up when I next call or there'll be consequences.'

CHAPTER FIFTEEN

Tiredness continues to elude me. I'm in bed now, lying in the dark, but there's no let-up to the onslaught of unpleasant memories.

I recall how my husband's temper became an increasing source of concern for me during those months leading up to his arrest. It never took much to set him off, and when he let rip, he frightened me.

Once, after another of Tommy's outbursts, I suggested he go on an anger management course and he reacted by shredding my old photograph album that contained many treasured memories of my earlier life and pictures of my former boyfriends. Afterwards, he said it was my fault because I'd purposely sought to wind him up.

Despite this, I still didn't tell anyone what was happening because I was too embarrassed and ashamed. I managed to conceal the truth from my friends and family, which wasn't that difficult because I didn't see that much of them. Plus, it wasn't as though he was like it every day. For most of the time, he was the Tommy I fell in love with. He'd be hearty and cheerful and go out of his way to pamper and spoil me. And that was the man everyone saw.

But his 'Mr Nice Guy' façade would slip as soon as things did not go his way, or when he felt I'd stepped over some imaginary line of his, or when he'd had too much to drink. One day I would be his 'beautiful princess' and the next I'd be a 'fucking bitch'. And he'd invariably give what he felt were reasonable explanations for his behaviour and insist he was acting in my best interest.

There's no question that I allowed myself to fall into a trap, and even before our first anniversary came around, my head was increasingly filled with thoughts of escape. I longed for the space to be my own person and the freedom to live a normal life beyond the shadow he cast. There wasn't any part of my life that he didn't try to control at this point.

Once I felt so desperate that I contacted a domestic abuse charity to ask for advice: was the most sensible course of action simply to leave him?

'That depends on your individual circumstances,' the adviser on the other end said. 'But you'd need to bear in mind that leaving an abusive partner or husband does not guarantee safety – in fact, it often escalates the violence. When the victim attempts or even threatens to leave, the abuser may feel they've lost control and this could prompt them to seek revenge.'

She went on to offer me advice on how to create a safety plan to leave my husband, what legal help I could get and information on the various support packages.

But what she said did not make me feel better or safer. And that was partly why I stuck with Tommy. I also convinced myself that my life wasn't all bad and that there were many other women out there who were trapped in marriages far worse than mine. I just needed to make the most of the positives, such as the luxury lifestyle and the fact that there was still a side to Tommy that was kind and generous.

I often wondered if us having a baby would improve things. He'd made it very clear from the start that he was in a hurry to have children, and I eventually had to tell him that I was keen too, even though it wasn't true. To keep him happy I agreed we should try, but thankfully I failed to conceive during those early months. And then when his bad behaviour escalated, I began to feel insecure about bringing a child into what had become an unsteady marriage. I resorted to taking the pill in secret, no longer trusting that he would understand my fears.

When he found the packet in my drawer, he went berserk; that was the first time he laid a hand on me, slapping my face. It hurt and it made me cry, but I wasn't as shocked as you might expect, because deep down I'd actually been expecting this to happen sooner or later. Still, I quickly apologised so that he wouldn't do it again and promised to stop taking them. But I didn't. I just hid them in a different place. By then, I couldn't bear the thought of him being the father of any child of mine.

For days after the slap, Tommy apologised countless times and went out of his way to be nice to me, all the while insisting that it had been my fault and that I'd provoked him.

'When I found those pills, it felt like you'd stabbed me in the back,' he explained. 'You made me believe that you wanted kids as much as I do.'

'I'm so very sorry,' I replied, even though it wasn't true. 'I just wanted us to spend time together as a couple before starting a family. I should have told you; it was a mistake.'

I feared the pressure on me would mount after that and Tommy would obsess even more about getting me pregnant. But that wasn't how it turned out because he was suddenly given something else to worry about.

And so was I because that was when I was confronted with the terrible truth about my husband.

CHAPTER SIXTEEN

Seven months ago

It's Sunday evening and we're coming to the end of what's been a rather pleasant day. Tommy took me for a drive around the Kent countryside and surprised me with a visit to the hotel where we got married.

We had lunch there and walked around the lake before visiting a local vineyard, where he bought me an expensive bottle of wine and a box of chocolates.

It was just the two of us, no Jack Fraser accompanying us for a change, and as we return to London, I feel happier than I have in a long time.

Three weeks have passed since Tommy slapped me and he no longer mentions it. For my part, I try not to think about it, and tell myself that Tommy meant it when he said he bitterly regretted it and that it wouldn't happen again.

Repeating this to myself over and over again doesn't

mean that I'm now comfortable in our marriage, nor that I no longer live in fear of my husband. But it does give me a small piece of hope to cling to; maybe he will change his ways and become a better person. And if so, then perhaps I'll stop inadvertently thinking about ways to leave him and our marriage will go on to survive against the odds.

'I've really enjoyed today,' he tells me as we descend the ramp into the car park beneath our block. 'We should make a point of doing things like that more often.'

'I agree,' I reply. 'It was fun.' It seems strange to me that everything feels so normal again. But I don't want to build my hopes up because I know full well how quickly things can change, and how little it takes to bring out Tommy's dark side.

'Are you happy to stay in for the rest of the evening or would you like to go out for dinner?'

I shake my head. 'I'd prefer to stay in and watch telly. We've got plenty of snacks in the fridge and we can open our new bottle of wine. Oh, and the chocolates, which I can't wait to get stuck into.'

He smiles. 'I was hoping you'd say that, Ems. I'm actually quite exhausted.'

After parking the car, we climb the short flight of stairs to reception. But when we get there, we're shocked because waiting to greet us are three uniformed police officers, plus two men in suits.

I hear Tommy curse under his breath as he grabs my hand.

'What the fuck are you lot doing here?' he demands and I'm surprised at the way he's talking to them.

'We've been waiting for you to arrive, Mr Driscoll,' one of the suited men responds and holds up an official-looking card. 'I'm Detective Chief Inspector Brannigan and my colleague is Detective Sergeant Fowler. We'd like you to accompany us across the river to the Yard so that we can interview you under caution. You can call your lawyer on the way.' The detective then turns to me. 'We'd also like to have an informal chat with you, Mrs Driscoll.'

'Leave her out of it,' Tommy tells him. 'She's going nowhere.'

I feel my muscles tighten and my jaw contract.

'Will someone tell me what's going on?' I blurt.

Brannigan pockets his card and says to me, 'You're among a large number of individuals we intend to question in connection with the government's latest crackdown on organised crime in London.' His eyes move from me to Tommy. 'And it will be in both your interests to cooperate fully with us.'

'But I don't understand,' I squeal as a cold chill washes over me. 'What's that got to do with us?'

He switches his gaze back to me. 'Come on, Mrs Driscoll. Do you really expect me to believe that you don't know how your husband makes the money that allows you to live in a place like this?'

I turn to Tommy, expecting him to explain to me what is going on, but he shuts his eyes and shakes his head, and I know then that I'm not going to like what I'm about to be told.

*　*　*

100

Despite Tommy's loud protestations, we're taken in separate police vehicles across the Thames to New Scotland Yard.

For me, it's like an out-of-body experience. I feel numb and hollow as I try to process what's happening. I'm expected to believe that my husband is a gangster and not a respected businessman like he's always claimed to be. And I'm confused as to why he didn't seize the opportunity to tell me that it's not true before he was ushered out of the building in front of me.

I've never been in trouble with the police before so I don't know what to expect or how to react. When we get to the Yard, Detective Brannigan explains that he'll be the one who'll be asking me questions.

'Your husband has called his solicitor and arrangements are being made for someone to come and represent you during our conversation,' he says. 'Before we begin, I'd like to make it clear that you are not under arrest, Mrs Driscoll. As I said earlier, we've launched a new crackdown on organised crime in the capital. You obviously know that for years your husband and his family have run one of the biggest illicit operations in London. We're now going to make it clear to him that we're closing in and his days are numbered. We also intend to make you, as his wife, aware that withholding information in respect of criminal activities may well lead to you being prosecuted.'

As he speaks, my heart is racing and my thoughts are churning. I have no idea what other nasty surprises are coming my way, but I don't doubt that they're going to plunge me deeper into the pit of despair.

It gets started once the lawyer arrives. Her name is Fiona Walsh and she looks about fifty years old. And the fact that Tommy felt it necessary to call her in makes me feel even more uncomfortable.

For nearly two hours, I sit in a small room and listen as Brannigan goes through a long list of allegations against Tommy, his brother and their father. My response to every question is that I don't know.

'I don't believe you, Mrs Driscoll,' he says, slapping the desk hard in frustration. 'It simply beggars belief that you were kept in the dark for so long.'

He claims that my husband is in charge of a criminal firm that generates huge income from activities including drug trafficking, counterfeiting and extortion. And that his legitimate enterprises are merely a front to launder his ill-gotten gains.

'You might wonder how he's got away with it for so long while managing to keep such a low profile,' Brannigan says. 'Well, it's because he's clever and devious, as well as being very, very lucky. Even the media haven't been able to expose him. But things are going to change for your husband and people like him. We now have the resources and the determination to lay waste to their grubby little empires and bring criminals like him to justice.'

I'm asked lots of questions that I don't know how to answer and eventually Brannigan gives up and calls an end to the interview.

When I finally get to leave the Yard, the lawyer drives me home. I remain silent in the car, what I've heard has knocked me right out of myself. It feels like my world has been torn to shreds and I find it hard to believe that Tommy has managed to keep so much from me for so long. But now that I've been given the real picture, various things suddenly make sense. I can see now why Jack Fraser is Tommy's constant companion; he's a henchman – not a colleague or assistant – and he's paid to protect him. It's also clear why Tommy never wanted to talk about his work – he didn't want me to know what he was really up to. And I realise why the men I was introduced to in pubs and clubs always appeared to have a dangerous air about them.

The lawyer drops me off just before ten that evening. Before I leave the car, I ask her when I'm likely to see Tommy again.

'That depends on whether they have enough evidence to charge him with anything,' she replies briskly. 'But we very much doubt that they do. This is essentially a fishing exercise for the police. They want to destabilise the Firm in the hope that mistakes will be made and people will come forward to disclose secrets.'

I clear my throat and shake my head. 'Please be honest with me, Miss Walsh. Is everything I was told back there true? If it is, then I really had no idea.'

She hesitates before speaking. 'You need to speak to Mr Driscoll about that. I'm in no position to say.'

'So it is true then.'

She doesn't answer, but she doesn't need to.

As soon as I'm back in the flat, I throw myself on the bed and lay there for almost an hour, my emotions in a hopeless tangle. I still can't take it all in and it feels as though I've lost all sense of reality. I berate myself over and over again for being so fucking stupid and gullible to have believed a single word that Tommy Driscoll ever said to me.

CHAPTER SEVENTEEN

The present

I'm still finding it impossible to sleep as so many thoughts are rushing around inside my head. I try in vain to stop myself dwelling on the past but it's like swimming against a ferocious tide.

That first encounter with the police may have taken place seven months ago, but it seems like it was only yesterday. The whole experience was so distressing and humiliating for me.

I recall that Tommy arrived home in the early hours of the following morning after being released. By that time, I'd got through half a bottle of vodka, but I was still wide awake and alert. He hadn't been charged with anything and appeared to be more angry than worried. When he tried to embrace me, I pushed him away despite fully expecting him to hit me in retaliation. But instead, he caught me off guard as he told me how sorry he was. He didn't try to deny what the police had said and instead launched into a long and emotional explanation as to why he had concealed the truth from me.

'I couldn't tell you at the start because I thought you'd probably be too scared to go out with me,' he said, and I'm sure I detected an element of guilt as well as anger in his voice. 'And then after I fell in love with you, I feared that if I came clean, you'd leave me. I just wasn't prepared to take that chance. As things progressed, I hoped you would never have to find out. My plan has always been to retire from the business once I've accumulated enough wealth and become a father. And that's what I still want to happen, Ems. You and me and our children can move abroad and lead a quiet, comfortable life in the sun.'

I was tempted to tell him that this wasn't something I could possibly contemplate now that I'd been made aware of who he really was. But I held it in.

Tommy went on to justify his actions by saying that growing up in a family of criminals made it impossible for him to walk a straight line and that's why he began breaking the law at an early age.

'It was what my dad expected of me,' he explained. 'And so, when he died, I felt I had no choice but to take over. And Mum encouraged me. I'm not proud of it, but I'm not ashamed either. We live in a tough world, and with my background I would have struggled to make ends meet with a shitty job.'

He refused to go into detail about the Firm's various operations when I asked, saying he had to keep as much information as possible from me for my own protection.

'All you need to know is that this doesn't change things between us,' he stressed. 'We carry on as though nothing has happened. So please don't try to use it as an excuse to leave me, I'll never let that happen. And don't worry about the coppers. There's no way they'll ever collar me. Most of them are bent and a good few are on our books anyway. This so-called crackdown on organised crime is all for show. They do it every few years.'

He was wrong to say that things wouldn't change between us. In the months that followed, he became even more controlling and I became more desperate. His behaviour towards me had a more chilling undertone, with veiled threats and unwarranted put-downs. And I got the impression that he was more insecure because I let it be known that I wasn't comfortable living with a notorious criminal.

'You'll get used to it,' he said one night, as he sliced through a blood-red steak with his knife. 'I'm still the same man you fell in love with and married. And at least you now know why it's so important that you always tell me where you are and who you're in contact with.'

Everything about my life was suddenly more intense and I withdrew further into myself. I felt trapped, isolated and more fearful about what the future held for me.

I didn't intend to tell my mum and sister what I'd learned, but it came out when the three of us next got together to celebrate Amanda's birthday.

They'd known for a while that I was no longer happy in my marriage so when the subject came up, I broke down and the whole sordid mess spilled out of me alongside my hot tears. They were both shocked, and it took me a while to explain how Tommy had managed to deceive me for so long. They urged me to leave him and Mum told me to report him to the police. They refused to accept that it wasn't as simple as that, and they weren't happy when I said I would sort things out – but in my own time. However, they did promise that they wouldn't confront him themselves and would keep my situation secret.

Tommy, meanwhile, became less guarded. He no longer felt the need to retreat to another room to make and take phone calls. And during the Sunday lunches at Ruby's house, the family no longer avoided talking about their nefarious activities.

By being more attentive and by eavesdropping on conversations, I learned more about what they did, including how they laundered money and trafficked drugs, and where some of the safety deposit boxes containing bundles of cash were located. I even dared to ask a couple of questions when they discussed in front of me such things as where to go in London to obtain illegal firearms. It was both bizarre and spine-chilling.

It also became apparent that there was a great deal of friction between Tommy and his brother.

'Liam has never been able to cope with responsibility,' my husband confided in me. 'That's why he hasn't been given much to do beyond acting as muscle and overseeing all our employees. I'm not confident that he'll hack it when he eventually takes over. If it wasn't for the fact that Liam's family, I wouldn't hesitate to get Jack Fraser to succeed me. He'd be more capable.'

The ringing of my phone wrenches me back to the present and I know instinctively that it's Tommy on the other end of the line. As I pick up the call, I remember the two angry voicemails he left earlier.

'Well, that makes a change,' he says as soon as I answer. 'You've decided to answer the fucking phone. Where have you been?'

My jaw goes tight, making it hard to speak. 'I'm sorry, Tommy. I had a late lunch with my sister and forgot to take my mobile with me. And then I went for a long walk before going to yoga class. I was desperate to keep busy.'

There's a long pause, during which I can almost hear his mind spinning.

'I'll give you the benefit of the doubt,' he says eventually. 'But don't let it happen again.'

I bite my tongue and suppress the rage that stirs inside me.

He asks me what I'm doing now and I tell him I'm getting ready for bed.

'Same here,' he says. 'Have you sorted out a visit yet?'

'I've put in a request,' I lie. 'I should hear back tomorrow.'

He asks me if I've seen anyone else today and I'm reminded of my conversation with Detective Brannigan outside the pub. But I don't mention it because that would be a bad idea.

It comes as a relief when the call ends without him raising the subject of the hidden camera. I wonder if that means he doesn't know that I found it or that it wasn't working anyway.

I find myself wrestling yet again with my awful predicament. And the same two questions continue to echo in my head: *How can I free myself from my husband's clutches? And how long before he discovers the secret that I'm keeping from him and everybody else?*

CHAPTER EIGHTEEN

I'm awake at six on Thursday morning, but I decide to stay in bed, curled up beneath the duvet. I just don't feel I can face the day ahead. My heart is beating uncomfortably hard and my head is already filled with too many unanswerable questions.

It's raining outside and I can hear it tapping at the window. The sound is soft and soothing and it brings to mind something that Tommy told me when he described what he has to listen to while lying on his prison bunk awaiting his hearing.

'The noise is off the fucking scale,' he said. 'Every day and every night, the nutters are shouting and screaming and banging on their cell doors. It drives me mad.'

I can't imagine what it's like to be locked up in prison. And for a man like Tommy it must be especially hard. On the outside, he lived like a lord and took orders from no one. He spoiled himself, did as he pleased, regardless of the consequences, and lived by his own set of rules. And he was arrogant enough to believe that the law would never catch up with him.

But, of course, it did eventually.

It was almost four months ago to the day when it finally did. I was by myself watching a film when Liam phoned out of the blue.

He was clearly shaken and told me that Tommy had been arrested after the police found a gun in his car. And he warned me not to say anything to the cops when they turned up at the flat.

He then hung up and before I could even take it in, the police were at our door. Detective Brannigan and a bunch of uniforms. I was told of Tommy's arrest and then shown a warrant giving them permission to search the flat.

They spent the best part of an hour going through our belongings and took stuff away in plastic bags. But thankfully they didn't find our hidden safe which contained cash and documents pertaining to some of the Firm's operations, along with information on various safety deposit boxes located across London.

Later that evening, Liam called again to inform me that his brother had been formally charged with being in possession of a firearm and would remain in custody to await trial.

'Jack wasn't with him today, so he was driving himself around town,' he explained. 'Whoever planted the gun in the glove compartment must have known that. They then tipped off the Old Bill, who stopped the car near our office in Vauxhall. Have you got any idea who could have done it? Have you spotted anyone acting suspiciously recently, Ems? You see, it could be someone who gained access to the car while it was parked under your block.'

'Well, I certainly haven't been made aware of anyone hanging around,' I told him. 'And only residents are allowed down into the car park.'

'So when was the last time you used the car?'

It sounded like a loaded question and I felt something cold move over my skin.

'I don't take the car out by myself, as you well know,' I replied icily. 'And the last time I was in it was when Tommy took me to your mum's house last Sunday.'

I wasn't sure I managed to allay his obvious suspicion of me, but I didn't care at the time. There were just so many other thoughts clamouring for attention in my mind. Foremost among them, the news that my husband was going to be held in custody at least until the start of the trial. How was I going to cope? What would be expected of me? Did I dare use it as an opportunity to break up with him?

Not having him around was strange at first. I had to be careful what I said and didn't say to people, especially to Liam and Jack Fraser. Tommy instructed them to keep an eye on me and one or both of them turned up almost every other day.

During one visit, Liam made me hand over my passport, saying that his brother didn't want me going on any trips abroad while he was inside. I was reluctant to comply but felt I had no choice.

113

Tommy insisted I go and see him in Wandsworth Prison and when I did, he explained that he felt he needed to prevent me fleeing the country in a panic. I told him that he was being ridiculous, but he insisted it was neccessary for his peace of mind.

'I know you must be going through hell, Ems, without me there,' he said. 'You're confused, scared and angry. And I fear you might be tempted to do something stupid. It's a fact that most wives whose husbands go to prison fail the ultimate test of commitment. I've heard that eighty per cent of those marriages end in divorce. Well, I'm not going to let that happen to us.'

From that day on, he became increasingly paranoid about what I might get up to without him being around. He made me tell him where I went, what I did and who I spoke to. But at the same time, he remained confident that evidence would emerge that would cause the case against him to collapse. Or, if it did go to court, that the jury would believe him.

'I swear to God that it wasn't my gun, Ems,' he said more than once. 'I wouldn't be stupid enough to have put it in the glove compartment if it was. But the police aren't bothering to investigate because they want to bring me down. My lawyer will use that against them in court. Meanwhile, our own people are on the case and I reckon they'll soon root out the bastard who is trying to frame me.'

But they didn't, of course, and now as I reflect on what he said to me back then, I realise that it was just wishful thinking. He'd been caught bang to rights and the police were able to offer up a solid case against him.

I remain in bed and manage to fall in and out of sleep. When I finally get up, it's almost ten o'clock. I feel cold and queasy, and my mouth is painfully dry.

I glance out of the window and see that the rain has stopped, but dark clouds still hang over London.

I make myself a cup of tea and after drinking it in the kitchen, I run myself a bath. I've got nothing planned for the day except to make arrangements to visit Tommy. I don't want to go to the prison but I know there's no way I can get out of it.

After the bath, I slip on my dressing gown and head back to the kitchen to pour myself another tea.

But just then the doorbell rings and I feel a ripple of unease. I suspect it's Liam and that he's here at the behest of his brother to find out why my phones are switched off again. And to check that I'm in.

But when I open the front door, it's not Liam who is standing there. It's Fraser.

'Let me guess,' I say. 'Tommy has told you to come and check up on me?'

He stares down at me, judgement in his eyes. 'We've been trying to contact you, Emma,' he says. 'There's something you need to know.'

'Really? What is it?'

'Tommy's been rushed to hospital. He was stabbed earlier this morning in the prison yard.'

CHAPTER NINETEEN

'One of our people in the prison called Liam minutes after Tommy was attacked,' Fraser says. 'We know he was stabbed in the stomach, but we don't know yet how serious it is.'

I feel the blood drain from my face and acid lodge in my throat.

'Which hospital is he in?' I ask.

'St George's in Tooting. It happened about three hours ago after a group of prisoners were allowed out for an early-morning exercise session in the yard.'

'But who would have done that to him?'

'A fellow prisoner,' Fraser replies. 'The finger is being pointed at one of the Albanians. The prison is full of 'em and they've been giving us problems lately, trying to muscle in on some of our operations.'

Fraser follows me into the kitchen and I ask him if he wants a cup of tea.

'I'd love one, thanks.'

The air wheezes in and out of my lungs as I fill the kettle again. I'm confused as to how I should feel about what's happened. I'm not so callous as to want my husband to die, but at the same time a small voice inside whispers that if he does, he'll no longer pose a serious threat to me.

'Are you okay, Emma?'

Fraser is standing to one side of me.

I turn towards him and nod. 'It's just come as such a shock, Jack.'

Fraser is a big, bad beast with a fearsome reputation, but I've never felt intimidated by him. He's always treated me with what I felt was genuine respect. And on those occasions when Tommy belittled me in front of him, I could tell it made him distinctly uncomfortable. So, I don't feel threatened now as I stand there, dwarfed by his height.

'Liam's already at the hospital and he's going to call me when he's got news about Tommy's condition. If he's well enough to have you visit, I'll take you straight there.'

I know there's no way I can get out of it so I don't bother to try.

'Does Ruby know?' I ask him.

'Yes. She was with Liam when he took the call and she's at the hospital too.'

I pour Fraser his tea and then switch my mobile on. The first thing I notice are the unanswered calls from both Liam and Fraser. And then I listen to a couple of voice-mails from Liam, who sounds angry as he relays the news about Tommy.

117

'I'd better go and get dressed,' I say and leave Fraser sitting on a stool at the breakfast bar as I head for the bedroom.

When I return to the kitchen a few minutes later, he isn't there. I walk along the hall and into the living room, where I find him inspecting the books on the shelving unit.

'The hidden camera is no longer there,' I tell him matter-of-factly. 'I found it and binned it.'

He looks embarrassed. 'I don't know what you're—'

I shake my head. 'Leave it out, Jack. I'm not stupid. Tommy must have put it inside the book to spy on me. So, don't insult my intelligence by denying it. And I'll be telling Tommy myself when I see him that I won't stand for anyone invading my privacy like that.'

He raises his brow and breaks into a grin. 'I can't say I blame you, but it had nothing to do with Tommy. He wasn't told about the camera. It was Liam's idea, but you'll be glad to know that since he installed it a couple of weeks ago, he hasn't been able to get it to work.'

This comes as a surprise and I can only think that Liam did it so that he could keep tabs on me without having to exert too much effort.

We don't have to wait long before Liam rings. Fraser puts his phone on speaker and tells him I'm listening in. Liam then informs us that Tommy is going to be all right.

'The blade missed his vital organs, so there was no internal damage,' he says. 'Luckily, the prison medics were on him before he lost too much blood. It was a single wound and it's been stitched up without the need for major surgery.'

'Is he conscious?' Fraser asks.

'He was and Mum and me were able to have a quick chat with him. But the doctor has given him medication to control the pain and he's now asleep.'

'Can he remember what happened?'

'He can. And he's given me the name of the guy who shafted him. As we suspected, it was one of the Albanians. A group of them surrounded him in the yard.'

'Has the guy been charged?' I ask.

'Not as far as I know, and there's every chance he won't be. Stabbings happen all the time inside and it's hard to get any prisoners to bear witness to them.'

Liam goes on to say that he's arranged for me to visit Tommy at one o'clock.

'Me and Mum will leave before then because they don't want too many people here at the same time. We'll catch up with you both later.'

As the call ends, I feel despair clawing at my insides. Sure, I'm sorry that Tommy has been hurt, but I can't help thinking that what has happened will only serve to make things much worse for me. He'll be even more paranoid from now on, which will probably mean he'll want to have more control over my life.

CHAPTER TWENTY

Before we leave for the hospital, I make us both some toast. I know that if I don't eat something now, I won't get a chance to until much later. I then switch on the TV to see if there's anything on the news about the attack on Tommy. And there is. His notoriety has prompted the BBC to carry a brief report. They show a photo of him and report that he's being treated in hospital after he was stabbed while exercising in the prison yard.

'His attacker hasn't yet been identified, but an investigation is under way,' the presenter says. 'Police have confirmed that the wound Mr Driscoll suffered is not life-threatening.' She goes on to remind viewers that just days ago Tommy Driscoll was sentenced to five years for possessing a gun. And adds a few lines about his alleged links to organised crime in London.

'It's good that Tommy knows who did it,' Fraser says when we're in his car. 'If the police don't sort the git out, then we will.'

'I don't understand how this kind of thing can happen in a prison,' I respond. 'Aren't inmates supposed to be searched and monitored and kept safe?'

He grins. 'Our jails have been dangerous shitholes for years and I speak from experience, having spent some time at Her Majesty's pleasure myself. They're overcrowded and too many staff are inexperienced. And it's bound to get worse. We're just fortunate that Tommy wasn't added to the rising death toll.'

It feels odd talking to Fraser without Tommy or Liam being around. In their presence, he has always kept his thoughts to himself, stayed in the background. I can't say I've ever been given a reason to dislike the man. And I don't feel ill at ease in his company. I know he's a brutal enforcer, and that he's committed God knows how many horrendous crimes. But he has never been anything other than polite to me, and unlike most of Tommy's other gangster mates, he's pretty articulate and doesn't use a profanity in every sentence.

I remember clearly the day that he won me over. We were at Ruby's house and she was praising her two sons to the hilt and saying how proud their father would have been of them. Fraser was sitting behind all three and we happened to glance at each other during the tedious mono-logue. He must have noticed how bored I was because he rolled his eyes and allowed himself a tight smile. I wanted to return the gesture, but I didn't dare because the others were all facing me and I feared I would land us both in trouble. But that moment stayed with me and made me feel a little less alone.

'Have you given any more thought to Tommy's list of rules?' he asks as we head towards Tooting.

The question takes me by surprise and I know I need to think before I answer.

'I'm not picking your brain for Tommy's benefit,' Fraser quickly adds. 'I'm just curious. And I can appreciate how hard it must be for you.'

I don't believe him, but I don't tell him that. He may not be as bad as Tommy's other gang members, but that doesn't mean I can put my trust in him.

'I still can't get my head around it,' I say. 'There's so much to take in and it's hard to see how it could possibly work.'

'Well, Tommy is hoping that you'll make it work, Emma. He really does love you and is terrified of losing you. I know what he's like, how controlling he is, but in that respect he's no different to other blokes I know who are used to getting their own way. It's who they are and they can't change.'

'But he's expecting too much of me, Jack. Surely you can see that. He wants me to be tied to him for five years while he serves his time in prison. That's a big ask.'

'Not to him it isn't. He takes the view that you're his wife and you took a vow to stick by him during good times and bad.'

I swallow hard, trying to moisten my throat, then turn to look out of the window. It's a dry but cold day and the sky is the colour of cement.

After a beat, I turn back to him and say, 'What do you think his reaction will be if I ask for a divorce?'

As soon as the words are out of my mouth, I regret saying them. What if he tells Tommy that I posed the question?

'If you've got any sense, you won't,' he responds without taking his eyes off the road. 'You've got too much to lose, Emma. And, for what it's worth, the last thing I want is for Tommy or Liam to order me to do something that I really don't want to.'

I don't sense any malice in his voice, but his words still send a shiver down my spine.

CHAPTER TWENTY-ONE

We arrive at St George's Hospital just before one. By then, my heart is in a sprint and a riot of emotions are running through me. Fraser's warning that I should not seek a divorce from Tommy has planted a lead weight in my chest. His words serve to emphasise the dreadful dilemma I'm faced with. They also remind me that I must never forget that Fraser is intensely loyal to his boss. He'll do whatever Tommy tells him to do, no matter how much pain it causes anyone else.

After that brief exchange of words in the car, we both lapsed into silence for the rest of the journey, which suited me.

Now, as I follow him inside, I try to steel myself for what's to come. My mind is reeling and I can feel the resentment brewing. I don't want to be here. I don't want to have to pretend to care about the man who is ruining my life. But I know I'll have to go along with the charade until I can find a way to release myself from the hold he has over me. Right now, I can't see how I can safely do that without having him turn on me or my family.

We go up to the floor where Tommy is being treated. There are two armed police officers standing next to the small reception desk. Fraser does the talking and tells the nurse behind it who I am. They're expecting me, but before going further, both me and Fraser are searched by one of the armed officers. My phone is taken away.

A doctor in a white coat appears suddenly and introduces himself. He tells me that my husband is awake and doing well but will need plenty of rest in the coming days.

'He was very lucky, Mrs Driscoll,' he remarks. 'The wound he suffered proved not to be fatal or that serious thanks to a combination of factors. The attack was rushed, the blade was short and thin, and it struck a rib before veering into muscle, thus avoiding any vital organs or arteries. Plus, a prison medic got to him quickly and stemmed the blood. So we repaired the damage with some stitches and I'm confident he'll make a full recovery.'

Fraser is then told he has to wait at reception and the officer who searched me takes me along a winding corridor to Tommy's private room. He leaves me in the hands of a uniformed prison officer who is standing outside.

The officer waits until the policeman is out of earshot and then speaks to me in a low, conspiratorial voice. 'Your husband is one of the inmates I'm prepared to do favours for, Mrs Driscoll. He's requested that I go against protocol and allow you to go in by yourself. I'm happy to oblige, but please don't mention it to anyone and bear in mind that I'll have to turf you out after fifteen minutes.'

It's another reminder of how much influence Tommy has, even in prison. Although unfortunately for him it's still not enough to keep him safe.

My husband is sitting up in bed with one arm attached to a drip. His face is grey and pallid and blood vessels bulge out of his temples. He no longer looks like God's gift to women and it's hard to believe that before I saw him for what he is we were once drunk with a passion for each other.

I walk straight over to the bed, take his hand and lean forward to kiss him on the forehead. I do it not out of affection, but because it's what he expects of me.

'I've been worried about you,' I tell him, trying to sound like I mean it.

He grins and places his other hand on mine. 'It's good to see you, Ems. You have no idea how much I'm missing you. It's not the same talking on the phone.'

I know that as his wife I should do my best to comfort him, to tell him what he wants to hear. But I can't. I won't.

This is all so messed up and as we look into each other's eyes, I feel a sudden urge to confess what I've done. At least then it will be out in the open and I can plead with him to forgive me.

But, of course, I resist, because I know he won't forgive me and that the punishment he'll inflict will be severe.

'How are you feeling this morning?' I ask him.

'I feel like shit,' he replies. 'But at least I'm not dead.'

'Do you know why the man attacked you?'

He bares his teeth suddenly and his eyes shine with a ferocious anger. 'The bastard saw what he thought was an opportunity to take me out of the picture so that his lot would find it easier to move in on the Firm's territory,' he seethes. 'But he fucked up and I'll make sure he lives to regret it.'

'But aren't you going to tell the police who he is? You told Jack on the phone that you—'

He puts a finger to his lips. 'You need to forget I said that, Emma. I want us to deal with the issue ourselves.'

I see the familiar gritty determination in his eyes, even though he must be feeling weak and vulnerable. The attack has knocked him for six, but it hasn't sapped all his strength or resolve.

'You've got to be careful, Tommy,' I say. 'The police will be on you like a shot if anything happens to him.'

'I'm not an idiot,' he says, with an edge to his voice. 'I won't be getting my own hands dirty. I don't intend to give the bastards any reason to extend my time behind bars. I promise you I'll be out in five years, Ems. And that's why I need you to hang in there. It'll pass quickly and when I'm released, we can start over again, have kids and enjoy life together.'

After a brief hesitation, I say, 'I'm not sure that—'

Tommy cuts me off by gritting his teeth and squeezing my hand. 'That's enough,' he snaps. 'I've told you I'm not going to let you go, so you need to accept that. You chose to marry me and I know you haven't fallen out of love with me. You're just scared and confused because of everything that's happened. That's why I'm having to take steps to keep us together.'

His words seem to suck the air out of the room and it's several seconds before I'm able to stammer out a response.

'But I'm my own person, Tommy. You can't expect me to abide by a set of rules you've drawn up to control me.'

He moves his face closer to mine and I can see the raw anger in his bloodshot eyes, the same eyes that once seduced me. I can't believe I was so wrong about him. 'You're living in La La Land if you think I'm going to let you walk away just because I won't be around for a few years,' he goes on. 'You're my wife, for fuck's sake. You should be ashamed of yourself. I've given you everything you've ever wanted and all I expect in return is loyalty.'

I consider telling him that all I ever wanted was to be loved and treated right. That the fancy flat and expensive lifestyle were never that important to me. But I hold it in for fear of how he'll react. Even as he lies in a hospital bed, I can't help feeling threatened by him.

He pulls his face back, but maintains his grip on my hand. 'I'll make sure you won't regret sticking by me,' he says. 'We're husband and wife and that will only change when one of us dies.'

A sense of unreality consumes me. I want to tell him that I don't love him any more. That I hate the thought of staying married to him. That he's a violent, abusive bully who is exactly where he belongs. But my brain won't let me form the words. So, I just stand there staring down at him, an uncomfortable tightness in my chest as I try to hide my loathing.

He loosens his grip on my hand and his features soften. 'You need to count yourself lucky that you've got someone who loves you as much as I do,' he tells me. 'All the while I'm inside, you'll be looked after. You'll have no money worries. My brother will make sure you're safe. And you and me will meet as often as possible to plan our future. Before you know it, we'll be back together and life will be good again.'

For a moment, I see myself through his eyes. The frail, submissive wife who is no match for someone as cruel and vindictive as he is. The air gets stuck in my throat and a bunch of conflicting thoughts and questions tumble through my mind. It takes all my self-control not to wrench my hand away from his and rush out of the room.

'You just have to have faith, Ems,' he says and gives me a smile that doesn't quite reach his eyes. 'As long as we love each other, things will turn out well in the end. And you do love me, don't you? Enough to stay the course?'

I force myself to smile back. 'Of course I do.'

It seems to reassure him, cheer him up and prompts him to go into a monologue listing all the places he wants to take me to when he's served his sentence.

I nod and feign interest, but it comes as a huge relief when the guard enters the room to tell me that my time is up.

CHAPTER TWENTY-TWO

I'm back in the car with Fraser, my heart pounding in my throat. He hasn't spoken to me yet, probably because he can see how shaken I am.

I close my eyes, breathe in deep through my nostrils, and fight to keep my emotions in check. We sit there for perhaps a minute before he breaks the silence.

'Do you want to tell me how it went?' he asks.

I open my eyes, clench my jaw and turn to look at him.

'There's not much to tell,' I say. 'He made it clear that I have to toe the line or else.'

'And what did you say to him?'

'That I would.'

'Sounds sensible to me.'

He starts the engine and we drive out of the car park.

'You look like you could do with a stiff drink or a hot coffee,' he says. 'The Firm's just taken over a new wine bar in Clapham. I think it'd be a good idea to stop there on the way back.'

I can't be bothered to object and I'm in no hurry to go home anyway.

'Fine by me,' I tell him, as he steers a course along the A24 through Tooting and Balham.

I continue to dwell on my encounter with Tommy. It's not right that I should be so unsettled by a conversation with my own husband, but that's what it's come to. How I wish I had never met the man. And what a mistake it was to rush into tying the knot with him. What is it they say? 'Marry in haste, repent at leisure.' I should have given myself more time to find out what he was really like. To realise that I was being sucked into a toxic relationship with a man without morals. But back then I made one bad decision after another and now I'm having to pay the price. It's as though I'm travelling along a tortuous road with no end in sight, and I'm clinging to my sanity by a thread.

The Firm's new wine bar is just off the A24 close to Clapham Common. It's small and classy-looking, with wooden benches out front.

Fraser parks the car at the kerb and we get out. I'm glad I've come and I'm tempted to treat myself to a glass of wine, even though I know it's not a good idea.

Thankfully, I don't feel uncomfortable in Fraser's company even though we've never socialised without Tommy being present. The strange thing is that even though I've known him for two years, he's still an enigma. I've no idea what he does in the privacy of his own home or if he has a girlfriend. I've never heard him speak about himself. But Tommy told me once that Fraser's mother was a prostitute who died of a drugs overdose when he was three. He never knew his father. He was in an orphanage until he was adopted at the age of seven by a couple who raised him on a council estate in Peckham. It was there he got involved with teenage gangs and ended up spending time in a youth detention centre. His criminal career progressed after his release and he did spells in prison for various offences, including causing grievous bodily harm, burglary and being in possession of stolen goods. He was recruited by Tommy six years ago and has been with him ever since, rising to the rank of his closest and most trusted henchman.

The door to the wine bar is ajar and Fraser leads the way inside. There's a small empty reception area and beyond it another door that stands open.

As I step through it into the bar area, I get an unwelcome shock. Just in front of me, sitting at one of the tables, is Liam Driscoll and his mother Ruby.

'They wanted it to be a surprise,' Fraser says without looking at me.

It is a surprise, just not a pleasant one. I feel a sharp spike of dread work its way under my ribs. The last time I sat around a table with these two, they made threats against me and handed me Tommy's cruel list of rules.

So, could it be they're about to ramp up the pressure even more?

'Come and join us, Emma,' Liam calls out. 'We need to have a chat with you.'

CHAPTER TWENTY-THREE

Ruby fixes me with a steely gaze as I take a seat at the table. Her skin is washed out and pale, and deep furrows have entrenched themselves in her brow. She doesn't look well; I can only suppose it's down to stress. I can sense the animosity coming off her in waves and my heart jumps. I feel a prickle of fear, a shot of adrenaline.

Liam suddenly draws my attention by asking me what I would like to drink. When I look at him, I see that his expression is composed, neutral, and not hostile like his mother's.

'You can have anything you want,' he tells me. 'Wine, spirit, coffee.'

I let out a breath between my teeth and opt for a glass of wine. I know I shouldn't, but I'm sure that one won't hurt.

'Do us a favour and open a nice bottle of Pinot,' he says to Fraser, who is standing behind me. 'And fill up a bowl with some savouries.' Liam looks back at me and adds, 'We won't be open officially under new management until next week. Tommy set his sights on this place before his arrest. We finalised the deal a few days ago and I thought I'd take the opportunity to show it to you and Mum.'

'It's a nice place,' I say, looking around at the bar and the collection of mirrors on the walls that make the room appear bigger than it is.

'It's about time we started acquiring some upmarket venues,' Liam says. 'I plan for this to be the first of many.'

He looks pleased with himself. I can tell that he wants to make his mark, to show that he knows what he's doing now that he's running the show.

Fraser places a glass of wine on the table in front of me and I avoid making eye contact with him.

Just as I go to pick it up, Ruby leans forward and speaks.

'I can't believe how lucky we are that Tommy is still with us,' she says, her voice husky with emotion. 'It broke my heart when I saw him this morning. Was he awake when you were there?'

'He was, and he was much better than I expected,' I answer. 'He was sitting up and very talkative.'

She nods. 'Thank God for that. I hope you didn't say anything to upset him.'

'Of course not. Why would I do that?'

She snorts dismissively. 'Well, from what I hear, you don't seem to care that your husband is having such a tough time of it.'

I feel my hackles rise. 'What's that supposed to mean?'

Ruby's about to respond, but Liam stops her by placing a hand on her arm and jerking his head in a small show of annoyance.

'You agreed to leave this to me, Mum,' he says. 'I don't want you to wind yourself up. It's not good for your heart.'

Ruby shoots her youngest son an angry look and lets out a frustrated sigh.

'Well, get on with it then,' she says to him. 'I want to go home. I have things to do.'

They're talking as though I'm not here and I feel my muscles tense.

'Look, what's all this about?' I ask, and I'm sure they can see that I don't want to be here any more than they do.

Ruby sits back in a huff and crosses her arms while Liam clears his throat.

'We've got you here because of the way you've been acting since the trial, Emma,' he says. 'You seem determined to make it difficult for us to ensure that you're following the rules and staying faithful to my brother. You don't answer his calls and you've even started switching your phone off. And all the time you fuck around like this, it means I have to stop what I'm doing to find out what you're up to. It's pissing me off as well as Tommy.'

'I've explained to Tommy why I didn't take his calls,' I say. 'But I don't see why I have to explain things to you.'

He shakes his head. 'Well, that's the problem. You see, you do have to answer to me. It's already been explained to you that me and Mum will act as Tommy's eyes and ears and you'll do what we tell you while he's banged up inside.'

'And is that why you hid the camera in the flat?' I ask him. 'So that you could spy on me?'

He shrugs. 'You weren't supposed to find it, but yeah, that's why it was there. Tommy doesn't trust you and he wants us to take steps to make sure you don't let him down. But don't worry, I can't be bothered to replace it.'

I can feel my heart banging against my ribs. A white-hot fury is building up inside me, but I know I can't afford to lose control. I don't know how far Liam will go to put me in my place. I have to accept that without Tommy around there's no one to rein in that unpredictable temper that Liam shares with his brother.

I pick up the wine glass and my hand shakes as I raise it to my lips. I take a sip.

'It's clear to us that you're not really taking this seriously enough, Emma,' he goes on. 'I think I need to remind you that if you don't follow the rules your husband has laid down, then there will be serious fucking consequences. Please believe me when I tell you that we won't hesitate to pay your sister's family a visit if you give us a reason to. Or maybe we'll get someone to drop in on your mum?'

I put my glass down on the table and sit there simmering, ready to blow.

'No one forced you to marry into our family, Emma.' This from Ruby, whose words are dripping with anger and contempt. 'If it was up to me, I'd have had Tommy leave you long ago. You're nothing more than a gold-digging deadweight. But he insists that without you he would rather be dead. And I'll do whatever it takes to keep my son happy. If that means keeping you in line for five years, then so be it.'

I can tell from the look in her eyes that she's enjoying my discomfort.

'But it's not right to do this to me,' I tell her. 'It's up to me if I decide to move on.'

Ruby shakes her head. 'That's not how it works. You're married to Tommy and he has every right to expect you to remain loyal, no matter how tough things get.'

'But when I married him, I didn't know what he was involved in. He lied to me. And you both know that he's been mentally and physically abusive to me.'

Her eyes flash and she jabs a finger at me. 'You're an ungrateful bitch. You ought to be thankful that my son loves you and wants to go on protecting you. I just pray that he eventually comes to his senses and casts you adrift.'

I feel tears stinging the backs of my eyes and the urge to tell her what I really think of her son is overwhelming. But I force myself to stay calm and get to my feet. 'You've made your point,' I say, my voice strained. 'Can I go now?'

It sounded like I was asking for permission and I wish I hadn't said it. I should have just stormed out.

It's Liam who responds. 'I think that's probably a good idea. I'll call you later.'

I rush out of the bar and into the street. Fraser follows and offers to take me home, but I turn him down and tell him to stay away from me.

'I need to be by myself,' I say. 'And don't worry, I won't turn my phone off.'

I'm no stranger to Clapham, so I decide to go for a walk to clear my head before looking for a taxi. The Common is only a couple of hundred yards away so I head there.

My mind is leaping all over the place and panic has seized my chest, making it hard to breathe.

Ruby has never spoken to me like that before and I'm convinced from the way the words seemed to flow right out of her that she must have been holding it in for some time. It's no surprise that she would like to see the back of me. But her determination to carry out her son's wishes is scary.

Her outburst is also a sobering reminder that all members of the Driscoll family share the same merciless trait. It's why my predicament is so dire – and why I fear it's likely to get much worse the way things are going.

CHAPTER TWENTY-FOUR

I stay on the Common for almost an hour, spending some of the time sitting on benches. There are a surprising number of people about, mainly joggers and mothers with small children. I envy them all and can't imagine that their lives are as fucked up as mine is.

I've been left in no doubt that I can't just end my marriage to Tommy. Unlike most men, he's in a position to stop me, through a combination of threats and brute force.

I recall my recent encounter with Detective Brannigan and what he said about providing protection for me and my family. It's tempting to believe that it's a way out, but I know in my heart that it's not. The Firm has more than a few coppers on its payroll and it would be virtually impossible for the police to ensure me and my family's safety. Plus, if I went down that road, I'd surely be ruining so many lives. Amanda and her husband would probably have to give up their jobs and move out of their home into some sort of witness protection scheme. And they'd always be worried that the Driscolls would seek vengeance somehow and that their girls would never be safe. My mother would also spend the rest of her life living in fear.

I call up an Uber and in no time I'm on my way back to the South Bank. Anger and frustration have settled in my chest like a sack of bricks. How can I be expected to hold myself together with so much pressure piled on me?

There's a part of me that now wishes Tommy hadn't survived the attack – not just because of what he's putting me through. The man is a shameless criminal and he must have been responsible for countless despicable acts of violence.

I once asked him if he had ever killed anyone and he responded with a grin, saying, 'No comment.' When I pushed him on it, he got angry and told me it was none of my business, which was all the answer I needed.

Once back in the flat, I make myself a mug of tea and a sandwich that I only manage to nibble at.

My nerves are frayed and I feel empty inside. The words that came out of Ruby's mouth have hit me hard, even though she's always been disrespectful towards me and, for that matter, anyone else she disapproves of. I once had the misfortune to see her swear at a waitress in a restaurant because the coffee she was served wasn't hot enough. It's no surprise to me that Tommy and his brother have ended up the way they are with her as a mother.

I slump down on the sofa and glance at the clock on the mantelpiece: 4.15 p.m. The prospect of a long, lonely evening by myself fills me with dread. I need to do something other than dwell on the fact that I've lost control of my life.

It suddenly occurs to me that I could go to my regular yoga class. I haven't been since before the trial and I miss it. It starts at five and takes place in a gym that's only a ten-minute walk from the flat.

I manage to push Tommy out of my mind as I change into my yoga outfit and pack my bag. Then I grab my coat and hurry out the door. I desperately need to work out because every muscle in my body is tense.

I arrive at the hall just as the class is about to start. I'm one of a group of fifteen people – eleven women and four men. The instructor, a young man named Ajay Singh, begins by getting us warmed up with some simple exercises. Then we spend the next hour bending, posing, stretching and folding our bodies, with soft music playing in the background. When the class ends, I do feel invigorated, which makes me glad I came.

I'm on first-name terms with most of the other pupils, but I've never let it be known who I'm married to. Before Tommy's trial, I went to great lengths to ensure my face did not appear in the newspapers. And while I can't be sure that none of the others saw me on the news or in the many reports of the trial, no one is saying anything.

The only person who does know about me is Ajay, and that's because he saw me with Tommy in a restaurant shortly before he was arrested on the gun charge. When the news broke, Ajay quietly approached me and asked how I was coping.

He does it again now, just as I'm about to exit the hall.

'It's good to see you, Emma,' he says. 'I can imagine you're having a very difficult time of it.'

He's standing in front of me, a tall figure with a bleached white smile and muscles bunched beneath a tight black T-shirt.

'That would be an understatement, Ajay,' I tell him. 'It feels like I have the weight of the world on my shoulders.'

His eyes spike with concern. 'Well, if you ever feel the need to talk about it with someone, I'm always here for you. Remember that.'

'I will and thank you, Ajay.'

I really do feel more relaxed and less anxious as I step out of the hall and head home. I hope it'll help me to get a good night's sleep.

Minutes later, I reach my block and enter the bright reception area. As I pass the front desk, Edward, the duty concierge, seizes my attention.

'Someone left this for you a short time ago, Mrs Driscoll,' he says. He's holding up a small white envelope and I step up to the desk and take it from him.

There's no address on the front, only – FOR MRS EMMA DRISCOLL, STRICTLY PRIVATE. It strikes me as odd that something like this would be hand-delivered and my mind starts to spiral with fresh fears and questions.

'Who delivered it?' I ask.

Edward shrugs. 'I'm afraid I don't know. I had to answer the phone in the back office and when I came out, it was here on the desk.'

I thank him and tear the envelope open as I go up in the lift, eager to know what it contains.

There's a single sheet of plain A4 paper inside and the words scribbled on it in black marker send a shiver down my spine.

I know you have a secret, Emma Driscoll. If you don't want me to tell your gangster husband and his family, then it will cost you. Be prepared to pay up. I'll be in touch. And if you know what's good for you, then you won't involve the police.

CHAPTER TWENTY-FIVE

When I'm back in the flat, I re-read the note and the words send a cold, crawling sensation down my spine again. I can't believe that I'm now being targeted by a blackmailer.

Questions rage in my mind. *Who the hell could it be? Is it a man or a woman? How could they possibly have found out? And what amount of money will buy their silence?*

At some point, I must have made a mistake, but I can't think when or where. I've been so bloody careful not to slip up, even to the extent of checking to see if I was being followed on those days when I might have given the game away.

Shit, shit, shit.

I feel the urge to have a drink, but I know I shouldn't. It takes a great deal of willpower to resist. Instead, I drop onto the sofa. I feel flat, disconnected, miserable and weighed down by dread. I find it hard to believe that this new threat has reared up out of nowhere. I feel more helpless than I ever thought possible.

I can't help wondering what has happened to the strong, confident woman I used to be. She would have been more resilient, better able to cope. But I'm no longer that person. My marriage to Tommy has made me weak and insecure. Oh, how I wish I could rewrite history.

I just can't think of who would seek to blackmail me like this. Is it someone I know? Or someone I've never met?

More questions pile up. When will I next hear from them? Will they just turn up and confront me in person or deliver another note? And if I do pay them, will that really be the end of it?

I draw a tremulous breath and close my eyes. I need to silence the voices in my head so that I can concentrate. But it's proving impossible, each one is demanding attention. And together they're creating so much noise, I want to scream.

I look at the clock and see it's 8 p.m. already. It's dark outside, but millions of lights sparkle across the city.

How am I supposed to get through the rest of the evening? I'm all by myself, a stream of tortured thoughts tearing through my head. All I want to do is close my eyes and shut them out. But I know that's not going to happen.

After about fifteen minutes, I get up and pour myself a lemonade, then put on some music in the hope it will lift my spirits and calm my nerves. But, instead, the songs serve only to stir the emptiness inside me.

I return to the sofa and try to get my thoughts in order.

I'm still sitting there thirty minutes later when my mobile rings. I see Amanda's name on the screen.

'Hi, sis,' she says when I finally pick up. 'Just wanted to make sure that you're okay.'

'Of course I am,' I fib. 'Just relaxing in front of the box.'

'Well, Chloe and Grace send their love to their favourite auntie. And they want you to know that they can't wait to see you again.'

'And I'm looking forward to seeing them too,' I say and feel the emotion rise in my throat. 'I'll make a point of coming over soon.'

'You'd better. And don't forget to stay in touch with Mum. She's been beside herself these past few days.'

'I won't. Promise.' I pause, and then continue: 'I thought you might have been calling to ask about what has happened to Tommy.'

'What do you mean?'

'Well, it's been on the news,' I tell her. 'He was stabbed this morning in the prison. He's in hospital and I went to see him there.'

I hear her draw a breath. 'Jesus Christ, Ems. I haven't seen the news today. How serious is he?'

'Not as serious as his attacker intended. It happened in the exercise yard. He was knifed in the stomach, but his wound wasn't too serious and has already been stitched up.'

'Blimey, that must have come as a shock.'

'It did.'

After a pause, she says, 'Well, I'd be lying if I said I feel sorry for him, Ems. In fact, I hope that whoever did it has better luck next time.'

I'm sure that if Amanda knew that Tommy was threatening to harm her own two daughters, she would happily plunge a knife in his gut herself.

We talk for another ten minutes or so and she urges me again to apply for a divorce. And again, I tell her it's too soon and I need to think it through some more.

After we end the conversation, my mind takes me back to the note from my anonymous blackmailer. It ignites a fresh blast of anxiety and my insides start doing somersaults.

I rack my brain again, trying to come up with a name, a face, a clue to their identity. But I draw a blank, and it's another five minutes before a thought pops into my head.

It strikes me like a slap around the face and I wonder why it hasn't occurred to me before now. I experience a flush of excitement as I hurry out of the flat, closing the front door behind me.

Edward is still behind the front desk, where he will be until his shift ends tomorrow morning. He greets me with a warm, generous smile and puts down the book he's been reading.

'I need a favour, Edward,' I say immediately. 'Would it be possible for me to have a look at the security camera footage?'

His eyes narrow inquisitively. 'May I ask why, Mrs Driscoll?'

'I want to know who delivered the note you passed onto me earlier. You said you were in the office when it arrived.'

'That's right.'

'Well, there's no indication who it's from and it's important that I find out.'

I can't see why he would object, but I'm ready to make a fuss if he does.

'I don't see a problem with that,' he says, to my relief. 'If you come into the office, Mrs Driscoll, I'll check the recording.'

The office is about the size of my walk-in wardrobe and the security camera recorder is on the small desk.

'I believe it was about five o'clock when the note was delivered, shortly after you left the building,' Edward says as he sits down and fiddles with the machine.

Within seconds, footage showing an empty reception area fills the screen on the attached laptop. I see myself enter from the left on my return from the yoga class and watch as Edward hands me the envelope.

He scrolls backwards through the tape until we finally see someone enter the reception carrying an envelope in one hand. I judge it to be a man from his build and the chunky trainers on his feet. He's wearing a knee-length dark parka with a fur hood covering his head.

'This must be him,' Edward says. 'But unless he looks directly up at the camera, I don't think we'll get to see his face.'

And we don't, because he keeps his head down as he walks up to the desk and drops the envelope on top. Then he turns and walks back out of the building without looking up.

'Damn it!' I blurt out.

'It seems like he doesn't want to be identified,' Edward comments. 'Is that a matter of concern to you, Mrs Driscoll?'

I don't want him to know how alarmed I am, so I shake my head. 'No, it's not a problem, Edward. I'll find out who he is some other way. Thank you for letting me see it.'

'Not at all. And before you go, please allow me to say how sorry I am about what's happened to your husband. If there's anything else I can do for you, then please don't hesitate to ask.'

'That's very kind of you, Edward,' I say. 'I appreciate it. Goodnight to you.'

I head back upstairs with the footage of the man in the hooded parka running on repeat in my mind. I still don't know who he is, but the sight of that sinister figure has turned my blood cold and sent my pulse galloping.

CHAPTER TWENTY-SIX

I have another restless night. Despite how tired I am, I get hardly any sleep. When I do drop off, the dreams taunt me.

One of them takes me back to the party to mark Tommy's thirty-fourth birthday. It was held in one of the clubs he owns and because he'd been out doing business, I had to meet him there.

I turned up in a low-cut, off-the-shoulder dress that I bought that afternoon and thought he would love. But as soon as I took off my coat, I could tell from his face that he wasn't impressed.

He leaned forward to kiss me and whispered, 'What the fuck possessed you to wear that? You look like a tart.'

He hardly spoke to me during the rest of the evening and showed me no affection. I managed not to cry or storm out because I didn't want to ruin the occasion or let my mum and sister know that something was wrong.

Instead, I played the part of the loving wife and pasted a smile on my face for everyone's benefit.

When we got home, he let rip and told me it was time that I stopped embarrassing him with my choice of clothes. He went through my wardrobe and threw some of my dresses and tops in a bin bag.

'We'll go out together and buy you some new clobber,' he said. 'I don't think it's too much to expect you to look smart and decent rather than frumpy and sleazy.'

I was shocked and angry and told him that it was up to me what I wore.

'Not now that we're married it isn't,' he replied.

As usual, he had convinced himself that his actions were justified and he wasn't being unreasonable. Even if he didn't believe that, he didn't care.

The following day, he took me to the West End and bought me some new clothes, but only ones that met with his approval.

I forced myself to act like I was grateful, but inside I was fuming. My marriage was becoming increasingly intolerable. I felt scared, trapped and helpless. I no longer had any autonomy. I couldn't make decisions or act without his permission.

And yet I still didn't leave him because I was too afraid of what would happen to me if I did.

And now I face a new threat from a mysterious black-mailer. Someone who knows what I've done and why I'm having to keep it a secret.

I wonder if I'll be contacted again today. If so, will it be through another note delivered to reception? Or will it be by phone – do they have my number?

The questions roll around inside my head as I shower, ready for the new day. By the time I'm dressed, my mind has conjured up various worst-case scenarios. What if the blackmailer is waiting to pounce on me when I next venture out? What if they ask for more money than I can lay my hands on? What if I pay up and they still tell Tommy what they know?

My phone rings at ten, making me jump. I suck in a breath and hold it until I see Fraser's name on the screen.

'Hello, Jack.' I relax a little.

'Morning, Emma,' he says. 'I'm ringing to say that Liam has had confirmation from the hospital that Tommy is allowed one visitor today and he wants it to be you. I can pick you up at eleven.'

My scalp prickles at the thought of seeing my husband again today. It was something I hadn't expected, but I should have. There's no way I can get out of it, so I tell Fraser I'll be waiting for him.

I spend the next hour trying to keep busy as uncertainty beats in my heart. I tidy the flat, put some clothes in the washing machine and tell myself that I can't give up hope, even though things are becoming more complicated and frightening.

Fraser calls me again when he's outside. I go downstairs and ask the concierge if any mail has arrived for me. Edward's shift has ended and a portly Scot named Sean is manning the desk.

'Not as yet, Mrs Driscoll,' he replies politely. 'Are you expecting something?'

'No, I'm not, but if someone does drop something off, could you please get their name for me?'

'Of course. No problem.'

Fraser is standing on the pavement with his back up against his car.

'Did you sleep well?' he asks.

'Not really. What about you?'

He shakes his head. 'A bad night. We've got a lot going on and I'm knackered.'

It occurs to me that I've never seen him looking so tired and worn out. His eyes are puffy and sandpaper stubble coats his chin. It's obvious that Tommy's sentence is taking its toll on all of us, but for different reasons.

As soon as we're in the car, he updates me on Tommy's condition.

'Liam spoke to him earlier this morning and he's doing fine. The pain is being controlled and he's looking forward to seeing you.'

'Have the police found out who attacked him?'

'Apparently not.'

'Which means that Tommy hasn't told them.'

'Correct.'

There's no point pursuing that particular issue, so I don't.

At the hospital, we go through the same procedure as before. When I enter Tommy's room, he's sitting up in bed and the drip is no longer attached to him.

We kiss, even though it pains me, and I pull over a

chair to sit next to him. He grabs my hand and squeezes it tight.

'They reckon I'm doing much better than expected and will probably be discharged in a couple of days,' he says.

I can't help being pleased about that because at least it means he'll be back behind bars.

'That seems a bit too soon,' I say.

He nods. 'I know, and it's a shame because it's much more comfortable in here. But they say I just need to rest and the medical facilities at the prison can handle that.'

I don't have much to say and he does all the talking, mostly about himself. Throughout, my mind keeps jumping back to the blackmail note. It occurs to me that Tommy might well know the man who delivered it. Could it be one of his own people? Perhaps Tommy got someone to start following me soon after he was arrested? And whoever it is might have decided to keep my secret from him – for now at least.

My thoughts are so loud in my head that as I come to, I suddenly realise I haven't been listening to Tommy at all and have no idea what he's just said. But as I tune in again, the words that spill from his mouth next cause me to bristle with indignation.

'. . . Anyway, Ems, we both need to adjust to this new reality,' he says. 'Since we've been married, I've done all I can to make you happy and comfortable, even though you didn't always seem to appreciate it. Now I have to ensure that you stay loyal to me because I love you and I'm not prepared to lose you.'

He pauses to draw in a long breath that he releases in a sigh. Then, after a bit of lip chewing, he continues without taking his eyes off me.

'The last four months have been sheer fucking torture thinking that you might be tempted to stray. I know that over the next five years the mental and emotional strain on both of us is going to be huge. That's why you need to understand that I'm going to have to be cruel to be kind. If I'm not, then what we have will be lost and that'd be a tragedy. I have no doubt that you'll thank me when I'm finally released and we can rekindle our relationship and start a family.'

I can tell he believes every word he just spoke. To him, it makes sense and is perfectly reasonable. But to me, it feels like I've just been given a harsh and undeserved prison sentence of my own. His sentence is five years. Mine will be a lifetime.

CHAPTER TWENTY-SEVEN

Thank Christ I was only allowed to stay with Tommy for fifteen minutes. Any longer and I might have got into trouble by saying something he didn't want to hear.

Fraser and I don't say much to each other on the drive back to the South Bank. He seems preoccupied and keeps checking his watch. I take a call from Amanda, who wants to know how I am and ask about my husband.

'As a matter of fact, I'm just leaving the hospital,' I tell her. 'Tommy is looking much better and I'm fine. Jack is taking me home, so do you mind if we talk later?'

'Of course not. Just look after yourself, Ems.'

'I will.'

Before Fraser drops me off, he tells me he'll let me know when I can see Tommy again.

'If you need anything, just give me or Liam a call,' he shouts as he drives away.

As I close the front door behind me, I feel a sob rising

in my chest. Oh, how I wish I could share my problems with someone, get their perspective on my wretched dilemma. But I can't because it would place them in danger too.

I spend most of the afternoon lying fully clothed on my bed feeling all kinds of messed up. Only when my rumbling stomach becomes too irritating to ignore do I force myself to get up and eat a ready meal from the fridge.

My head eventually gets to the point where it feels like the walls are closing in on me and that's when I decide to get out of the flat for a while. I decide to go to a yoga class again. Hopefully, a workout will relieve some of the stress that has me in its grip.

It's another busy class and I go through the motions, along with everyone else. But this time my heart isn't really in it. I find I'm too distracted.

When it's over, Ajay approaches me with a concerned look on his face.

'I hope you don't mind me saying this, Emma, but I got the impression you didn't enjoy this evening's class. Am I right?'

I nod. 'You are, Ajay, and I'm sorry. It's been a bad day and I found it hard to concentrate.'

He glances at his watch. 'Look, I've got a bit of time before I have to be anywhere. Why don't you join me for a quick drink? You can tell me as much as you want to or just chill out and say nothing for an hour or so.' He smiles. 'I'll do the talking for us both.'

I instinctively want to say no, but as I check my watch and see that it's still only six o'clock, I change my mind.

The thought of spending another night on my own is too hard for me to bear.

'You're right,' I tell him. 'It'll probably do me good.'

We go to a familiar pub not far from my block. It's quite busy, but we find a corner table and Ajay asks me what I want to drink. I opt for a non-alcoholic beer and so does he. Like me, he's been steering clear of the booze.

'I want you to know that as well as being your yoga instructor, I'm also your friend,' he says once he's seated. 'So, if there's anything I can do to help you through this, you only have to ask.'

'That's kind of you, Ajay,' I tell him. 'And I want you to know that I appreciate the fact that you're not at all judge-mental. I know that a lot of people regard me with contempt because I'm married to a notorious criminal.'

'Just because you're married to him doesn't mean you're like him, Emma.'

During the conversation that follows, I refrain from giving much away. I don't tell him about Tommy's rules or that I'm being targeted by a blackmailer. I simply explain how hard it is for me to adjust to this new life and how I can't decide what to do with myself. I convey the impression that I intend to wait for my husband and that, to fill the time, I'll probably get a job. He's a good listener and doesn't ask many questions, which I'm grateful for.

After another beer, he has to go. As we get up, I assure him that I have every intention of continuing with the yoga classes.

'That's great to hear, Emma,' he says. 'It will help you to get through this terrible time. Trust me on that.'

Once back outside, we give each other a brief hug before we go our separate ways.

Walking back to my flat, a wave of tiredness crashes over me, although the prospect of sleep still seems distant.

I'm halfway home when I start to feel the hairs on the back of my neck stand up, while at the same time I suddenly experience a deep sense of unease. And then it hits me: I think I'm being followed. I stop abruptly and look around, but I appear to be the only person on the street. I can't see anyone lurking in the shadows.

You're imagining it, I tell myself. *Your mind is playing tricks.*

Nevertheless, the feeling that I'm being followed stays with me long after I walk into my building. And the thought that it might be my blackmailer adds to the crippling anxiety that again keeps me awake for most of the night.

CHAPTER TWENTY-EIGHT

On Saturday morning, Tommy's patronising voice from yesterday is still in my head. The more I listen to it, the harder it is to see how I can ever be free of him. He has a hold over me that is as tight as a hangman's noose

But, right now, I don't know who I should be more afraid of – him or the person who has decided to blackmail me.

I shake my head to dislodge the image of the note I received, but my mind flicks straight back to the words.

I know you have a secret, Emma Driscoll. If you don't want me to tell your gangster husband and his family, then it will cost you. Be prepared to pay up. . .

I decide not to lie in bed because I'll just keep mulling on everything and that will only make me feel worse. Instead, I choose to go out for breakfast and plan to pick up a few things from the local convenience store on the way back. Since Tommy's arrest, I haven't had to make sure that the cupboards and fridge are stocked up. I don't eat much, but even so, there's hardly any food left in the flat, though there are typically plenty of unopened bottles of wine and spirits in the bar.

Being by myself again has taken some getting used to and even after four months, it still feels strange. There are things I really miss, including those times when my husband was on his best behaviour and even managed to make me feel good about myself. Tommy would take me to expensive restaurants for lunches and dinners, and to classy casinos, where he'd let me squander hundreds of pounds on the tables and then still be able to laugh about it. And there were the regular visits to the shops in Knightsbridge, including Harrods, where he would buy me things I didn't need and sometimes didn't even want.

There's no doubt that he spoiled me rotten, and sometimes I couldn't help but feel guilty. But I now suspect that his aim wasn't just to make me happy. It was also to give me lots of reasons not to leave him.

It's a pleasantly sunny day, but as I walk towards Borough Market, I'm reminded of the previous evening when I sensed that I was being followed. A dark unease pushes its way into my mind and I have to keep looking behind me. There are lots of people around, but it doesn't appear like any of them have their sights set on me.

I go to a café I know and order a cup of tea and a large pastry. Then I check my phone browser to see if there are any fresh stories about Tommy, but there aren't.

Just as I put the phone back in my pocket, it pings with a text message from Fraser. He tells me that I won't be able to see Tommy today because he's still only allowed one visitor and Liam needs to go. I message back thanking him for letting me know, and of course I refrain from saying what a bloody relief it is.

After breakfast, I go to the store and fill a plastic bag with a few groceries. Then I walk slowly back along the South Bank.

As I enter our building, Sean, today's concierge, is behind the reception desk. When he sees me, he waves me over. As I approach, he holds up an envelope, causing my stomach to flip.

'This arrived for you, Mrs Driscoll,' he says promptly. 'A man dropped it off not long after you went out. I asked him his name as you requested, but he didn't respond and rushed straight out. I couldn't even see his face because he didn't look up and his head was covered by a hood.'

He hands me the envelope and the expression on my face must make him hesitate and he asks if I'm okay.

'Yes, Sean. Just tired.'

I clutch the envelope tightly in my hand as I go up in the lift. I don't open it until I'm in the flat and when I do, it chills my blood. Inside is a single colour photograph.

As soon as I lay eyes on it, I feel an icy chill in my gut because I now know who is blackmailing me.

CHAPTER TWENTY-NINE

The photo was taken ten weeks ago on a rare night out on the town with two friends I hadn't seen in a very long time. I'd decided to make the most of being free from Tommy because I didn't know how long it would last. Plus, I'd grown tired of being cooped up in the flat and only leaving it to visit him in prison, where he was on remand awaiting the trial.

I put my hair up for the occasion to try to make me look different from my usual style – I didn't want anyone to recognise me as the wife of a notorious gangster who had been all over the news recently. My pals, twin sisters Sonja and Kim, were sworn to secrecy and perfectly understood why I didn't want anyone else to know that I was going on a girls' night out. It was agreed that I'd use the name Bella and remove my wedding ring. I trusted them implicitly because we had grown up together and been best friends at school. The only reason that we'd lost touch was because eight years ago they had moved to

America with their parents. But after moving back to London they were keen to reconnect despite the recent news about Tommy.

The evening started with a pub crawl and ended up at a house party in Southwark. Sonja, Kim and I were invited to the party by a group of four guys we met at one of the pubs. They were celebrating someone's thirtieth birthday and wanted some female company. We were happy to oblige and they struck me as a good-natured bunch even as they were throwing back the booze.

By then, I was on my fifth cocktail and enjoying letting my hair down. It made me realise that I'd forgotten what that was like, how much fun and liberating it could be.

The house was a three-storey terraced affair close to the Old Vic and only about a fifteen-minute walk from my home. To this day, I have no idea who lived there, but when we arrived, the place was already packed.

We weren't the only ones who didn't know the host or most of the other guests and that made us feel comfortable. It wasn't long before the three of us were mingling and helping ourselves to drinks from the free bar that was set up in the kitchen.

It was approaching midnight when I found myself in the small back garden wondering where Sonja and Kim had got to. I was sipping Prosecco under a starlit sky and thinking about all the nights out I'd spent with Tommy, usually at bars and clubs run by the Firm. During our first few months together, I really enjoyed them. But that changed when he began encouraging me to wear clothes that met with his approval, and he monitored what I drank, both of which I found infuriating. The one time I got tipsy he accused me of being an embarrassment and got one of his guys to take me home.

He would also make a huge fuss whenever I wanted to go out with friends. It would trigger him into a state of paranoia. The few times that I did go out, he pestered me with phone calls and text messages, and insisted on having me picked up at the end of the evening. Sometimes he would even tell me when that should be. I would then be questioned about where I'd been and who I'd spoken to. His possessiveness was off the scale, and so too was the level of insecurity he displayed.

So being at this party without him knowing was an experience to be savoured. I was even able to appreciate some male attention without worrying that it would lead to Tommy blowing a fuse and threatening anyone he thought was showing an interest in me.

I was thinking how great it was to have regained at least some of my independence when a guy suddenly stepped forward and introduced himself as Ruben. He handed me a fresh glass of Prosecco and said, 'I saw that your glass was empty and thought I'd save you the trouble of going inside to get a refill.'

I'd spotted him earlier in the living room and it had occurred to me that he was the best-looking bloke there. He was a lean thirty-something, wearing a pale green shirt and tight black trousers. His dark hair was spiky and quiffed, and his eyes were vibrantly blue.

I took the glass from him and we started chatting. I told him that my name was Bella and I lived in Chelsea.

At this point, I had no intention of stepping over the line and being unfaithful to my husband, even though I was no longer happily married. But the longer we talked and the more I drank, the more I struggled to resist the obvious spark between us.

Ruben told me he was a financial adviser in the city and a close friend of the man throwing the party. I warmed to him immediately and I was so enjoying his company that when Sonja and Kim came over at one in the morning and said they were leaving, I told them I was going to stay a little longer and would find my own way home.

Kim gave me a wink, while Sonja told me that I deserved to have some fun after all the crap I'd been through.

I was having such a good time that I soon found myself acting like an uninhibited singleton. Truth be told, I saw it partly as a way to get back at Tommy for all the pain and humiliation he had subjected me to. And for lying to me for so long about who he really was. Surely if it was okay for him to keep things from me, then it was okay for me to keep things from him?

On that night, I was back to being the person I used to be – fun-loving, outgoing, impetuous and tactile. One thing led to another and I let Ruben steer me back into the house by hand. Then I let him kiss me. Then I sat on his lap on the sofa and I even let his mate take a photo of us on his phone. It didn't occur to me that any of what I was doing would ever get back to Tommy and what it would mean for me if it did. I was just so caught up in the freedom, the revelry, that I just let it happen.

This was the photo that was delivered by the hooded man. On the back was scrawled the message: *This is one of several pics I have of the night we spent together while your crime lord husband was languishing in jail. How do you think he'll react if he gets to see them? And if I let him know that we fucked? You'll hear from me again soon, so be prepared to pay up.*

It shames me to say that soon after that photo was taken, I went on to have sex with Ruben in one of the upstairs bedrooms. For the first time in almost a year, I didn't have to fake an orgasm.

I was guilt-free while it lasted – I was drunk, turned on and carried away by the sheer magic of the moment. It wasn't until I was dressed and back downstairs that the enormity of what I'd done finally hit me. But even though I was still giddy with drink, I at least had the sense not to compound my mistake by telling Ruben the truth about myself. Instead, I continued the lie that I was Bella Haskins and fobbed him off with a fake phone number. I also told him that my brother was staying with me so he couldn't come and spend the rest of the night at my flat.

Ruben said he would love for us to meet again and I lied and nodded, telling him to ring me. He then called me a cab and accompanied me outside when it arrived. He informed the driver that I wanted to go to Chelsea and handed over a twenty-pound note. As I got in, he leaned into the car and gave me a long, lingering kiss on the lips and said he'd had a wonderful evening. In truth, I had, too, and I told him so. If it hadn't been for my situation, I would have been keen to see him again. But, of course, that was out of the question.

As soon as the cab pulled away, I told the driver that I'd changed my mind and wanted to go to the South Bank instead. 'You can keep the twenty quid,' I added.

CHAPTER THIRTY

So, the man I had a one-night stand with is the person who is blackmailing me. Ruben the financial consultant. But I don't know if what he told me about himself is true, of course. He may well have lied just as I did.

It's hard to believe that the same sweet-talking man who charmed me into sleeping with him the very first night we met would stoop so low. I haven't seen or heard from him since then because I gave him a fake phone number. But I have thought about him a lot. I can only assume he saw me on the TV news, realised that I had lied to him and took the trouble to find out where I really lived. Now he's seizing on what he believes to be an opportunity to screw some money out of me.

In a strange way, it's come as a relief that he obviously doesn't know the real secret I'm desperate to keep. If he did, I'm sure he would be threatening me with that rather than just a bunch of compromising photos.

But that's not to say that I won't do whatever I can to stop Tommy from seeing them. I don't want my husband to know that I lied to him, that I cheated on him, that he's right not to trust me. Tommy will carry out his threat for sure against me or my family. And he'll feel justified in doing so. I'll have no excuse, no way of mitigating my actions in his eyes.

This latest unsettling development in the ugly, twisting saga that has become my life makes me want to kick, punch and hit out at the walls around me. I'm being smothered by a dark blanket of despair and I have no idea how to crawl out from under it.

I go over to the balcony doors, clamp my arms around myself, and stare out across London. The sun is peering through the clouds and shedding its glow on the surface of the Thames.

I cast my mind back to that fateful night at the party and realise how stupid I was. How thoughtless. How wrong. I gave myself to a man who won me over with his charm and smooth chat-up lines. But just as with Tommy, it was all a front, concealing another heartless monster behind the mask.

I'm still trying to get my head around this latest discovery when Tommy calls. He wants me to know that he's sorry I won't be able to visit him today.

'Liam is coming this afternoon,' he says. 'He's got some business he needs to discuss with me.'

'Not to worry, I understand,' I reassure him, and I'm so pleased that I won't have to face my husband with this new cloud hanging over me. 'How are you doing?'

'I'm improving all the time. What are you up to?'

'I had to pop out to get some shopping. I'm thinking of doing some painting this afternoon to pass the time.'

Fortunately, it turns out to be a short conversation because the doctor appears in his room to check him over.

'I'll call you later if I can,' Tommy concludes. 'You have a good day, Ems. And I'll be thinking of you.'

It's a huge weight off my chest to know that I won't have to visit him. Yesterday was hard enough, and I know that each time I see him, it's going to get increasingly harder. I'd pinned my hopes of a new life on Tommy going to prison for a long time, leaving me free to divorce him so that I could move on. But that's not how it's turned out and I'm now being forced to contemplate a number of wretched scenarios. If I file for divorce, go to the police or simply refuse to follow his outrageous demands, then I have to accept that he'll make sure I live to regret it. If I confess to what I've done and throw myself on his mercy, it's unlikely he'll show any.

And then there's the added complication of the one-night stand who has come back to haunt me. The man who I suspect was watching me last night when I left the pub.

It feels like I'm operating on autopilot. I'm only half aware of what I'm doing and what's going on around me.

There was a time when I looked forward to weekends: shopping, nights out, visiting friends, binge-watching box sets. But now I mostly spend them alone because Tommy succeeded in isolating me from almost everyone I cared for and who cared for me.

There's nothing on the news that interests me, so I switch the TV off and try to decide what to do for the rest of the day. I could sit here in the flat and dwell on my problems, including how to respond to being blackmailed. Or I could go for a walk and try to take my mind off them. Eventually, I come to the conclusion that I need some company otherwise my mood will plunge me to a new low.

I grab my phone, call my sister and ask her if she'd mind if I pop over.

'That's really freaky,' Amanda says. 'I was just about to ring you and invite you to lunch. Mum's coming over and the girls would love to see you!'

'In that case, I'll be there as soon as I can.'

I take a taxi to my sister's home in Kennington. It's an end-of-terrace house close to the Oval cricket ground.

As soon as I walk through the door, I feel a sharp tug of love for the people who I care about the most in the world. They're all there – Amanda and her husband Jacob, my two lovely nieces, Chloe and Grace, and my mother.

I put on a show for their benefit, acting like I'm on top of things, happy and not struggling emotionally.

The girls are all over me and it's a joy to see them. Eight-year-old Chloe with those impossibly light freckles scattered across her always-smiling face. And ten-year-old Grace with her sparkling green eyes set in soft olive skin. I love them as though they're my own and I can't bear to think of them being harmed in any way because of me.

My mum is all smiles, though she can't quite conceal

the fact that she's been worried about me. I can tell from the way she keeps holding my hand and hanging on to my every word. She looks older than the last time I saw her. Her eyes are pouchy and raw and I'm sure she's lost weight.

During lunch at the dining table, we all avoid talking about my husband. But that changes after Jacob takes his daughters on what I suspect is a pre-planned visit to the shop for some sweets. As soon as they're gone, Amanda and Mum start asking questions, their faces pinched with concern.

I tell them again that I'm still considering my options and that divorcing Tommy is one of them. But as the lies tumble out of my mouth, I feel a twist of guilt in my stomach.

There's so much I want to tell them. Why I can't just walk away even though he's going to be behind bars for years. That he's threatened to hurt them if I do. That, only days ago, he got someone to take a photo of Amanda and the girls leaving the house just to make a point. And that even if I go to the police, their lives will be upended and they still won't be safe from the Driscoll family. I don't suppose they would ever forgive me, even though they know that when I married Tommy I wasn't aware of his true nature.

In response to my empty promises, they both make clear their frustration, their disappointment, their surprise that I'm not more proactive and decisive. All I can do is try to reassure them that I know what I'm doing.

Thankfully, Jacob and the girls are soon back from the shop and the grilling ends.

For the next hour, we force ourselves to talk about other things, including Christmas, their holiday plans for next year and how Chloe and Grace are doing at school.

Just before I leave to go home, my sister takes me to one side, gives me a hug and thanks me for coming.

'I know there's something you're not telling us, Emma,' she says. 'If Tommy is still giving you grief, then you should go to the police. They'll do something about it.'

'There's really nothing for you to worry about,' I tell her.

She shakes her head. 'I just don't buy it. I know what Tommy Driscoll is like and I'm sure that being locked up won't stop him trying to control you. Threaten you even.'

'Of course he isn't. You're letting your imagination run wild.'

Moments later, I bid everyone farewell. As I walk out to the taxi that's waiting for me, my stomach is churning and I can feel the sting of guilty tears in my eyes.

CHAPTER THIRTY-ONE

I'm back in the flat by four thirty and wishing that I'd stayed longer at my sister's. I didn't because the guilt was dragging me down and making me feel uncomfortable.

I hate how pathetic I've become and how easy I now find it to lie to my own family. And my hatred for Tommy is growing by the minute because he's put a chain around my neck with his dark threats and willingness to ignore all moral boundaries.

After I remove my coat, I take a moment to check myself in the hallway mirror. It's like looking at someone I hardly know and I have to swallow down a surge of self-pity. My face is grey, the skin tight, and the light in my eyes is gone. It's striking how much of an impact this is all having on me physically as well as mentally.

Ten minutes later, just as I'm powering up the laptop to check my emails, Tommy calls. He sounds tired, his voice low and croaky.

He begins by asking me if I managed to paint a picture.

'No, I didn't,' I answer. 'I went to Amanda's for lunch instead. Mum was there and it made a nice change. I've only just got back.'

'Do they know what happened to me?'

'They do, and they asked me to pass on their best wishes.'

His sneering response is not unexpected. 'I find that hard to believe, Ems. I reckon they're gutted that I survived.'

'That's not fair, Tommy. Granted, they've never put you on a pedestal, but they would never want you to be harmed,' I lie.

'Yeah, right. Have you told them that you're going to stick by me?'

My spine goes rigid, but I manage not to hesitate. 'Of course I have. I had that conversation with my sister and mum straight after the trial.'

'And how did they react?'

'They said it's up to me what I do, but they pointed out that it's going to be difficult for both of us.'

'It doesn't have to be difficult,' Tommy responds sharply. 'If you put your heart and soul into it like I will, then there's no reason for there to be too many problems. You just have to accept that things will be different for a few years, but as long as we both stay committed to the marriage, there'll be a bright light at the end of the tunnel.'

I squeeze my eyes shut and pinch the bridge of my nose with my free hand. I'm not sure how to reply and fortunately I don't have to.

'Look, I have to go,' he says. 'My officer friend has just

poked his head through the door to warn me that the doctor is on his way. I'll call you tomorrow.' There's a short pause, then: 'In the meantime, make sure you don't do anything else to fuck me off. If you do, you'll be taught another lesson.'

He hangs up before I can ask him what prompted that last remark. His voice had suddenly taken on an angry tone and there was malice in every syllable. Was he referring to something specific when he said 'another lesson'? Have I done something since we last spoke that's upset him? I can't think of anything and that confuses me, triggering another bolt of panic. I start pacing the floor, chewing my lips, feeling the pressure building within me.

It's not long before I realise that I need a distraction, something to stop my brain from exploding. Yoga springs to mind and I'm just glad that Ajay holds weekend classes. Perhaps we can even go for another drink together to break up what will otherwise be a long, lonely evening.

Something bad has happened. That much is obvious as I approach the hall. There's a police car parked out front alongside an ambulance. A number of people are also gathered close to the entrance and among them are several of my fellow yoga class members.

One woman, who I recognise as Iris Chambers, looks visibly distressed while speaking to a uniformed police officer who appears to be making a note of what she's saying.

As I draw closer, another woman beckons me over. Her name is Cindy Maddox and she's clearly eager to pass on some news.

'You'll never believe what's happened,' she says. 'Poor Ajay has been attacked in the hall. Iris found him because she was the first to arrive for class. Ajay was lying on the floor. Apparently he's been badly beaten. There's lots of blood and at first she thought he was dead.'

I recoil in shock and a pulse starts beating high up in my throat.

'Who would do such a thing?' I demand to know.

Cindy shakes her head. 'God knows. Iris did say she saw two men walking out of the hall just as she got here.'

I swallow the saliva that has gathered in my throat and then watch in stunned silence as two paramedics emerge from the hall carrying a stretcher. I'm close enough to see Ajay lying on it, and his face is covered in blood. He's quickly put into the ambulance, which races off with its siren wailing. Someone says he's being taken to the nearby St Thomas' Hospital.

A couple of police officers then proceed to take statements from various people and I hang around long enough to hear one of them say that Mr Singh's condition is serious but not critical. It's a relief, but it doesn't stop my heart from thudding in my ears.

I eventually drag myself away from the scene and head home. When I close the front door behind me, I go straight to the kitchen and make myself a mug of tea. The image of poor Ajay on the stretcher is seared onto my retinas and I pray that no lasting damage has been done to him.

* * *

I'm still reeling from the shock an hour later and haven't moved from the sofa. I decide it's time to call the hospital to check on Ajay's condition. I'll claim to be a worried relative.

But just as I pick up my phone, it rings with an incoming call. I thumb the green button without checking the caller ID.

'Hello.'

'It's Liam here, Emma.'

He's the last person in the world I want to talk to, so I tell him I've got my mother holding on the landline.

'You sound upset,' he says. 'Is that because you've heard what's happened to your yoga instructor?'

His words take my breath away.

'How on earth do you know about that?' I blurt out.

'Well, because the two guys responsible were acting on my orders,' Liam says. 'I gather they did exactly what was expected of them.'

'Please tell me that's not true, Liam.'

'Oh, but it is.'

I feel a cry gather in my throat, but I refuse to let it out.

'Why, Liam? Why would you hurt him?'

'Surely you must know, Emma. You went for a drink with him last night. I know because someone was following you on my behalf. And Tommy was furious when he saw the photograph of you two hugging outside the pub.'

I feel a sudden tightness in my throat. 'But we were just saying goodnight to each other. It was completely innocent. I was back home by nine.'

'Come off it, Ems. Tommy's been inside for two minutes, and you're throwing yourself at the first man you see. It's pathetic, and you needed to be taught a lesson. Don't worry, Mr Yoga wasn't told why he was targeted.'

'You're fucking sick, and so is your brother!' I shout into the phone, losing control.

Liam chuckles, which makes me realise that he's having fun at my expense. 'And you're a stupid, naive bitch if you think we'll let you go chasing cock while your husband is in prison,' he says. 'Let this be a warning to you that you're married to Tommy so you're not free to do whatever you want. That's been made clear to you enough bloody times. It seems to me that you're just not prepared to listen.'

'But I haven't done anything wrong.'

'You might want to believe that, but it's not true. And by the way, don't even think of going to the Old Bill. There's nothing to link me to Mr Yoga, and I'm sure you wouldn't want the same thing to happen to one of your pretty little nieces.'

CHAPTER THIRTY-TWO

If there had been even a scintilla of doubt in my mind that Tommy would follow through on his threats, then it's gone now. Suddenly I know what he was alluding to when he warned me over the phone not to do anything else to fuck him off. And I also know that it wasn't my blackmailer who followed me from the pub last evening. It was one of my husband's henchmen.

It's been fifteen minutes since Liam's chilling phone call and my heart is still beating rapidly. I blame myself for what has happened to Ajay and the guilt weighs heavy on my conscience. I should never have allowed myself to go for a drink with him. I should have known there was a chance that Tommy was having me watched.

I can just imagine his reaction when he was sent the photo of Ajay and me hugging. And I don't doubt that he was quick to instruct his brother to make sure it didn't happen again. It's another salutary reminder of why I must never underestimate their capacity for cruelty.

I want desperately to go to the police, but there's no point. I don't know the identities of the two men who attacked Ajay and Liam would of course deny that they were acting on his behalf.

I'm sure that Detective Brannigan would believe me, but there's no way he'd be able to prove it. Even if the attackers were tracked down, there's no chance that they would place their boss in the frame, not if they valued their own lives.

Once again, my mind flashes to the image of Ajay on the stretcher, the blood on his face. An icy shiver runs down my spine and I'm forced to blink back tears of anger and frustration. I wonder how he is.

Picking up my phone, I search online for the number of the A & E department at St Thomas' Hospital. It takes me seconds to find it and a further five minutes or so to get through. I pose as the sister of Ajay Singh, who was taken to the hospital by ambulance a short time ago.

After a short wait, I'm told he's being assessed by the team and that he's fully conscious and able to speak. That's the extent of the information they're able to impart at this stage and suggest I call back tomorrow.

After hanging up, I start pacing the floor again, willing the evening to pass quickly. But it doesn't, and the longer it goes on, the more tempting it is for me to pour myself a stiff drink.

Eventually I decide to go to bed even though I know that sleep won't come easily. I switch off my phone, along with the lights, and head for the bedroom. After cleaning my teeth, I peel off my clothes and slip beneath the duvet. As soon as the darkness consumes me so does the sheer hopelessness of my situation. I turn on my side, hug the pillow, try to close my mind to it.

But, of course, there's no way that's going to happen and it's only a matter of minutes before the tears break free.

Sunday morning arrives with heavy showers across London, which is all the excuse I need to stay in bed. Sleep eluded me for most of the night so I'm limp with fatigue and feeling as though my world is falling apart.

I lay on my back, staring at the ceiling, wondering where I'll be this time next week, next month, next year. I'm no longer in control of my own destiny and that's a petrifying thought.

It's been over four months since I shared the bed with Tommy, but sometimes I still sense his presence, as though he's here beside me. There's the warmth of his body, his boozy breath, the way he was always so restless.

It's hard for me to believe that I used to love sleeping with him. I felt so lucky, so wanted, so deliciously comfortable. But all that changed when he turned me against him. Then I had to pretend to enjoy it when he ran the tips of his fingers across my naked flesh and thrust his dick between my legs.

I think he honestly believes that if he can hold on to me for five years, we'll get back to how we first were when he gets out. That may well happen in marriages where love is reciprocated, but I already detest the man and the feelings I once had for him can never be resurrected.

It's ten o'clock when I finally haul myself out of bed. The first thing I do is switch on my mobile so that I can phone the hospital to check on Ajay. But there's an email waiting for me from Rebecca Fleming, who also works at the hall as a yoga instructor. She and Ajay cover for each other and everyone suspects they're in a relationship.

The email is an update on his condition and has been sent to all his students.

> Ajay wants to thank you all for your concern. I spoke to him this morning and I'm glad to say that he's receiving excellent treatment from the doctors and nurses. He has a broken nose and a fractured rib, plus some cuts and bruises. His two attackers wore masks and he has no idea who they are and why they did it. I'll make sure to keep you updated and FYI I'll be taking over Ajay's classes from tomorrow until he's well enough to get back to them.

It's a relief, but it doesn't make me feel any better or less guilty. The attack on Ajay was barbaric and unwarranted, and I'll make that clear to Tommy when he calls me. But I'm sure he won't care what I say or think, and he's bound to lay the blame squarely at my feet.

* * *

Tommy doesn't phone me until midday. By then, I'm show-ered and dressed and wondering how and where I'm going to spend the afternoon and evening.

Before I accept the call, I tell myself I must not lose my temper. That would only encourage him to lose his, and perhaps prompt him to teach me another lesson.

When I answer, I let him speak first and he gets straight to the point, no holding back.

'Liam has told me he spoke to you about what happened yesterday,' he says. 'But apparently you don't think you did anything wrong by going out drinking with that yoga prick. Well, you did, and I expect a fucking apology.'

I stiffen my spine and take a deep breath before responding.

'You're the one who should apologise.' My words drip with ice. 'What you did was out of order. It was just a friendly chat after yoga class. There was nothing else to it.'

'The photograph that was taken of the pair of you tells a different story,' he retorts. 'If you see him again, I'll know, and next time, he'll end up in the mortuary instead of the hospital.'

'But I will see him again because he's my instructor.'

'Not any more he isn't. I've added a new rule to the list. You're not to attend those classes again. There's no need anyway. You can do that stretching shit in the flat. All you need is a mat.'

I feel my mouth open, but I'm too shocked to say anything.

'Right now, I'm really upset and annoyed,' Tommy continues. 'But I'm prepared to forgive you because we all

185

make mistakes. Just don't let it happen again. And don't ever forget that you're still married to me even though we can't be together right now.'

I manage to find my voice, but it doesn't sound like it belongs to me. 'But you can't run my life from inside prison, Tommy. I need to be free to be myself, to do my own thing.'

'And I'm not stopping you. All I'm telling you to do is follow a few rules which will give me peace of mind and help ensure that our marriage survives. It's not a lot to ask, for Christ's sake. I don't understand why you have to make a fuss.'

I can see there's no point in trying to convince him otherwise. His mind is made up. I'm his possession, his puppet, and he's determined to go on pulling my strings regardless of how I feel about it.

'I'm sure you'll see sense once it properly sinks in,' he says. 'You just need more time. And luckily for you I'm a patient man.'

I can't listen to this any more so I tell him I have to go, I need to use the loo. I'm sure he doesn't believe me, but he doesn't object.

'I've got to hang up anyway,' he says. 'I'm due a visit from the doctor. And just in case you're interested, I'll probably be going back to prison tomorrow. So, you'd better arrange a visit.'

The turmoil raging in my head continues to make it impossible for me to relax. I'm angry, deflated, worried and miserable.

Once again, I go without lunch because I just don't have an appetite. Then I shuffle around the flat trying to find jobs to keep me occupied.

I'm at the window, watching the rain lash the capital, when I decide to phone the national domestic abuse hotline. It's been months since I last contacted them and my circumstances have changed since then so I want to know if the advice will be different now.

'My husband is in prison and will be for five years,' I tell the person I'm put through to, a softly spoken woman with a Scottish accent. 'But he won't agree to a divorce and has even drawn up a list of rules that he expects me to abide by.'

'What's on the list?' she asks.

I've committed it to memory so I reel them off.

'That's totally unacceptable,' she says. 'Can you speak to your husband about how this is making you feel? Is it safe to do so?'

'I've told him that I'm not happy, but he's threatened to hurt me and my family if I don't go along with it.'

'Then perhaps it's time to speak to the police about it.'

'But my husband is a career criminal and his family run an organised crime gang here in London. He has an army of men who will do whatever he tells them.'

The woman hesitates before replying and I sense she realises that my predicament is more serious than she first thought.

'All the more reason to involve the police,' she says after a beat. 'They will know what to do. And they have the manpower and resources to put a stop to it. You might also want to consider resorting to an emergency shelter if things get really bad and you find yourself in imminent danger.'

She goes on to offer more practical advice, including confiding in someone I trust who can check in on me every so often.

'But from what you've told me I really feel you should contact the police in the first instance,' she finishes.

I decide it's not worth telling her that my husband has contacts in the Met, and I don't want to be drawn into revealing his identity. So, I thank her and end the call. I don't know what I expected her to tell me, but I should have known that she wouldn't have a ready-made solution to my problem. In any other situation the advice offered would be of great help, but with Tommy Driscoll as my husband I have to tread oh so carefully.

I go into the kitchen to make myself another tea. When it's poured, I take a sip and feel the warm liquid slide into my stomach. I just wish there was a magic potion I could take that would make everything right again.

I'm about to leave the kitchen when the phone on the wall buzzes. It's the internal service linked to the reception desk and is used by the concierge to let residents know when we have visitors.

'Hello there, Mrs Driscoll.' Edward's warm voice calls from the other end.

'Good afternoon, Edward. What's up?'

'A chap just popped in and left an envelope for you,' he tells me. 'He asked me to let you know about it straight away. I'm sure he's the same man we saw on the surveillance camera delivering that other note. I did ask him for his name, but he rushed out without giving me an answer.'

I feel my heartbeat quicken.

'Would you be kind enough to bring it up, Edward?'

'Of course, Mrs Driscoll.'

CHAPTER THIRTY-THREE

The envelope is similar to the others I've received, but this one doesn't contain a photograph. Instead, there's a short message scrawled in pencil on a piece of paper.

Meet me at Ben's Café on Temple Street in an hour.
And make sure you come alone.

I know Ben's Café because it's not far from where I live and was opened only about six months ago. I decide to go because I need to confront Ruben, or whatever his name is. There are questions I have to ask him, including how much I'll have to pay to stop him. After what happened to Ajay it's all the more imperative that I stop these compromising photos of us at the house party from reaching Tommy or any members of his family.

I'm guessing it will be impossible to persuade him to drop the threat and leave me alone without any recompense.

He's clearly put a lot of thought into planning it. First he would have had to get the photos from his friend who took them and then he would have had to find out where I lived to be able to deliver them in person. Finding my home address would have been very difficult because Tommy is careful about keeping it private, so I know he's determined and resourceful.

And I also know he won't go away until he gets what he wants.

The rain has stopped by the time I leave the flat at half five. It's dark already and the evening feels heavy and subdued. I walk at a leisurely pace, but I keep looking around to see if anyone is following me. The last thing I want is for one of my husband's henchmen to witness me meeting up with another man. But I don't see anyone acting suspicious or showing an interest in me, so maybe he's called off the hounds for now, believing I wouldn't dare make the same mistake again. I keep my fingers crossed.

It will only take me about ten minutes to get to the café and, on the way, I think back to what happened between me and Ruben. There's no question I was attracted to him. The perfect-teeth smile, the dark spiky hair, those come-to-bed eyes. I wish now I'd got him to tell me more about himself: his surname, for instance, where he worked, if he had any children. But I suppose even if he had told me, I wouldn't have taken it in, let alone remembered it since I wasn't exactly sober and focused at the time. I do recall noticing that he wasn't wearing a wedding ring, but I can't remember asking him if he was married.

Suddenly, the café is ahead of me and, as I approach the entrance, my pulse begins to pound and the noises around me seem to fade away. It's one of those smart, trendy establishments that attracts a young clientele. But it's not very busy when I enter. I count three couples and two guys by themselves, and Ruben is not among them.

I order a tea at the counter and take a seat next to the window. My nerves are as taut as guitar strings and I feel butterflies in my stomach.

After ten minutes of staring out the window and at the door, I start to wonder if he's going to show.

Another five minutes pass and the lady who served me comes over to my table.

'Are you Emma Driscoll?' she asks pleasantly.

'I am.'

'Well, the man you're waiting for just called to say there's been a change of plan. He said his name was Ruben and he wants you to meet him at the Anchor pub on Bankside instead. It's only a short walk from here along—'

'I know where it is,' I interrupt her. 'Thank you!'

I don't bother to finish my coffee and walk out of the café wondering what the hell he's playing at.

The Anchor is a pub I know well. It's in a prime location overlooking the Thames and has an outside seating area.

On the way there, I remain vigilant, frequently checking to see if I'm being watched or followed. But I don't sense that I am, unlike the other night when I walked home after saying goodbye to Ajay.

The fact that Ruben didn't come to the café has enraged me. Did he never intend to? Was it a ploy to exert more pressure on me? To make it clear that he's the one calling the shots?

My heart picks up speed and I can feel my body trembling from the inside out.

I'm about halfway to my destination, walking along a quiet street, when a white Transit van pulls into the kerb just ahead of me. As I get closer to it, the offside door is thrown open and a voice calls out: 'Hi there, Bella.'

I stop walking and panic squeezes the breath out of me. Peering into the van, I see a shadowy figure behind the wheel. The dashboard lights are bright enough to illuminate the features of the man I know as Ruben.

'Jump in,' he says. 'Don't be afraid. I'm not going to hurt you or drive off with you. I promise.'

As if to prove his point, he turns off the engine.

'You can leave the door open if you like,' he adds.

Fear clutches at my stomach, but I don't let that stop me from climbing into the passenger seat. I leave the door wide open with one leg hanging out.

'I'm sorry I made you wait in the café,' he says and I'm surprised how friendly he sounds. 'I wanted to make sure that you came alone. So, I followed you there from your block and watched you leave after making the phone call.'

'I can't believe you're doing this,' I tell him through tight, trembling lips. 'And you're insane if you think you're going to get any money out of me with your absurd threat.'

He smiles, cocky and confident, and I flinch as his gaze sweeps over me. It's obvious that he can tell I'm bluffing.

'You lied to me at the party and you're lying to me now,' he says, his voice sharp and no longer friendly. 'If you had no intention of paying up you wouldn't be here. So, let's dispense with the bullshit, shall we? I've done a lot of research into you and that scumbag husband of yours. I know about him and his family and it's clear he won't be happy if he discovers that his wife started screwing around as soon as he was banged up.'

'What happened at the party was a mistake.'

He shakes his head. 'Bollocks. You were up for it as much as I was. And the thing is, I really liked you and wanted to meet you again. I called the number you gave me and found out it was a fake. To be honest, that hurt. But then I saw you on the news during your husband's trial and found out that your name isn't Bella and you're not single. It suddenly all made sense.'

'And so you thought it would be a good idea to blackmail me?'

'I saw an opportunity, Emma. I lost my job five weeks ago and I'm up to my eyes in debt. And now I'm presented with a way to make some money. I'd already got my pal to send me the pictures he took so I decided to make use of them. It wasn't easy to find out where you lived, but I got there in the end. I haven't been able to get your mobile number, though, so I'll need that to set up the next meeting.'

'What makes you think there will be another meeting? And how do you know that I haven't already told my husband what I did?'

'Because you don't strike me as being that stupid,' he replies coolly. 'Tommy Driscoll has a reputation. And a friend of mine who's a copper has told me what he's like. No way will he take kindly to you disrespecting him like that.'

It's hard to believe that this is the same man who beguiled me with his charm. He seems so different, as though he's had a personality transplant. And he looks different too. Those eyes I found so attractive at the party are now filled with a fierce intensity. His hair has grown long and covers his ears, and his jawline is rough with stubble. I note he's wearing the dark parka he had on when he walked into reception at my block.

'What exactly do you want from me?' I ask him.

He shrugs. 'Cash, obviously. In return, I'll get rid of the pictures, hubby won't know we fucked, and you'll never hear from me again.'

'How can I be sure of that? What's to stop you coming back for more?'

He shakes his head. 'This is a one-off. I'm taking a big risk and I know it. I don't intend to push my luck. One payment is all I'm asking for.'

'How much?'

'Ten thousand. It's a reasonable amount and I reckon you're good for it. That flat you live in must be worth millions and I'm sure you can lay your hands on some of your husband's ill-gotten gains.'

It's less than I expected him to want and he's right, I do have access to a safety deposit box containing in excess of a hundred thousand pounds.

'But why should I trust you?' I demand.

'Because you don't have a choice, Emma, not if you don't want your husband to find out that you've been unfaithful to him.'

'And what makes you so sure it would bother him that much? He's going to be in prison for a long time, so he's not expecting me to remain celibate.'

He responds to that with another roguish grin. 'That's more bullshit, Emma. A bloke like Tommy Driscoll wouldn't be happy to know that his wife is fucking around. So, stop taking me for a fool and let's get this done so that I can be on my way. Are you going to pay up or are things going to turn ugly?'

I want to leap across the seat and scratch his eyes out, but instead I gulp in some air and give a small nod.

'You'll get the money, but believe me when I say that it'll be a big mistake if you think you'll be able to squeeze any more out of me. Being married to Tommy means that I know people who will hurt you if I ask them to.'

He smirks. 'They'd have to find me first. You know nothing about me, Emma. I'll use a burner phone to call you and it'll get dumped after the money is handed over.'

I expel a puff of air. 'When do you want the money?'

'As quickly as possible. I'll call you tomorrow. When you've got it, we'll meet up and that will be the last you hear from me. I swear.'

He takes his mobile out of his pocket. I give him my number. After tapping it into his phone, he asks me if I have any more questions.

I bite my lip and shake my head because the last thing I want to do is prolong this conversation.

I can't get out of the van quick enough and I slam the door behind me.

He starts the engine straight away, and as I watch him drive off, I let out a gasp of relief.

It's true he has me over a barrel, and I'm going to have to pay him the ten grand. But the situation could be far worse. At least he doesn't know my big secret – the secret that I have to keep from him at all costs – that I'm pregnant and that he's the father of my child.

CHAPTER THIRTY-FOUR

I'm lying on the bed, curled into a ball, arms wrapped around myself. I'm still shaking from the encounter with Ruben and there's a dull, deeply embedded ache behind my eyes.

The experience has left me traumatised, so much so that I'm struggling to force air past the knot in my throat. But I have to admit that it would be so much worse if he knew about the baby.

Thank God he doesn't.

Just under two months have passed since I discovered that I was pregnant, and as my stomach swells, it's going to become harder to keep it secret, which is why I wanted to be out of Tommy's life as soon as possible. Nobody knows except my GP and the staff in the hospital maternity unit. I've longed to tell Amanda and my mother, but I can't. Not yet.

Tommy had been in prison for two weeks when I stopped taking the pill because I didn't think I needed to. But when

I had sex with Ruben I was too tipsy and too excited to think about protection.

The next morning, there was a lot I couldn't remember, although I somehow managed to convince myself that before we got started I'd heard him say that he would use a condom. It turned out that I must have imagined it or else he lied to me.

So it blew my mind when the pregnancy test came up with a positive result. And since then, I've struggled with what to do and how to handle it.

My first reaction was to have a termination. I even booked an appointment at a private clinic, but at the last minute I backed out. I couldn't go through with it. Couldn't bring myself to kill the baby that's growing inside me. I made myself believe that if I held my nerve, things would turn out all right. Tommy would go to prison for a long time and he'd grant me a divorce. I could then move out of London, to a safe place far away from the Driscolls, and give birth. Tommy would never have to know about the baby and I could start a new life.

But it was a mistake to think that he would let me go and abandon his dream of us starting a family together.

I can't even pretend to him that the baby is his. He's no fool and would question the dates, probably demand a DNA test. The thought of how he'd react on finding out the truth leaves me cold. I wouldn't put it past him to try to hurt both me and the baby.

I can't let that happen. I already love my child and it doesn't matter to me that the father is such a scumbag. It's the reason I've stopped drinking alcohol and coffee. I've read that they're both bad for unborn babies.

It's amazing to think that he or she is already five or six millimetres. And I've read online that the foetal development is now on fast-track and making large leaps in size from week to week.

I stifle a sob and uncurl myself, then I roll onto my back. My mind continues to race, seeking a way out of the darkness, trying to find answers to the questions that are causing me so much grief. What am I going to do? Could I flee the country with the money I can lay my hands on, assuming I'm able to obtain another passport? What would happen if I did? Would the Driscolls use all their considerable resources to find me? Would Tommy seek revenge against my sister, mother and nieces? And dare I take that chance?

Suddenly the urge to vomit rolls through my stomach. I jump out of bed and rush into the en suite, where I throw up into the toilet bowl. Afterwards, I clean my teeth and slip out of my clothes, then shower and prepare for bed.

I'm walking through the flat, turning off the lights, when my mobile rings. I hurry into the kitchen and pick it up. When I see that the call is from an unidentified number, I assume it's Tommy.

But it isn't.

'Hi, Emma. It's Ruben here. I thought I'd ring to check that you've given me your real number this time.'

I feel a tight spasm in my chest. 'You could have done that earlier.'

'I know, but I thought a little late-night reminder wouldn't hurt.'

'I've told you I'll get the money,' I say through gritted teeth.

'That you did. And I just hope that for your sake you mean it.'

I hang up before he can say any more and the ferocious anger that rises up inside me robs me of air. It takes a while for me to stop shaking, but the tension in my limbs stays with me throughout the night.

CHAPTER THIRTY-FIVE

I'm awake at the crack of dawn on Monday morning, but the lack of sleep has worn me out before the day even begins.

I get a fright when I look in the mirror. Is that really me? My face is pasty and drawn, with dark rings hanging beneath my eyes.

I look only marginally better after I've showered and applied some make-up. But at least I'm able to focus on what has to be done during the coming hours.

First off, I've got to visit the bank and take ten thousand pounds from the safety deposit box. Only Tommy and I know what's inside and even Liam doesn't have access to it. That's because Tommy wanted us to have our own personal stash of cash to break into in the event of an emergency. Paying off a blackmailer is an emergency as far as I'm concerned.

After I receive a call from Ruben, I'll take the money to him. And then hope to God that he keeps his word.

It feels like I'm playing a part in a crime movie, only this isn't fiction, it's actually happening, and the fear that's pulsing through me is real. I'm worried that what I'm going through will have a negative impact on the baby. I've read that high levels of stress can lead to preterm delivery, a lower birth weight and even health problems for the child later in life. It all adds to the maelstrom of conflicting thoughts and emotions inside my head.

I make myself a tea and drink it while standing on the balcony. It's a dry start to the day, but windy. Fast-moving clouds are casting shadows over the buildings on the other side of the river.

I force down a slice of buttered toast with my second cup of tea, then call the bank and make an appointment.

I still don't know if I'm doing the right thing by allowing Ruben to extort money from me so easily. If the stakes weren't so high, I'd tell him to go to hell. But I'm in no position to do that. I don't know the man, so I have no idea how he'd react or what he's capable of. I can't be sure that he isn't as ruthless as my husband. Or even a grade A psychopath.

Most of the money generated by the Firm's various businesses is laundered and then reinvested. But significant amounts of cash are syphoned off and hidden in bank accounts, safety deposit boxes and secret locations where the police can't lay their hands on it.

Tommy and Liam have built up their own personal fortunes over the years. I'm not privy to where Tommy has hidden most of his money, but I have access to a joint bank account, as well as to the safety deposit box. Plus, I receive a regular income from the Firm's legitimate business accounts, where I'm listed as a personal assistant even though I don't actually do any work.

The bank with the safety deposit box is in Kensington and I arrive there by taxi just after 2 p.m. I've been there before with Tommy so I know what to expect. I have to go through stringent security checks to get to the vaults.

There are three different size boxes available at the bank and ours is one of the largest. It's filled with nothing but dirty money, but that doesn't bother me in the circumstances. I've brought a leather rucksack and I carefully place the cash inside it. I take out bundles of £20 notes amounting to £10,000, and then help myself to a further ten thousand in case I need it in the coming days or weeks. When the rucksack is zipped up, I get out of there as quickly as I can and take a taxi back to the flat.

The afternoon crawls by as I wait anxiously to hear from Ruben. I can't relax and my thoughts are spinning in all directions.

At six o'clock, my mobile rings and I feel my stomach contract. I'm ready to tell Ruben that I have the money, but it's Tommy on the line. He wants me to know that they're keeping him in hospital for another night.

'The wound has developed an infection so they're having to treat it,' he says. 'I'm not complaining, though. I'd rather be here than in my cell. What have you been up to?'

I have to be careful what I say in case he knows that I've been out.

'I felt like treating myself so I got a cab to Kensington and bought a pair of shoes in Harrods,' I tell him. 'And I had lunch while I was there.'

'What about tonight? I assume you'll be staying in.'

'Of course. I thought I'd do some cleaning and then watch a film.'

'That's what I like to hear, Emma. Keep yourself busy and the time will pass much more quickly.'

This is what he wants. To know where I'm going and what I'm doing. All day and every day. And he believes he can achieve that over the next five years through a combination of threats, the fact that his family will be keeping tabs on me and his ability to use a mobile phone to contact me whenever he wants to.

He tells me his mother is not very well and wants me to go and spend some time with her.

'And what I'd really like is for you and her to have a better relationship,' he says. 'It'd mean a lot to me.'

'The problem is your mother doesn't like me, Tommy,' I say.

His tone changes suddenly, and his voice rises an octave. '*You* don't like *her* and you never have. But while I'm in here you're going to need each other. So make more of a fucking effort for my sake.'

I swallow hard. 'If you say so.'

'I do. And while I'm at it, try not to keep pissing Liam off. I don't want him distracted from running the business.

I've told him to look out for you, but he's already complaining that it's taking up too much of his time.'

There's a challenge in his voice, but I don't rise to it because I know that if I do, it'll encourage him to pick more faults with my behaviour and attitude. And that will only serve to drag this out while creating more opportunities for me to put my foot in it by saying something I shouldn't.

He rants on for a while about the stabbing in the prison yard, but then reveals to me that those responsible are about to receive payback.

'Spare me the details, Tommy,' I say. 'I really don't need to know.'

The conversation ends abruptly after that because Tommy has to go. He tells me he'll call again tomorrow and when he hangs up, I breathe a sigh of relief.

But within minutes my phone rings again and this time it's Ruben.

'I've been trying for bloody ages to get through,' he moans. 'What's going on?'

'I was talking to my sister,' I lie. 'I didn't know when I'd hear from you.'

'Well, you're hearing from me now. Have you got the money?'

'I have.'

'Right. Do you know where Laxton Street is?'

I have to think about it before telling him I do.

'Then meet me there at half seven and don't be late,' he says. 'You'll see the van parked up. Come alone or you'll be sorry.'

He ends the call and I stand there fuming. The more I hear from this guy, the more I'm convinced that he's cut from the same cloth as my git of a husband.

CHAPTER THIRTY-SIX

Once again, the location Ruben's chosen for the meeting is within walking distance of the flat. Laxton Street is lined on both sides with small commercial properties, most of which are disused and boarded up. Several years ago, the council closed it off at one end when the area just beyond it became a building site. Since then, pedestrians have avoided it because it leads to nowhere interesting and attracts rough sleepers and druggies. So I approach it with mounting trepidation. I can't deny it's the perfect place for handing over a bag of dirty money in secret. But it's also poorly lit and seedy, and the last place I want to be on a cold, dark night.

The street is short and run-down, and as soon as I turn into it, I spot the van because there are no other vehicles there. It's parked against the kerb about halfway along and its lights are off.

I stop and look for any sign of life. But I can't see anyone and there are no lights coming from the properties that aren't boarded up.

I'm tempted to turn around and return to the flat, and when he phones, to tell him that I want to meet in a more public place. But I plough on because I'm desperate to get this over with even though I'm scared and my breath is coming in short, nervous gasps.

When I reach the van, I expect the side door to be thrown open as it was the previous day. But it remains closed and when I peer through the window, I see that the front is empty.

'I'm behind you, Emma.'

His voice startles me and when I spin round, I see him standing in a narrow alley between two of the buildings. Behind him is a large wheelie bin and some discarded cardboard boxes.

'I needed to pee,' he explains. 'I'm sorry if I made you jump.'

My heart is pumping furiously and it feels like a dead-bolt is being twisted in my stomach.

Ruben steps forward and I notice that he's wearing jeans and a jumper but no coat. The sombre sodium glow from the nearest street lamp reaches his face and I see a smile tugging at the corners of his mouth.

His eyes shift from me to the rucksack I'm carrying. 'Is the money in there?'

I nod. 'Exactly what you asked for.'

His tongue slithers between his teeth as he takes another step towards me and holds out his hand.

'Don't leave until I've counted it,' he instructs.

He snatches the rucksack from me, then moves over to the van, pulls open the door and places it on the passenger seat.

I watch as he takes out the bundles of notes and asks me how much is in each.

'A thousand pounds,' I tell him.

He counts the bundles and flicks through each of them. As I watch him, my chest is tightening and it's becoming more difficult to breathe.

When he's satisfied, he piles them all back in and puts the rucksack in the footwell in front of the seat. Then he closes the door and before turning around he uses the key fob to lock it. I can't help feeling alarmed that he's not about to get straight into the van and drive off.

'You did good, Emma,' he says.

My body is rigid, jaw clenched.

'That's all I'm able to lay my hands on,' I say. 'So, don't come asking for more. And I expect you to delete those photos.'

I shove my hands in my coat pockets and turn to go. But I manage to take only one step before he grabs my arm and pulls me around to face him.

'Not so fast, Emma,' he rasps threateningly. 'We need to have a conversation.'

My eyes are drawn to a large commando knife that's suddenly appeared in his other hand. I instinctively open my mouth to scream, but before I can, he hurls himself onto me, forcing me back against the side of the van with a painful thud. In a heartbeat, he has me in a vicelike grip, his free hand clamped over my mouth and the tip of the knife blade inches from my left eye. Then he pulls me away from the van and pushes me towards the alley. I try to break free, but he tightens his grip and punches me roughly in the back of the head, which hurts like hell.

'The more you try to resist, the rougher it will get,' he warns me.

Pure terror rises in me and the breath is squeezed from my lungs like air from a paper bag.

He forces me into the alley, past the rubbish bin into a small enclosed yard where he releases his hold on me before stepping back.

I turn and face him and he points the knife at my throat.

'I've had a change of mind, Emma,' he says.

'What?'

He inhales, puffing out his cheeks. 'Since you managed to come up with the ten grand so quickly and easily, I'd be a fool not to expect a bit more.'

I feel a twist of panic. 'But you told me you wouldn't do this. And I believed you.'

'I know and I'm sorry. But this is too good an opportunity to pass up. But I promise that if you get me another ten grand, that will be the end of it. The photos will be destroyed and it will be the last you ever hear from me.'

I shake my throbbing head. 'I don't believe you. So, no way will you get any more out of me.'

He takes a step forward, his stare intense and full of aggression. 'Then I'll have to show you what a big fucking mistake that would be.' Before I can try to run for it, he's close enough to grab my left arm with his free hand. He holds the knife beneath my throat again and says, 'If you don't come up with another ten grand by tomorrow, I'll send the photos to your husband. And I'll tell him you've already given me some of his dosh.'

Instinct takes the place of caution and I react by throwing my head back and knocking the knife away from my throat. I then follow through with a hard kick to his groin.

He cries out and stumbles backwards, at the same time dropping the knife.

I see my chance and reach down to pick it up so that he doesn't get to it before me. But as my fingers close around the handle, he recovers his balance and rushes towards me.

I just have time to raise myself, knife in hand, and thrust out my arm in the hope that it will stop him in his tracks.

But instead, he lurches straight into the knife. The full length of the blade punctures his stomach and I scream because I didn't mean it to happen.

He staggers sideways with the knife still in him. And as pain contorts his features, he finds the strength to grip the handle with his right hand and wrench the blade out of his belly.

'You fucking bitch,' he gasps.

As he starts moving towards me, an ugly gurgling sound comes out of his mouth along with a spurt of blood. But he manages only a couple of steps before he falls to the ground.

I'm left standing there, looking down at his body as the life oozes out of him.

CHAPTER THIRTY-SEVEN

Everything inside me has turned cold and my chest is so tight I can barely breathe.

My unborn baby's father is lying dead at my feet with blood pouring from his belly. I killed him and I struggle to keep the panic in as I stare down at his face. The wide-open mouth, the eyes staring blankly ahead like dark holes, the blood frothing between his lips.

I push my fingers through my hair and shake my head. It feels like my mind is coming apart and I know that if I can't hold it together, I'm going to be in deep trouble.

I have to get away from here, but not before I take steps to make sure there's nothing to connect me to what just happened. This wasn't my fault. After all, he threatened me with a knife and I'm convinced he would have used it had I not stopped him. All I did was defend myself. I had no choice. It was him or me.

Despite that, guilty feelings stir inside me which I try to ignore. I close my eyes and count to ten. After I open them, I run through in my mind what I need to do and then go back to the mouth of the alley. I look up and down the street. It's still empty, thank God, and creepily quiet.

By now adrenaline has taken hold of my body, but at the same time a curious detachment has set in. It's all about covering my tracks as fast as I can. If Tommy was here with me, he would know what to do. And I don't doubt that he's been in this same position himself, more than once. But I haven't lived a life of villainy and this is definitely the first time I've killed someone. So, I'm having to think on my feet about how not to leave behind any traces of myself.

I don't have any gloves with me, so I need to be extra careful. My fingerprints are on the knife so I'll have to clean it here and take it with me. And I need to retrieve my rucksack with the money, which means taking the keys from Ruben's pocket. I manage to do this with a shaking hand. There's nothing else in his other pockets except a hanky, so I take that and lay it on the ground. Then I carry out the gut-wrenching task of picking up the knife. I use his trousers to wipe the blood from it and then wrap it in the hanky before placing it in a deep pocket of my coat.

Before leaving the scene, I check to make sure that I haven't dropped anything. Then I look at Ruben's body one last time and feel a cold shudder ripple through me.

New questions suddenly rear up in my mind. Will

anyone miss him? Was he married? Did he have children? How long will he be here before someone finds him?

I can't afford to dwell on these matters now, so I turn and rush out of the alley. I use the key fob to open the van. I lift out my rucksack and as I do, I notice Ruben's coat lying on the driver's seat. I take that out too and sift through the pockets. I find a leather wallet and two mobiles. I assume that one is the burner phone. I drop both phones and the wallet in the rucksack, along with the keys. Finally, I use his coat to wipe my prints from the door handle and leave it on the seat.

As I exit Laxton Street, I start looking for CCTV cameras and spot several. I just have to hope that I haven't been captured on any of them. But I know I probably have, which means that the police might be able to identify me. So, I'll have to come up with a plausible explanation for going for an evening walk carrying my rucksack.

I return home via the Embankment and throw the knife and Ruben's keys in the Thames when I'm sure that nobody is watching. His two phones I drop into separate drains after smashing them under my shoe. The wallet I leave in the rucksack because I want to see if it will tell me anything more about the man I killed.

Then I pray that I've done enough to ensure the police can't link me to the body they'll eventually find in the alley, the body of my unborn child's father.

CHAPTER THIRTY-EIGHT

When I arrive home, my thoughts are swimming in feverish circles. I feel dizzy and nauseous, as though I'm about to pass out. I sit on the sofa and mentally rewind through everything that happened this evening.

It's still hard to take it all in even though the sight of Ruben's body keeps pushing itself into the front of my mind. I tell myself that he got what he deserved and that if I hadn't killed him, it would be me lying back there in the yard.

I'm just glad I had the presence of mind to cover my tracks. No way will the police find the knife or the phones. I've made sure of that. And even if they do, they won't lead them to me.

I remember that I need to check my clothes. I get up and examine my coat, I spot no traces of blood, but that doesn't mean there aren't any, so I decide to chuck it. It'll be no great loss because I've got one that's identical but a size smaller. I stuff it into a black bin liner along with the trousers and jumper I was wearing. I'll also make sure to polish my shoes later.

I've seen enough films and documentaries featuring scene of crime teams to know they're very thorough and many murders are solved thanks to them. But I'm as sure as I can be that I haven't left behind any clues for them to find.

I take the cash from the rucksack and decide that it will go in the wall safe that's hidden behind the fuse box in the hall. It's only when I pick the rucksack up that I remember dropping Ruben's wallet into it. I lift it out and place it on the coffee table, then take the rucksack into the hall and put the cash in the safe. There's already a large sum of money inside the safe, along with various documents, so it's a tight fit adding the cash from the bag.

I go back to the living room and turn my attention to the wallet. Blood thunders in my head as I open it up. In the pockets are three ten-pound notes and various cards. Among them are two credit cards from well-known high-street banks. From these, I learn that his full name was Ruben Swift. There's also his driving licence, which gives his date of birth and his address. He was thirty-three and lived in New Cross, South London. But there's nothing else to indicate anything more about him like where he worked and if he had a family.

Curiosity compels me to grab my phone and tap his name into the browser. It shows up scores of men with that name, so I narrow the search to 'Ruben Swift

London'. There's still a long list, so I switch to the image search bar and go through the photo results instead. That's when I spot the familiar face. It's a head-and-shoulders shot of Ruben and it leads me to a news story that was published online by the *London Evening Standard* five weeks ago.

A London man got drunk and 'went berserk' in a pub hours after he was sacked from his job for inappropriate behaviour towards female colleagues.

Ruben Swift, aged 33 and unmarried, lost his temper after the pub landlord refused to serve him any more drinks. Swift reacted by throwing an empty beer bottle at the shelves behind the bar. He then pushed over a table, smashed several glasses and was verbally abusive to other customers.

Staff members managed to restrain him before he caused any more damage and he was held back until police arrived to arrest him.

In court, he pleaded guilty to being drunk and disorderly and it emerged that earlier in the day he had been fired from his job as a financial adviser for an investment company based in the City, following an internal investigation looking into claims that Swift had sexually harassed several female colleagues over a period of many months. He was accused of making unwanted physical contact and sexual harassment, with one colleague apparently describing him as a 'serial groper'.

Swift told magistrates that he had gone to the pub to drown his sorrows after losing his job and he drank too much.

He has been fined £2,000 and ordered to cover the cost of the damage he'd caused.

It gives me some comfort to know that the man I killed was a serial abuser of women and it goes some way towards ameliorating my guilt. At least I can put a positive spin on what I did, knowing the man who blackmailed me is dead and he no longer poses a threat.

But my husband still does, of course.

CHAPTER THIRTY-NINE

I wake up wet and shivering on Tuesday morning, having had about two hours sleep. My eyes are heavy, my joints stiff and my scalp prickles when I think about what the future holds.

After I get out of bed, I stand naked in front of the wardrobe mirror and check my baby bump. It's still not large enough for others to notice, but it's growing by the day and it won't be long before I have to buy some new clothes.

The foetus is now the size of a big juicy raspberry and its ears, nose and eyelids are developing. I just wish I could enjoy and appreciate what's happening to me, this miracle that's taking place in my womb. But I can't. And I can't even be sure that I'll carry my baby to term.

Last night, I could have lost my life and I fear that if there's a next time, I won't be so lucky. The sense of foreboding grows as I shower and dress, and I try to focus on what I need to do today.

In the kitchen, I put on a pair of rubber gloves and lay out the contents of Ruben's wallet on the worktop. Then I carefully clean everything with a wet cloth to get rid of my prints. Afterwards, I cut up all the cards and the three ten-pound notes. I stuff the pieces in the bin liner with my clothes and take it to the chute. Luckily, there's a rubbish collection tomorrow.

It's a bright day outside and the sky is a perfect, uninterrupted blue. So, I decide to go for a stroll, and while outside, I stop for a coffee at a café nearby.

On the way back, I can't resist checking out Laxton Street again. I'm half-expecting Ruben's body to still be undiscovered, but when I get there, the street is closed off by a taut ribbon of police tape. Beyond it are several police cars and figures in high-visibility jackets, some of whom are gathered around Ruben's van, while others are walking in and out of the alley.

Suddenly there's a roar in my head that feels louder than a jet engine. I don't even initially notice when a uniformed officer approaches me asking if I'm all right.

'Er, yes, of course,' I say eventually, flustered. 'I was just wondering what's going on here?'

'I'm not at liberty to say, madam,' he replies. 'Do you need to reach one of the buildings?'

I shake my head. 'No, I was just passing. I'm on my way home.'

'Well, you have a good day,' he says.

'I'll try to.'

* * *

I spend the afternoon holed up in the flat with the silence pressing against my ears.

In between drinking cups of tea, I spend much of the time pacing the living room, trying to run from my thoughts. But it proves impossible. There's just so much to think about. So many questions that I can't answer. Plus, my mind keeps falling backwards to the night before and I picture the scene in the yard with unwelcome clarity.

I know now that Ruben's body has been found and the police investigation is under way. They're looking for the person who killed him. They're looking for me.

Being married to a brutal gangster hasn't prepared me for this. I feel a strange mixture of emotions ranging from guilt and shock to outright fear. But, above all, I feel an intense wave of protectiveness for my unborn child. He or she will only survive if I do and, right now, I don't know if I will.

The only thing I'm certain of is that I will not have an abortion. But that creates a problem that I need to confront. Do I tell Tommy the truth and trust that he won't have me killed? Do I run away and hope that he won't take revenge on my family? Or do I go to the police and tell them everything I know about my husband's illicit business empire in return for a dubious level of protection? There's no easy answer and my head is going round in circles.

After a while, I go into the study and fire up the laptop because I want to know if the discovery of Ruben's body has made the news yet.

It has, and the coverage is more extensive than I expected. The story has made the BBC website and it includes photos of Ruben and the police presence in Laxton Street.

A murder hunt has been launched after a man was found dead with a knife wound to the stomach in South London this morning.

Ruben Swift, 33, is believed to have been attacked last night.

His body was found in a small enclosed yard off Laxton Street, Southwark by a homeless man passing by.

Police believe the motive was robbery as Mr Swift's pockets appear to have been emptied. It's not known what he was doing in the alley but, according to police, his van was parked close by.

Mr Swift was unemployed and lived in New Cross. Police would like anyone who was in the Laxton Street area last evening to contact them.

As I finish reading the article, I feel a corkscrew twist in my gut and I start to cry.

Tears are still slipping from my eyes ten minutes later when Tommy phones. My croaky voice makes him immediately suspicious.

'Is something wrong?' he asks me.

'No, Tommy,' I reply. 'I'm just tired. I was dozing on the sofa.'

'So, what have you been doing with yourself?'

I gulp in air and squeeze my eyes shut. 'Not much. I got up late and went for a long walk. Then did some painting before sitting down to watch TV. I think I might have to get a job. I know you don't want me to, but I'm finding it hard to fill the time.'

'A job is out of the question,' Tommy immediately tells me. 'You've got all the money you need. Just take your painting more seriously and find another hobby. And you can keep yourself busy by visiting my mum on a regular basis. She's struggling and it'll be good for both of you.'

When I don't respond, he adds, 'I'm not asking you to make an effort with her, Emma, I'm telling you. I thought I'd already made that clear. As you've said you've got plenty of time on your hands so there's no reason why you can't keep an eye on your own mother-in-law. She's going to need you as much as you'll need her.'

He then tells me that he's being moved back to the prison tomorrow and I ask him if he's worried that he'll be attacked again.

'Not a bit,' he tells me. 'I'll be better protected than the Pope from now on.'

We talk for a few more minutes before he says he has to go.

'Sleep tight, Ems, and remember that I love you and what I'm doing is all for your own good.'

'I know, Tommy.'

'And do you still love me?'

I pause, and have to force the words out, 'Of course I do.'

CHAPTER FORTY

It turns out to be another long, rough night, my mind bedevilled by too little sleep and too many dark thoughts.

The conversation with Tommy before I went to bed served to compound my anxiety. It made me angry when he told me not to get a job and to basically act as a part-time carer for his mother. I so wanted to tell him the truth when he asked me if I loved him. But I chickened out, just as I've always done. And when he wanted to know what I'd been doing with myself, I was so tempted to reveal the whole sordid truth, *'Well, actually, Tommy, I had to go to the bank and take out money to pay off a man who was blackmailing me. The same man whose baby I'm having. And when he threatened me with a knife, I accidentally killed him.'*

Even before I rise from my bed the next morning, a cloak of dread has wrapped itself around me. I'm faced with another day of feeling lonely, helpless, scared and angry. Another day of trying to remember what it felt like to be happy.

As soon as I'm dressed, my thoughts turn to Ruben Swift and a cold shiver sweeps through my body despite the warmth of the flat.

After pouring myself a coffee, I switch on the TV news. I have to wait a few minutes before the story appears on the BBC London news. Nothing much has changed overnight. The police are still appealing for witnesses and a forensic team remains at the scene in Laxton Street.

But there's a brief interview with the detective in charge of the case, a DI Carl Berry, who says, 'We're still trying to determine what Mr Swift's movements were on Monday evening. What we do know is that he was driving a white Ford Transit van that he'd borrowed from his father. We've ascertained from CCTV footage that he drove to Laxton Street just before seven o'clock. The van was parked at the kerb close to the yard where he was murdered.'

I feel a rush of air into my lungs and have to resist the urge to yell at the screen that it wasn't murder. That I killed him in self-defence. I know I won't be able to distance myself from what I did, and the guilt is still swirling around inside me. And that's why I almost want the truth to be known: Ruben Swift was not the innocent victim of a callous killer.

I'm still finding it impossible to come to terms with how my life has suddenly spiralled out of control. At least before Tommy was arrested all I had to contend with was being trapped in an abusive relationship. Now I'm pregnant with the child of a man I killed. And my husband – who has no idea of everything that's gone on – is determined to hold on to me while he resides behind bars for the next five years.

I know that I'm where I am because I've made too many mistakes. The first was to fall in love with a monster. The second was to marry him. The third was to go to a party and sleep with another monster. And the fourth was to stab that man to death. Perhaps in time I'll be able to forgive myself. After all, we all make mistakes. But forgiveness can't come before I know the consequences of my actions.

Getting through the day is going to be tough. It doesn't help that there's no structure to my life. I don't have a job to keep me busy and I'm avoiding the few friends I have because I don't want them to get wind of my predicament. The fewer people who know the less chance there is of it getting back to Tommy.

At the same time, I'm aware of how fast the pressure is building as time runs by. My baby is growing and it will soon be obvious to everyone that I'm expecting. And Tommy is becoming more frustrated and aggressive. If I don't respond to his demands, he'll take steps to ensure that I do.

At least when I check my phone there's one piece of good news. Ajay is recovering well from the beating inflicted by Tommy's thugs. Rebecca has emailed, saying he's been discharged from hospital. She's attached a photo of him sitting up in bed and smiling for the camera.

I cringe when I remember that he suffered a fractured rib and broken nose as well as various cuts and bruises. And all because I went for a drink with him.

I reply to the email and pass on my best wishes, that I hope to see him soon even though I'm not sure I'll ever see him again in truth.

Then I decide that the only way to shake the stiffness from my bones is to go for a walk.

It's another bright day and London is at its bustling best. But I'm in no mood to appreciate it. My heart leaps every time I hear a siren or see a uniform. I'm on edge the whole time, a dull beat thudding in my chest.

I go for a tea in Borough Market and scoff a pastry to stop my stomach from gurgling like a sewer.

When I return to the flat an hour later, I try to decide how best to destress. Should I embark on a new painting or would it be better to do some yoga?

I'm still trying to make up my mind when the internal service phone buzzes.

Now that Ruben is no longer around to blackmail me, I assume it's just Edward calling to tell me that a letter or parcel has arrived for me and he wants to know if he should deliver it to the flat or put it in my mailbox. But, instead, what he says shakes me to the core.

'I'm sorry to bother you, Mrs Driscoll. There are two police officers here in reception and they'd like to speak to you. I've told them you're in, so shall I send them up?'

CHAPTER FORTY-ONE

The bell rings a few minutes later. I have to brace myself before I open the door and let them in.

I was expecting uniformed police officers so I'm surprised that there are two detectives. One of them I recognise from seeing him on the television earlier. He's the officer leading the investigation into Ruben Swift's murder.

'Hello, Mrs Driscoll,' he says, holding up his warrant card. 'I'm Detective Inspector Carl Berry and my colleague here is Detective Sergeant Linda Warwick. Thank you for agreeing to see us.'

My eyeballs tingle as I shift my gaze between the pair of them.

'Why do you want to talk to me?' I ask.

'I'd rather we spoke inside,' DI Berry says. 'May we come in?'

'Of course. I'm sorry.' I step to one side and wave them through, while trying to ignore the fact that I'm shaking all over.

I close the door behind them and they follow me along the hall and into the living room.

'What a lovely place you have, Mrs Driscoll,' DI Berry says, looking around. 'And that view of the Thames is spectacular.'

I invite them to sit on the sofa and plant myself on the armchair facing them.

DI Berry is a slim, wiry man with chiselled features and fair hair that is parted with surgical precision. His colleague looks about ten years younger, with a pleasant face and thoughtful dark eyes.

'We're here to ask you what you know about a man named Ruben Swift,' DI Berry says without preamble.

I feel my face overheating and try not to let them see how nervous I am.

'I've never heard of the man,' I say. 'Who is he?'

DI Berry aims unblinking eyes at me. 'Sadly, Mr Swift was murdered not far from here on Monday evening, Mrs Driscoll. The story has been in the news.'

'I've not seen the news so I wouldn't know,' I tell him. 'But what has it got to do with me?'

The detective takes a photo from his pocket and shows it to me. 'This is the man we're talking about. Ruben Swift. Until recently he was a financial adviser working in the city. Do you recognise him?'

I study it carefully and shake my head. 'I've not seen him before.'

'Are you sure?'

I feel I have no choice but to plead complete ignorance,

so I glance at the photo again for good measure and this time give an emphatic nod.

'I'm positive,' I insist. 'I never forget faces. And I can assure you that he hasn't been in contact with me by phone, through social media or in person.'

'Well, that's odd. You see, we carried out a thorough search of Mr Swift's flat in New Cross. Among the objects we took away and examined was his laptop. And we discovered that for several weeks he'd been searching for information online about you.'

I try to stem the panic that's rising in me by taking a long, deep breath.

'But I don't understand,' I say. 'Why would he do that?'

'We were hoping you'd be able to tell us.'

'Well, I'm afraid I can't. Like I said, I didn't know him.'

The detective makes a thoughtful noise in his throat as he takes a notebook from his pocket. He flips it open and taps a finger against the first page. 'It appears he was keen to find out as much as possible about you,' he says. 'He searched for your address and saved to his laptop two photographs of this very building. He also saved photos of you, Mrs Driscoll, and it was your name he put into his search engine. He also closely followed your husband's trial up to the day of the verdict. We're checking to see if he actually went to the Old Bailey and sat in the public gallery at any point.'

'That's all very creepy,' I say, relieved that they haven't come across the photo taken at the party. 'Perhaps he was one of those people who becomes obsessed with high-profile criminal cases?'

'That's one theory, I suppose. But it doesn't explain why he downloaded pictures of you and not your husband.'

His colleague, DS Warwick, then leans forward and asks, 'Is it possible that Mr Swift knew Mr Driscoll?'

'I wouldn't know, but I doubt it,' I tell her. 'Can't you check the man's phone contacts and emails?'

'Unfortunately, his phone is missing and we're assuming it was stolen by the person who killed him. Neither you nor your husband are listed as email contacts.'

It suddenly occurs to me that if I don't ask about the murder itself, they might assume that I lied when I told them I'd not heard about it.

'You said this murder took place near here,' I say. 'Where exactly?'

It's DI Berry who answers. 'Laxton Street. Do you know it?'

'Of course. How was the poor man killed?'

'He was stabbed.'

'And do you have any idea who did it?'

'Not yet. But it's early days and I'm confident we'll find the killer, or killers.'

Another thought occurs to me and it causes the back of my neck to prickle. What if they ask to check my own phone and laptop? They'll see in my browser history that I've been searching for information on Ruben Swift and the killing.

'We will be asking your husband if he knew Mr Swift,' the DI says.

'Tommy is in hospital,' I tell him. 'He himself was stabbed while in the prison yard.'

'We're aware of that, Mrs Driscoll. But it's our understanding that he's being transferred back to Wandsworth later today.'

'Yes, that's right.'

Much to my relief, the two detectives exchange a glance and then get to their feet.

'I don't think we need to keep you any longer,' DI Berry says. 'However, if we do find out why Ruben Swift was so interested in you, I'll be sure to let you know.' He hands me one of his cards and adds, 'Please get in touch if you think of anything that might help us.'

I see them to the door, but before they step outside, the detective turns to me and says, 'I do have one final question for you, Mrs Driscoll. Can you please tell me where you were on Monday evening?'

'I was here for most of the time,' I reply because I know that if I appear on any CCTV footage I'll be caught out in a lie. 'I did go out for a short walk to get some exercise, but I can't remember what time it was.'

'Did you go anywhere near Laxton Street?'

'I don't think so, but I can't be sure.'

'And were you by yourself?'

I nod. 'I've been living here alone since my husband was first taken into custody over four months ago. And I don't get many visitors.'

CHAPTER FORTY-TWO

As soon as I close the door behind the two detectives, a wave of nausea engulfs me and I have to rush to the bathroom to throw up.

When I return to the living room, my throat burns and my eyes water. I find it a struggle to get air into my lungs and my whole body feels like it's humming with electricity.

The thought that they might not have believed me is terrifying. What if I'm now their prime suspect? Will they check out what I told them? Will they ask to see the security footage from reception which will show Ruben delivering the envelopes? Will I show up on CCTV between here and Laxton Street? Did I leave a trace of myself in the alley along with Ruben Swift's body? And will they want me to hand over my phone and laptop?

Then there's the fact that Tommy is also going to be questioned. He'll be asked if he knew the murder victim. And when they tell him that Swift had been searching for information on me, his suspicions will be aroused, especially since the man's body was found so close to our apartment building.

He'll probably get his brother to find out if what I told the police is the truth. And I really don't need that.

It occurs to me that I should delete the calls I had from Ruben on my phone along with the searches I carried out on my browser. After it's done I sit there on the sofa for what seems like an eternity, my stomach churning with dread, my mind freewheeling. The air in the room is warm, heavy – claustrophobic.

I get up and walk over to the window, push it open and breathe in the cold air. The sun is still shining, but some benign clouds have started to gather in the sky over North London.

I hear a voice in my head telling me I made a huge mistake by not calling the police after I killed Swift.

Surely they would have believed that you had no choice and struck him in self-defence?

But it's followed by a more convincing voice, that says I was right to flee the scene.

You couldn't take that chance, Emma. You would have had to explain why you stabbed him, what you were doing there and why he was blackmailing you. And it would have got back to Tommy...

I leave the window open and go into the kitchen. It's lunchtime already, so I see no harm in pouring myself a glass of wine. But before I drink it, I look down at my tummy and say to my unborn baby, 'Please bear with me little one. One of these won't hurt you and it'll help me to get through the day. And I promise I'll find a way out of this mess so that when you eventually come into the world, everything will be okay.'

I chug back the wine even though I know I shouldn't. But how else am I going to shift the unease in the pit of my stomach and stop my thoughts from burning like a fuse?

The problem is, I've already tried to come up with a workable solution to my predicament. A way of moving on with my life and becoming a mother without incurring my husband's wrath. But, so far, I've failed, and that's not good because I know that my day of reckoning is fast approaching.

The afternoon passes slowly and I spend most of it sitting on the sofa or lying on the bed. My gut is fighting off more waves of nausea and I have to keep swallowing back the bile that rises in my throat.

I check my phone browser from time to time, but there are no further updates on the murder investigation. However, I do learn that a man has been stabbed to death in Wandsworth Prison and two other men have been badly beaten. They're all Albanians according to the reports and I wonder if it means that Tommy has got his revenge against those who attacked him.

I'm reminded of the occasional conversations I overheard between Tommy, Liam and Jack Fraser after I found out what they did. I'd hear them discuss how someone had been 'sorted' or 'got rid of' or 'made to pay' for whatever it was they'd done.

Occasionally a name would be mentioned and then days or weeks later, I'd read in the papers about a man with the same name going missing or turning up dead. And I'd know in my heart that the Driscolls were behind it.

I dealt with it by convincing myself that those who were targeted were no angels themselves. That Tommy moved on them before they made a move on him. I wonder if it will be any easier to justify his behaviour in the future now that I'm a killer myself.

When I notice that it's five o'clock and dark outside, I decide to go for a walk. Having sat around for most of the day, I feel restless and my body is rigid with tension.

But as I head into the hall to get my coat, the internal service phone buzzes for the second time today. When I answer it, Edward tells me that I have another visitor.

'It's a Detective Chief Inspector Brannigan, Mrs Driscoll. He says he needs to speak to you urgently.'

CHAPTER FORTY-THREE

Brannigan is by himself when I open the door. A week has passed since he came up to me while I was having a drink outside the Old Thameside Inn. I don't want to talk to him again, but I need to find out if he's got anything new to say. If he hasn't, then I'll send him packing, repeating my threat to report him for harassment.

'What do you want with me now, Detective Brannigan?' I ask as I try to keep the anxiety out of my voice.

'I've got a few questions that I need to ask you in relation to what's happened since your husband's trial ended,' he says. 'I promise it won't take long.'

He follows me into the kitchen and I notice that his suit carries a heavy stench of cigarette smoke. My throat is as dry as sand, so I put the kettle on and ask him if he wants a tea or coffee.

'That's kind of you, Emma. I'll have tea please. Milk, no sugar.'

His use of my first name has always annoyed me. It started when he first came here with a team from Scotland Yard's Serious and Organised Crime squad to search the flat after Tommy's arrest. I reckon it's his way of trying to build a rapport with me in the hope that I'll eventually provide him with incriminating evidence against the Firm.

'I gather you had a visit from two of my colleagues in the Met today?' he says as he takes a seat at the breakfast bar.

I feel the blood stir inside me, a hot flush through my veins.

'That's right,' I tell him.

'Detective Inspector Berry informed me that you weren't able to help them.'

'No, I wasn't. I never knew the man who was killed and I've no idea why he was searching for information online about me.'

The kettle boils and I make the teas. Brannigan waits for me to place his cup in front of him before he speaks again.

'The murder of Ruben Swift on Monday evening was of no interest to me until your name was flagged up,' he says. 'It struck me as odd – and suspicious – that it took place so close to your home.'

I fix him with a hard stare across the breakfast bar. 'Are you seriously suggesting that I had something to do with it?'

He pushes a faint smile onto his lips. 'Not at all. From what little I know about you, I don't think you have a murderous bone in your body. But the same can't be said for your husband, can it?'

'In case you haven't heard, my husband is in hospital after he was stabbed.'

'Oh, I know about that, Emma. But it doesn't mean he didn't arrange for Mr Swift to be killed in that yard off Laxton Street.'

I'm taken aback. 'Surely you can't be serious? Why on earth would he do that?'

'That's the million-dollar question,' he replies. 'But let's consider the facts.' He spreads out a hand and begins to tick off a list with his fingers. 'We know that Mr Swift was looking you up on the internet. Perhaps he'd developed an obsession with you or he thought you'd be fair game now that Tommy will be in prison for a while? He even downloaded photos of you along with two of this building. That suggests to me that he was planning to come here. Did he turn up one night? Maybe he scared you and you told your husband, who then dealt with it the only way he knows how.'

I shake my head. 'That's ridiculous and you know it.'

'Then you're sticking to your story that you never met the man?'

'Of course, I am. I hadn't even heard of him before today. That's the truth. I swear!'

He doesn't believe me. I can tell. I suddenly feel completely helpless, vulnerable and defenceless. I'm worried where this will go if Brannigan insists on pursuing it. If he works in tandem with those investigating the killing, then the pressure on me will be ramped up even further. Christ only knows what they'll manage to unearth.

'How much do you know about what happened to Mr Swift?' he asks. 'I assume you've looked up the news stories out of curiosity.'

'Yes, I have. But they don't really say much.'

I sip at my tea and as I do so, I sneak a look at my watch. I'm aware that Tommy is likely to call me at any minute and I dread to think of how he'll react if he finds out that Brannigan is here.

'Have you discovered much about Mr Swift himself?' he presses.

'No, I haven't.'

'Well, it may interest you to know that he wasn't squeaky clean. He was recently sacked from his job as a financial adviser for sexually harassing women in his office, and then he got drunk and smashed up a pub.'

I raise my brow. 'In that case, isn't it likely that he had quite a few enemies and one of them did it instead?'

'That's the conclusion DI Berry and his team jumped to before they found the stuff about you on Swift's laptop.'

'The more you go on, the less sense you make, inspector,' I tell him. 'Neither me nor my husband had anything to do with that man's death. I know it's not what you want to hear, but it's true.'

'My gut tells me otherwise, Emma,' he says. 'I don't think you're being totally honest with me. Look, if Tommy got his heavies to attack Mr Swift, and you can help us prove it, then we can take steps to keep you out of it.'

'Is that right?' I snap and feel a spurt of irritation. 'Well, it sounds to me like you're grasping at straws because you're so desperate to bring down the Driscoll empire. And you're convinced that the way to do it is through me. But you're wasting your time. And let me repeat what I've already said: I didn't know Ruben Swift and I never met him.'

He pulls back his lips, exposing his teeth. 'Nice try, Emma. But as far as I'm concerned, it's all too much of a coincidence that the man who was stalking you online should suddenly turn up dead just a few streets away from here.'

'Come off it, detective. There are probably dozens of weirdos out there who have an unhealthy interest in me because I'm the wife of a high-profile gangster. And I don't doubt that some of them live or work within a few miles of this building.'

He drinks some of his tea and runs a knuckle across his lips. Then, after a long pause, he says, 'Okay, Emma, we'll leave it at that for now. But be warned that if you've lied to me, I will find out. And the consequences for you will be serious. So are you sure that—'

'That's enough, Brannigan!' I shout, cutting him off. 'I want you to go before I pick up the phone and call my lawyer. This is the second time you've harassed me in a week. If you approach me again, I intend to make a formal complaint. And then you'll be the one facing the consequences.'

He shrugs his shoulders and gets down off the stool. Then he shakes his head at me, his eyes intent under dark brows. 'I hope for your sake that I'm wrong and that you've told me the truth, Emma,' he says. 'But if you are covering for that amoral husband of yours, then you might well end up behind bars too. And that really would be a shame after all the shit you've already had to deal with.'

A new wave of panic courses through me after I close the door behind the detective. My heart is racing and it feels like my head is going to explode.

My situation is going from bad to worse at a rate of knots and I don't know how much more of it I can take. It was bad enough being at the mercy of my controlling husband while trying to keep my pregnancy secret. Now it's possible that I could soon be facing a murder charge. I can only hope that the police won't be able to prove that I've lied about not having met Ruben Swift. There are so many ways I can come unstuck. And if I do, I fear the police will never believe that I killed the man in self-defence.

I also have to consider what Tommy's response will be when they talk to him. Or maybe they already have. I've got to be careful what I say when he calls me. All I need is for him to suspect that I'm hiding something. If he does then he won't rest until he finds out what it is.

Before long, I'm cloaked in a deep sense of despair and find myself shedding tears of self-pity. I get quite a shock when I realise it's ten o'clock. I've been so wrapped up in my own agonising thoughts that I was unaware of the time passing.

I'm not sure if I've dozed off, so I check my phone to see if I've missed any calls from Tommy. But I haven't.

And that's a relief. It must mean that he's not been able to call me, probably because of the move back to prison from the hospital.

I feel like I've drunk too much and my eyelids are heavy and drooping. But that doesn't stop me popping a sleeping pill.

I switch off the lights and slope off to the bedroom, where I slip out of my clothes. I don't bother to remove my mascara or clean my teeth. Instead, I crawl under the duvet and pray for an end to this nightmare for the sake of my baby. Then I close my eyes and eventually drop into the icy embrace of oblivion.

CHAPTER FORTY-FOUR

It's mid-afternoon and I've spent another day feeling that my life is about to implode. Every nerve in my body is buzzing and wave after wave of misery washes over me. I feel bereft, empty of everything, and my sense of self-worth has been completely shattered.

Tommy just called to tell me that he's back in Wandsworth.

'I didn't have a phone yesterday, so I couldn't call you,' he explained. 'How was your day?'

'I had a weird experience,' I told him. 'Two detectives came here to ask about a man who'd been murdered nearby.' I decided to reveal this because I suspected he already knew, but I didn't tell him about Brannigan's visit.

'They came to see me as well,' he said. 'I told them I'd never heard of any Ruben Swift.'

'Same here. I can't think why he was looking us up online.'

'It was you the guy was interested in, Emma. The coppers told me he downloaded photos of you and our apartment block.' There's a note of suspicion in his voice and it unsettles me.

'That's right. It's all really strange.'

'Are you sure you didn't know him?'

'Of course, I'm sure. The name means nothing to me and I can only think that he was following the trial and wanted to find out more about me.'

'So, was that the highlight of your day?' he asked me, and I felt relieved that he didn't sound overly concerned.

'I'm afraid so. I did some cleaning and then some yoga, but mostly I sat and watched television.'

'Did you see anyone else?'

'No, I thought about going to my sister's but decided to do that at the weekend instead.'

He said he hadn't got much time before he'd be disturbed again so he asked a few more mundane questions and then cut the conversation short.

'I'll call you later if I get the chance,' he told me. 'Take care and know that I love you.'

'Love you too, Tommy.'

More lies, more deception, more reasons to feel like I'm making an already bad situation much worse.

Tommy sounded deeply suspicious when he was asking about Ruben. Perhaps he doesn't believe that I didn't know him. If so, then he might get his brother to look into it on his behalf, and Liam would likely make things even more difficult for me. I already know that my husband doesn't

247

trust me, following my visit to the pub with Ajay. And it's so hard to convince him that I'm his loyal and loving wife when I don't want to be.

My view of the man now oscillates between a 'controlling monster' and a 'pathetic excuse for a human being' desperate to cling onto his most prized possession.

Dark memories of our time together suddenly surface in my head and remind me why I'm so glad that he's locked up.

I always knew that marriage would entail some loss of my liberty, but what I've gone through is nothing less than ruthless subjugation. The stress of it all is making my skin clammy with dread and panic, and I feel hot tears threatening once again.

I don't want to cry, so I heave myself up off the sofa and head to the kitchen in search of a distraction. I put the kettle on, force down a couple of digestive biscuits, and check my phone. There are no new messages or emails and I haven't missed any calls.

I go online and use my browser to search for updates on the Ruben Swift murder investigation. But there aren't any, and I have to assume that's a good thing.

As the evening draws in, the last thing I expect is a visitor. So, I feel the breath catch in my throat when I hear the doorbell ring. I'm pretty sure it can't be the police again because the concierge would have called up to tell me. That means it has to be either Liam or Fraser, and when I peer through the peephole, I see that it's both of them. I really don't want to let them in, though I know I have to.

'We need to have a talk, Emma,' Liam says as he brushes past me into the hall.

Fraser is at least polite and smiles as he gestures for me to follow his boss while he closes the door behind us.

It's long been a source of resentment to me that Liam acts like he has as much right to be in the flat as I do. If I'm going to be stuck here for a while it's one of the issues I want to address when I get the chance.

Liam goes straight through to the living room and up to the bar, where he opens the Scotch and pours some into a glass.

'Help yourself why don't you?' I say with as much sarcasm as I can muster.

He turns to me, his mouth pinched and drawn in tight. 'As long as the Driscolls are paying for this flat, I'll do as I please when I'm here, Emma. You need to get used to that.'

His tone is sneering and condescending, and I know he would never have spoken to me like that before Tommy went inside.

'What do you want, Liam?' I ask. 'I was just about to go to bed.'

He downs some Scotch and then carries the glass over to the sofa and sits down. Fraser moves across the room and stands behind him with his arms crossed.

'Tommy asked us to drop by,' Liam says. 'He wants to

know why you've been meeting up with Detective Brannigan. Are you feeding him information about the family?'

I swallow hard and splutter my words. 'What? Of c-course not. He came here to ask about the man who was murdered. Ruben Swift.'

'Then why didn't you tell your husband when you spoke to him?'

I shrug. 'It slipped my mind. Plus, he wasn't able to speak for very long.'

'What about when you met with Brannigan a few days ago? Did that slip your mind too?'

The question catches me out, but I manage to control my reaction. 'He appeared suddenly when I was sitting by myself outside a pub having a drink. I told him to piss off, that I had nothing to say to him.'

'Then why keep it secret?'

By now, there's a pounding in my head and I have to pause to breathe in some air.

'I didn't mention it to Tommy because I didn't think he needed to know,' I say. 'He's got enough on his plate as it is.'

'And we're supposed to believe that, are we?' he scoffs.

'You'll have to, Liam, because it's the truth. Why would I lie?'

He stares at me, his eyes cold. 'That's what I want to know, Emma. I also want to know what went on between you and that Swift bloke.'

I feel my stomach clench. Him asking about Brannigan is bad enough, but he can't find out about Ruben.

'Jesus, Liam. I've already told Tommy that I never met the man and I have no idea why he was searching for information about me. I wish I did, but I don't.'

'The cops think you do and they believe Tommy might have arranged for him to be dealt with.'

'Well, that's not my fault.'

He clucks his tongue. 'Look, Emma. Since the trial, you've done nothing to convince us of your loyalty to the family. First, you gave us the impression that you don't intend to abide by Tommy's rules, and then you go out boozing with a bloke the first chance you get and force us to put him in hospital. Now by having secret conversations with Brannigan, you're making Tommy think that you're plotting with the Old Bill behind his back.'

'But that's total nonsense. You must realise that,' I snap.

'The only thing I know for sure is that you want to abandon your husband when he most needs you. And you seem to think that we'll let you do that.'

I stare back at him, not trusting myself to speak. I can feel a chill creeping through me, and once again I curse myself for marrying into this demonic family.

Liam sips at his drink and then breaks eye contact with me to look at his watch.

I remain standing in the middle of the room, my body shaking, a ball of fury building up inside me.

'Would you like me to pour you a drink, Ems?'

This from Fraser, who I'm guessing feels some sympathy for me.

I'm just about to respond when my phone rings. It's lying on the coffee table and I can't decide whether to pick it up because I fear it could be Tommy.

'You should answer it, Emma,' Liam says. 'It'll be your mum.'

His words send a shock wave through me. 'How do you know that?'

A cruel smile plays on his lips. 'I just do. And I also know that she wants to thank you for the gifts she's just received.'

Panic squeezes the breath from my lungs as I reach for the phone and discover that it is indeed my mother and she's FaceTiming me.

'Hi there, Mum.' I try to sound calm and unflustered, but Liam's words have me rattled. 'Are you okay? Is anything wrong?'

'Far from it,' she replies. 'I'm over the moon with the presents you sent over and your friend Max wanted me to call you to say they'd arrived.'

Max? I don't know anyone by that name.

'Just go along with it,' Liam mouths at me as he gets up from the sofa.

On the screen, I see my mother sitting at the kitchen table in her flat, a big smile on her face. She's holding a bunch of flowers in one hand and a large box of chocolates in the other. 'Max said you wanted to show me how much you love me,' she says. 'And you've certainly done that. Thank you so much. It's such a lovely surprise.'

A man I've never seen before steps into view behind

her. He's tall and broad-shouldered with a square jaw and thin mouth.

'I got exactly what you asked me to get, Ems,' he says to the camera, and the tone of familiarity in his voice makes me cringe. 'And I'm really glad I've met your mum at last. She's a gem. I'll be off now.'

My mother then thanks me again and tells me that she loves me.

'I'm so lucky to have you as a daughter,' she says. 'Will I be seeing you at the weekend?'

'I hope so, yes.'

'That's great. You can help me eat the chocolates.'

Liam snatches my phone from me and switches it off.

'What the fuck was all that about?' I yell at him, losing my temper.

'Surely it's not hard for you to guess, Emma,' he responds calmly, the smile back in place. 'Tommy wanted to remind you just how much you've got to lose if you carry on treating him with contempt. Next time our man Max pays your old lady a visit, it won't be to deliver presents.' He hands me my phone back and adds, 'We'll be off now and you can go to bed. And while you're lying there in the dark, I suggest you reflect on how fucking easy it will be for us to make you suffer if you're disloyal.'

He nods at Fraser and they both head for the door. I want desperately to cry, but I fight against it because I don't want to give him the satisfaction of knowing how shocked and scared I am.

* * *

253

After Liam and Fraser leave, I feel mentally fried, but at least I manage not to cry.

Instead, I hurriedly call my mother back. I want to know that she's all right and that the man calling himself Max has gone.

To my immense relief, he has, and Mum tells me she's getting ready for bed.

'Of course, I'm okay,' she says. 'Why wouldn't I be? I've just put your lovely flowers in a vase. It was such a nice gesture, Ems.'

'I'm glad you like them. Did Max say much?'

'Not at all. I asked him if he would like a cup of tea, but he had to rush off. It was kind of him to bring them over for you. He said you wanted to do it yourself but something came up and you couldn't.'

'Er, that's right,' I lie. 'I had a meeting with the lawyer. Just a routine thing.'

'So how do you two know each other? I didn't get a chance to ask him.'

I say the first thing that comes into my head. 'He's an old friend of Tommy's.'

'Is that right? Well, he seems a very nice man.'

If only you knew! The guy probably wouldn't think twice about cutting your throat if Tommy or Liam told him to.

'And how are you coping, my love?' she asks.

'I'm taking each day as it comes, Mum,' I say, tears pricking my eyes. 'Things need to settle down before I can focus on the future.'

'What's the latest on Tommy? Is he still in the hospital?'

'No. He's back in prison and on the mend.'

'Is he leaving you alone?'

Once again, I resist the urge to reveal what I'm going through. Instead, I lie and tell her that he hasn't been bothering me. And that she has nothing to worry about. Which is true as it's me who has everything to worry about.

After Mum and I say goodnight to each other, I make myself a tea. The flat suddenly feels suffocating despite its size, but it's too late to go for a walk. Plus, it's started to rain outside.

I sit on the sofa grinding my teeth as a rush of adrenaline sears through my senses. Before long, my brain is aching with the effort of thinking and worrying.

Even after I climb into bed, Liam's words echo in my head.

Next time our man Max pays your old lady a visit, it won't be to deliver presents.

I want to believe that it's an empty threat, but I know it isn't. Liam wouldn't think twice about ordering someone to hurt my mother, or any other member of my close family.

In that sense, he's just like his brother. They're both psychopaths who lack empathy and morals. And they have hearts of stone. It's why so many people fear and respect them, and why they're so successful at what they do. It's also why I'm in such an impossible situation. The only way I can think of to stop them wreaking further havoc in my life is to abort my baby and live by Tommy's rules for at least five more years.

But I'm not willing to entertain this option, which means, as impossible as it seems, I have to find another way out of the mess I'm in.

CHAPTER FORTY-FIVE

I wake on Friday morning at six after a fitful night's sleep, but I can't be bothered to get out of bed straight away. I've got nothing to do and nowhere to go, and I know I'll spend another day torturing myself with thoughts of impending disaster.

My eyes are dry and heavy, so I keep them closed in the hope that I'll drop off again. But that proves to be wishful thinking and I'm still awake almost an hour later.

When I finally get up, I put some music on, hoping it will drown out those destructive thoughts while I make myself a coffee.

I drink it as I look out of the kitchen window. The day is grey and oppressive and a dark mass of clouds hangs over the city. It does nothing to make me feel any better. And my mood doesn't improve as the morning progresses.

It requires a monumental effort to shower and dress, and then I make myself eat some cereal, which I just about manage to keep down.

I go online to see if there's anything new on Ruben's investigation, but it seems not. The story itself has been relegated by most of the news providers, partly because another gruesome murder has taken place in London. A young woman was beaten to death last night while walking home from a late shift at an East End restaurant. She hasn't been named and at this stage police have no idea what the motive was.

It serves as a chilling reminder of what could happen to me. Hardly a day goes by when someone isn't shot or stabbed or badly roughed up in the capital. And it's in part down to people like my husband, crime lords who traffic drugs and people and don't care how much damage they cause.

I feel guilty thinking about it because it's the money from all the pain and suffering that pays for this flat and the other luxuries that I've enjoyed over the past two years. I wonder if I'll ever be able to forgive myself.

By eleven o'clock, I'm feeling stir-crazy and decide I need to get out of the flat, at least for a short while. I put on my coat and shoes and grab my handbag. I'm just about to pull open the front door when my mobile goes off.

I pull it from my pocket and see that there's no caller ID, which makes me think it's Tommy. And it is.

'I wasn't expecting you to call this early,' I answer.

'Something has happened, Ems, and I need you to do me a favour.'

I feel a shiver of anxiety, which causes my throat to thicken. I have to cough to clear it before responding.

'What is it, Tommy? What's happened?'

'It's my mum. She's been rushed to hospital with a suspected heart attack. Liam got word to me and he reckons she's in a bad way. I want you to go to the hospital. It's important to me. Are you at home?'

'Yes, I am.'

'Then go and wait downstairs. Jack is on his way to pick you up. He won't be long.'

'Er, right.'

'Do you have a problem with that?' he asks sharply.

'No, of course I don't. I just hope Ruby pulls through.' And it's true despite my feelings towards her.

'We all do,' he says. 'You can now see why I wanted you to keep an eye on her. I've been worried for a long time that something like this might happen. She hasn't been herself for ages.'

'I'll go and get ready,' I tell him.

'You do that. And make sure I'm kept informed.'

'I will.'

He hangs up before I do and I'm left surprised by this turn of events and I can't help wondering what it might mean for my future.

CHAPTER FORTY-SIX

Minutes later, I'm waiting in front of the block for Fraser to turn up. My thoughts are with Ruby. Even though she never warmed to me, I don't want her to die.

I recall how rough she looked the last time I saw her in the Clapham wine bar just a few days ago. But even then, she was still feisty enough to admonish and threaten me. I would never have guessed that she was only days away from having a heart attack.

It strikes me as bizarrely ironic that only yesterday her two sons issued a stark warning to me in respect of my own mother. But it's not something I'll dare to bring up with them.

Fraser pulls up in the familiar black Range Rover after about ten minutes. As I climb into the passenger seat, he says, 'Was it Tommy or Liam who rang you, Emma?'

'Tommy.'

'And how much did he tell you?'

'Only that Ruby has suffered a suspected heart attack and that he wants me to go to the hospital.'

He pulls away from the kerb and lets me know that our destination is King's College Hospital in Camberwell.

'It happened just after eight this morning and she was lucky in the sense that she wasn't alone in the house,' he tells me. 'Her cleaner had just arrived to start work. Ruby called to her when she started getting chest pains and was having trouble breathing. The cleaner phoned the emergency service, but Ruby collapsed before the ambulance got there and a paramedic had to administer CPR.'

'My God.'

'I was with Liam when he was told and then I took him straight to the hospital. He managed to get word to Tommy through the official channels and Tommy called him half an hour later to tell him that he wanted you at the hospital to show support for the family.'

'It's come as a shock, Jack,' I say. 'We can only hope that the trauma team can work their magic.'

Fraser shakes his head. 'Liam told her to go for a check-up weeks ago, but she wouldn't. You know what she's like. She just kept telling him not to fret, that she was in good health for her age. So, we don't know if she'd been experiencing any symptoms.'

Memories come rushing back and swirl through my mind. I remember Tommy telling me how active Ruby was when she was younger. She played tennis and golf and attended Pilates classes. As recently as six months ago, she was going on regular walks around Dulwich Park.

'When was the last time you saw her?' I ask.

'That would be when I took you to the new wine bar. I gather Tommy has been urging you to get more involved with her?'

I nod. 'That's right. I expect he'll up the pressure after this.'

'You should know that Liam doesn't think it's a good idea,' he says. 'And assuming Ruby gets through this, I don't think she'll be too keen to have you around.'

'That's what I told Tommy. I know she doesn't like me, but he thinks I can win her over.'

'He's desperate for you to have a better relationship with both Ruby and his brother. He thinks it'll make it easier to keep you tied to him while he's banged up.'

I'm surprised that Fraser is being so open and honest with me, and it makes me wonder if his loyalty to the family is flagging now that things have changed and Liam is at the helm.

I'm eager to ask him, but I accept that now is not the time. So, I hold it in and we both stay silent as we make our way through South London.

King's College is one of the city's major trauma centres and I know it well because it's where my own father passed away after a long battle with cancer. I haven't been back there since and I feel a surge of blood rush to my face as we approach it.

'They'll both take it hard if she doesn't survive,' Fraser says. 'She's been their rock since their dad died.'

I nod. 'Tommy worships her and he loves the fact that he's clearly her favourite.'

Fraser grins. 'It's been a source of friction between the brothers ever since I've known them. Tommy liked to wind Liam up about it and more than once Ruby has had to step in and insist that she doesn't have a favourite. But we know she does.'

I recall one occasion when I actually felt sorry for Liam. We were at Ruby's house and over Sunday lunch she told him that he needed to be more like his older brother if he wanted to make a success of his life. Liam retorted that he was happy with himself the way he was and then got up and stormed out of the room.

'That's why Ruby has always had a problem with you, Emma,' Fraser continues. 'She feels that no woman is good enough for her eldest son. And she hates the fact that he's not prepared to let you go. She just doesn't get it.'

'And yet she's prepared to go along with it.'

'Tommy is insistent. I've heard the conversations he's had with her and Liam. He's made them promise not only to keep you in line, but also to take care of you. Letting you go is not an option.'

'And what about you, Jack?' I ask. 'What do you think of what he's doing to me and his set of fucking rules?'

He shakes his head. 'It's not for me to say. I work for him. If I took a view on all that shit, I wouldn't be able to.'

I continue to stare at him but he looks straight ahead and it's clear that's the end of the conversation.

Liam is no longer in the emergency department so Fraser has to ring him to find out where he is. We then make our way to a small waiting room close to the cardiac operating theatres.

Liam is by himself, his pale, chubby face stricken with shock and bewilderment.

'How is she?' Fraser asks him.

He turns down the corners of his mouth and shrugs. 'I'm not sure. All they've told me is that she had a massive heart attack and was in a critical condition when they brought her in. They're now operating on her and all we can do is wait.'

'Well at least she's in good hands,' I say.

Liam turns and I flinch as his gaze sweeps over me. 'I don't know why Tommy wants you to be here, Emma,' he says. 'We all know that you can't stand my mum and you're probably glad that this has happened to her.'

I feel my jaw drop. 'That's a terrible thing to say, Liam. You can't possibly mean it.'

He looks straight at me, his face unreadable, and I can almost hear the wheels turning in his head as he forms a response.

But before he can get it out, the door to the waiting room opens and a man wearing a surgical gown walks through. He introduces himself with a heavy Irish accent as cardiac surgeon Paul Slattery.

'Is the operation over?' Liam asks. 'I'm her son. Please tell me she's going to be all right.'

The surgeon meets Liam's stricken gaze. 'I'm afraid we did not manage to save your mother, sir,' he says solemnly. 'We spent almost two hours fighting to keep her alive, but tragically there was simply too much damage to her heart. I am so very sorry.'

Liam presses his eyes shut and takes a deep breath. I feel a sob rise in my chest and I want to reach out and place a hand on his shoulder. But I don't, sure he won't want me to.

CHAPTER FORTY-SEVEN

What Liam said to me moments ago is still reverberating in my mind, but despite that, I feel his pain. And I know that Tommy is going to be heartbroken.

I'm not sure what to do so I just stand there biting my lip. I'm sad and shocked, but I don't feel an overwhelming urge to cry, and I can't force tears out.

Ruby wasn't someone I'll miss and her passing won't leave a gaping hole in my life. But I expect there will be implications that haven't yet become obvious. And it remains to be seen how they'll affect me.

Liam puffs out his chest and wipes at his eyes with the back of his hand. Then he tells the surgeon that he wants to see his mother.

Fraser and I stay in the waiting room and when we're alone, I ask him who he thinks should break the news to Tommy.

'Liam's been given the number of the mobile that Tommy's

using,' he says. 'I expect he'll send a message and Tommy will ring back.'

'And what do you think I should do, Jack?'

'Let's wait and see what Liam wants. I've an idea he'll be keen to go to Ruby's house, so I'll have to take him. And he may or may not want you to go too.'

My stomach is tied in knots and I'm suddenly desperate to be anywhere else but here. I'm pretty sure that Liam won't want me around to see him grieve, and my continued presence will in all likelihood make him angry.

I find myself reflecting on my various encounters with Ruby and how she never showed me any genuine affection. She often acted as though I wasn't in the room and never made me feel welcome when I visited her house with Tommy. And the last time I came face to face with her in the Clapham wine bar she made her feelings towards me plain.

'You're an ungrateful bitch, Emma. You ought to be thankful that my son loves you and wants to go on protecting you. I just pray that he eventually comes to his senses and casts you adrift.'

It's hard for me to remember Ruby as anything other than a nasty old woman who passed on her obnoxious genes to her two sons. She was sixty-five when I was first introduced to her so maybe she used to be nicer and less formidable before life finally wore her down, but I doubt it.

Tommy never had a bad word to say about her and he basked in the adulation she lavished on him. I've often wondered if she encouraged him to treat me like his possession rather than his wife. Perhaps that's why he continues to believe that his behaviour towards me is acceptable.

When Liam returns after fifteen minutes or so, his eyes are red and the tendons in his neck look as if they might burst through the skin.

'At least she looks at peace,' he says to Fraser rather than to both of us. 'I've sent a text to Tommy along with a photo of Mum. He hasn't responded yet, so I suspect he can't get to his phone.'

'What now, boss?' Fraser asks him. 'Are there things you need to do?'

'First off, I'm gagging for a fag,' he responds. 'Let's go outside while I get my thoughts together.'

He turns to me then and his eyes narrow as he searches my face.

'I wasn't sure you'd still be here,' he says, his voice suddenly hostile.

Before I can summon up a response, he pushes past me and strides back out of the waiting room.

The sun has broken through the clouds by the time we get outside. I'm determined not to let my emotions get the better of me so I don't walk off in a huff. Liam is in shock and it wouldn't be right to take offence at his attitude towards me. So, I follow meekly behind him and Fraser as they find a quiet spot on the pavement close to the entrance to the emergency department.

They both light up and I'm not offered a fag because

they know I've given up smoking. I feel tense and awkward and Fraser obviously senses my discomfort because he unexpectedly asks me if I need to be anywhere.

I shake my head and put my hands in my pockets, not knowing what else to do with them.

Liam closes his eyes for a few seconds and then sucks so hard on his fag that it makes his cheeks bulge. When he opens them again, he looks at me and says, 'There's no point you hanging around, Emma. You obeyed your husband's instruction by coming here even though I know you didn't want to. Now you can go home, but you'll have to make your own way because Jack is not paid to be your fucking chauffeur.'

I'm unable to supress a surge of anger. 'I've had enough of this, Liam,' I say. 'I'm really sorry about Ruby, but there's no need to treat me like this. I didn't kill her, for God's sake.'

His eyes grow large, like those of a startled animal. 'I'm not so sure about that. You've caused her nothing but stress. She knew from the start that you weren't right for my brother and that's why she pleaded with him to get shot of you. If only he'd listened, he wouldn't be where he is now.'

'What do you mean by that?' I snap.

'You know what I mean. I'm convinced that you put that gun in his car to fit him up. You wanted out of the marriage and that was the only way you could do it. Or so you thought.'

My breath stalls and it feels like icy fingers are stroking my spine. 'That's an outrageous accusation to make and you know it. How the hell would I know how to lay my hands on a gun?'

'Because Tommy told you. It came up during a lunch at Mum's house. I mentioned how easy it had become to buy all kinds of weapons. It sparked your interest and you asked a couple of questions. Tommy answered them and even let slip a name or two.'

'That's ridiculous, Liam. I wouldn't have. . .' I trail off, speechless.

He shakes his head and tuts. 'Oh yes you would, Emma, because you think you're so fucking clever, but you're not. You couldn't wait to get Tommy out of the way. As soon as he was banged up, you started playing around. There was the yoga guy and I'm sure you must have had something going with the bloke who was found dead. Maybe it was even you who killed him. I wouldn't put it past you. After all, it's fucking obvious that you're a cold-hearted bitch. That's why you're now working with Brannigan to put us out of business.'

I'm trembling uncontrollably and my insides are on fire. The bastard is determined to blame and belittle me, and I'm not prepared to take it any more.

I don't bother to respond, though, because I know that if I do, I'll probably choke on my words. Instead, I squeeze my lips together, push my shoulders back and walk away from there as fast as I can.

CHAPTER FORTY-EIGHT

It's almost three miles from Camberwell to the South Bank, but I decide to walk it. I'm hoping it will help me to calm down and restore my equilibrium. My heart is beating hard and heavy beneath my ribs, and too many thoughts are colliding inside my head.

Liam's tirade has unnerved as well as upset me. I wonder if he actually believes that I was responsible for Tommy's arrest or he's just saying it to hurt me. As much as I wanted to see the back of my husband, I would not have had the guts to plant a gun in his car and then tip the police off.

I'm still not a hundred per cent convinced that he wasn't a victim of his own stupidity. We only have his word that he didn't know the weapon was in the car until he opened the glove compartment and found it. The jury didn't believe him, so why should I?

I feel nothing but dread as I hurry away from the hospital.

The streets are busy with traffic and pedestrians, but I'm mostly oblivious to what is going on around me.

Ruby's sudden death is shocking enough, but I'm also having to process what Liam said. Those accusations are a little too close for comfort and the fact that he seems genuinely to believe that I'm colluding with the police to bring him down worries me. It's clear that he's eager to make things difficult for me, to turn my husband against me. He wants me gone because to him I'm a burden as well as a perceived threat.

He needs to prove himself in his new role as the syndicate boss and I'm adding to the pressure he's under. I'm a problem that has to be solved and that makes him extremely dangerous, especially now that there's no one to keep him under control. His mother's dead and Tommy is locked up.

As I walk on, it feels like I'm carrying a huge weight. I have to bite my lips to contain my emotions.

I know this area of South London well, but it's been a long time since I ventured through it on foot. This is part of the Driscoll manor. They control most of the drug trade, the prostitution and the fencing of illegal contraband here. Tommy used to spend a lot of his time doing business around here, and just beyond Camberwell Green are the council flats where he lived during the first fifteen years of his life. I give them a cursory glance as I stroll past and it occurs to me that if he'd begun life somewhere else, he might have turned out to be a very different person.

Beyond the flats, I carry on walking along Walworth Road and then continue to the Elephant and Castle. All the while, I've been expecting my phone to ring, but it doesn't until I'm on Southwark Bridge Road several minutes later. I answer it because I suspect it's Tommy and I'm right.

'Where are you, Emma?' he demands to know, his voice scratchy.

'I'm walking home from the hospital,' I tell him. 'I'm really sorry about your mum. Liam told me he sent you a message.'

'He did, and I'm gutted. I'll miss her so much, and I'll always regret being stuck in here when it happened.'

'It's a terrible shame, Tommy.'

'But Liam also told me that you and him had words, Ems.'

'I wouldn't put it that way, Tommy. Your brother had a go at me and basically told me to piss off. He also accused me of killing Ruby by causing her so much stress.'

I hear him suck in a breath.

'I can only apologise, Ems. He just said that he could tell you didn't want to be there and it annoyed him, so he thought it best if you didn't go back to Mum's place with them.'

'That's not what happened. You can ask Fraser. He was there.'

'I can believe it. But this is all I need today of all days. Liam's a prick and he was out of order. I'll speak to him.'

'There's no need. It's not the first time he's said nasty things to me.'

273

'Well, you shouldn't have to put up with it. He's supposed to be looking after you, not slagging you off. I know now that I was right to be worried about how he would handle things. And with Mum gone, he's bound to act up even more.'

'He doesn't want me around,' I say. 'He even accused me of planting that gun in your car.'

'Ah, well, I've tasked him with finding out who really did it and he hasn't been able to.'

'Well, he's starting to scare me, Tommy. You told me plenty of times how reckless and unpredictable he can be. Without you around, I don't feel safe.'

'You don't have to worry about him hurting you, Emma. He wouldn't dare because he knows what will happen to him if he did.'

I start to ask Tommy if he expects me to get involved in his mother's funeral arrangements, but he interrupts to say that someone is about to enter his cell before he abruptly hangs up.

My mind chews over what he said as I carry on walking. But his words do not reassure me. Despite what Tommy likes to believe, his brother is now the main man and will be for at least five years. And no doubt he'll have the full support of Jack Fraser, whose loyalty is first and foremost to the Firm.

As Liam's confidence grows, the hold my husband has over him will weaken. If he decides to take me out of the picture there'll be nothing or no one to stop him doing so. He could make me disappear, arrange for me to have a fatal accident, or force me to run away. If he bides his time,

Liam will eventually discover that I'm pregnant and he'll have no trouble then persuading Tommy that I'm an unfaithful slut who needs to be got rid of.

The panic builds up inside me during the last leg of my journey home.

Almost an hour after leaving King's College Hospital, I see my flat block. But when I reach the entrance, I'm in for yet another unpleasant surprise. Two familiar faces come out through the doors at that very moment.

Detective Inspector Berry and Detective Sergeant Warwick.

'Well, there's a coincidence,' DI Berry says, grinning. 'We came here to speak to you and the concierge said you'd gone out.'

'What do you want?' I respond nervously.

'We need to ask you some more questions relating to the murder of Ruben Swift, Mrs Driscoll. We can do it here in your flat or you can come to the station. It's up to you.'

CHAPTER FORTY-NINE

I feel a rush of despair as the two detectives follow me into the building.

Edward is the duty concierge and he smiles at me as we walk past the desk, but I don't smile back.

I can't believe this is happening. It's as though some dark force is working against me, doing its best to ensure that there's no respite from the unrelenting pressure.

Going up in the lift, DI Berry tries to make polite conversation by asking me if I've had a pleasant day so far.

'Not really,' I reply. 'My mother-in-law died this morning and I've just come from the hospital.'

He cocks an eyebrow, clearly shocked. 'Do you mean Ruby Driscoll?'

I nod. 'She suffered a massive heart attack and they couldn't save her.'

The two detectives exchange a look and Berry pulls out his phone and taps in what I assume to be a text message.

'I take it you're spreading the good news,' I say.

He looks up, a flicker of embarrassment in his eyes. 'I'm sorry for your loss, Mrs Driscoll, but I'm sure you can understand why I feel compelled to pass the information on to my superiors.'

I don't bother to respond because at that moment the lift stops and the doors open and I feel myself starting to shake. I wonder what it is they want to ask me. Have they found evidence linking me to what happened in Laxton Street? Do they know that I met Ruben Swift just over ten weeks ago? And that he was blackmailing me?

The fear is beating in my chest as I exit the lift and walk up to my flat. Once inside, I offer to make them tea or coffee, but they decline and this makes me think that this is not going to be a casual, friendly chat.

I lead them into the living room and invite them to be seated. My stomach does a slow roll when Berry takes out his notebook, and Warwick reaches for her phone.

'Have you made much progress with the investigation?' I ask them.

It's Berry who answers. 'Unfortunately, we haven't, but it's early days. We have established that Mr Swift was in considerable debt and owed money to some not very nice people. However, we still don't know why he was seeking information on yourself or if he had any links to your husband.'

'So, what new questions do you want to ask me that you didn't ask before?'

Berry glances down at his notes before meeting my gaze.

I suddenly wish I'd made myself a drink because my mouth is as dry as burnt toast.

'You told us that on Monday evening you went out for a short walk,' he says. 'But you didn't think you went near Laxton Street and you couldn't be sure of the exact time.'

'That's right.'

'Well, we'd like you to view a clip of CCTV that we've obtained, Mrs Driscoll. It shows a woman we believe to be you.'

He turns to DS Warwick. She gets up and holds out her phone so that I can see the screen.

'It only runs for a few seconds,' she says as she starts the clip.

As I watch it, I feel my heart grow heavier. The footage is slightly blurred, but it's definitely me walking along the pavement on the screen so I see no point in pretending that it isn't. Thankfully, it doesn't show me dropping anything into a rubbish bin and I'm clearly not in a great hurry to get to where I'm going.

'It certainly looks like me,' I say as cool as I can. 'Where was it captured?'

'On Cornwall Road, which is only a few streets away from where Mr Swift was found dead.'

'Then it confirms what I told you about going for a walk.'

'Indeed, it does, Mrs Driscoll,' Berry says. 'But because this was so close to Laxton Street and around the time we believe Mr Swift was killed, it also means we have to take it further.'

'What does that mean?'

'Well, for starters we would like to subject the coat and shoes you were wearing that evening to a forensic examination. We'd also request that you allow us to take your fingerprints and a DNA swab. We need to compare them with prints and DNA deposits found at the crime scene.'

I can feel my jaw drop in shock, even though this is just what I feared might happen. I know that if I don't cooperate, it will make them more suspicious.

'Does this mean you're going to arrest me?' I ask.

Berry shakes his head. 'We're not arresting you, Mrs Driscoll, and at this stage we're simply seeking to eliminate you from our inquiries. You won't even have to come to the station. We can take the coat and shoes with us and we can acquire your prints and DNA while we're here.'

Visions of a blood-covered Ruben Swift lying on the ground in the small enclosed yard fill my head suddenly and guilt tugs at my chest. Did I do enough to cover my tracks? Will they discover another CCTV clip that is far more incriminating?

'So how do you want to play it, Mrs Driscoll?' Berry asks me as his eyes search mine.

After a pause, I say, 'I'll go and fetch my coat. And I'm happy for you to do what you want to do here. I've got nothing to hide.'

I've already trashed the coat I was wearing that night, but I've got the smaller replica one. Tommy bought them both because he wasn't sure of my size. I always planned to take one back but never got round to it. Now I'm fervently glad I didn't. So, I give it to the detectives along with my shoes, which I carefully cleaned using polish and a knife to extract debris from the ridged soles.

Then they put a cotton bud in my mouth to obtain the DNA and use a mobile scanning device to take my prints. While they do this, I somehow manage to stay calm and swallow down my emotions.

'One final question,' Berry says. 'Do you often go for a walk in the evening carrying a rucksack?'

For a split second, I don't know how to respond, but then I find the words.

'Always. It's a habit. It comes in handy if I decide to get some shopping and when I'm carrying my yoga kit.'

His only reaction is to raise his brow, before asking me if they can take that with them as well.

After they've gone, I rush into the bedroom and throw myself on the bed, where I lay gasping like a landed fish.

CHAPTER FIFTY

I know I'm going to have a bad night so I take a sleeping pill to help me through it. The conversations I had today with the police, with Liam, with Tommy, are replaying continuously in my head, each one causing my heart to pound harder.

At the same time, my thoughts keep returning to Ruby and it makes me feel guilty because although I didn't want her to die, I'm so very glad that she will no longer play such a destructive role in my life.

It's almost ten o'clock by the time I properly get into bed, rain is hammering at the windows. I feel slightly woozy, and the voices in my head are now barely discernible, which is a good thing overall. But it still doesn't stop me crying silent tears of despair into the pillow as I find myself consumed by the darkness.

I can't help thinking that things are going to get much worse. The police are closing in, I'm sure of it. They have my coat, my shoes, and proof that I was close to where Ruben Swift was killed on Monday evening.

It's also clear to me now that Tommy's brother poses a growing threat. He doesn't like me or trust me and I'm effectively at his mercy. He arranged for two of his henchmen to beat up Ajay and then he sent another to my mother's house to scare me. Granted, he was acting on Tommy's orders, but I fear that it's only a matter of time before he stops being at my husband's beck and call. It would make his day to find out that I'm pregnant and it would give him the perfect excuse to inflict the most severe punishment on me.

Eventually, sleep pulls me under, but I keep waking during the night, tossing and turning, my body drenched in sweat. Each time I wake, I'm reminded yet again that I still haven't come up with a way to escape from my ever-worsening predicament.

Daylight is creeping through the cracks in the blinds. When I roll over to check the bedside clock, I see that it's 8 a.m. on Saturday morning.

I close my eyes again in the hope that I'll go back to sleep. I don't feel ready to get up. I'm still drowsy and my head is aching. I'm also dreading the prospect of having to deal with another unwelcome surprise. They've been coming thick and fast since the trial ended nearly two weeks ago and I'm almost in the habit of expecting them now. My life has become the stuff of nightmares and there's no reason for me to believe that my torment is coming to an end.

I decide that when I do get out of bed, I'll call my mum and sister. I should have told them yesterday about Ruby, but I had too much else on my mind. I wonder if they already know that she's dead. Would it have been considered newsworthy enough to have featured on the TV last night? Probably not, but I'm sure it will appear as a story in some of the morning papers and online sites.

The funeral will come next and Tommy will be hoping he'll be allowed to attend. I know I'll be expected to make an appearance, but I'd really rather give it a miss if I can. I'm sure that Liam won't want me there anyway.

It then occurs to me that I'm due to go and see Tommy on Monday for a visit. It's a gut-wrenching reminder that I'm going to have to find a way to stop seeing him soon. I can't go on hoping that my problem will solve itself. Unless I can distance myself from Tommy, he'll soon discover that I'm pregnant with someone else's child. And I cannot let that happen. But how in God's name can I prevent it?

I know now that I'm not going back to sleep. Too many disturbing thoughts are crashing through my mind. I open my eyes and push back the duvet.

But that's when I notice that something isn't right. The sheet over the mattress is supposed to be pristine white. But there's a large red stain beneath me that's unquestioningly blood.

My blood.

CHAPTER FIFTY-ONE

The sight of the blood on the sheet sends my heart into overdrive. I immediately throw my legs off the bed and stand up.

The blood is wet and fresh, and covers an area about the size of my hand.

I check and see that it's also dripping down the inside of my left thigh. It confirms what I already know – that the blood has come from inside me.

Fuck.

I tell myself not to panic, that bleeding and spotting are not uncommon during the first trimester of a pregnancy. But I also know that it can be the early sign of a miscarriage.

I have a choice. I can phone my doctor or the midwife and get their advice. Or I can follow my instinct and go straight to hospital.

I decide it's a no-brainer. St Thomas' Hospital is only a

ten-minute walk away. It has an emergency department and a maternity unit, and I know they'll examine me as a matter of urgency.

Thankfully, it appears that I've stopped bleeding now, which comes as a relief. I leave the blood stain on my thigh and rinse my face, but don't bother to take a shower or apply any make-up. I pull on some clothes – a pair of trousers and a loose jumper – and grab my phone, bag and coat.

My breathing is getting quicker by the second, in line with my racing heart. I'm also being ravaged by guilt because of the pill I took last night to help me sleep. Is that why I've been bleeding? Is it my own bloody fault? If so, and the worst happens, how can I ever forgive myself?

These questions taunt me as I hurry out of the flat. As I am going down in the lift, it occurs to me that I might be making things worse by rushing around instead of resting. But it's too late now. I'm already on my way to the hospital and I'm determined to get there as quickly as I can.

Sean is the duty concierge, he's on the phone as I pass so we just flash smiles at each other although mine is forced.

The weekend has begun with clear skies and there are only a few puddles left from the overnight rainfall.

As I step out of the building, I spot a black taxi pulling into the kerb to offload a passenger. I'm about to dash over, but a woman with two small children beat me to it. I don't want to waste time by explaining to the woman why she should let me have the taxi so I turn, throw my shoulders back and take assertive strides in the direction of the hospital.

I'm slightly comforted by the fact that I'm not experiencing any pain or cramping in my stomach. That has to be a good sign, I tell myself.

I walk fast, but I don't run, and it's not long before I'm panting heavily. At one point, I stop and look behind me because I suddenly feel like I'm being followed. There are lots of other pedestrians, but none of them appear to be showing any interest in me.

I shake my head, concluding that it's just my frazzled mind playing tricks and I continue to plough on, all the while praying that my baby is safe and sound within me.

When I approach the hospital, I'm reminded that it's where Ajay was treated after the Driscoll thugs beat him up. The memory piles on another layer of guilt because I've pushed him to the back of my mind and I shouldn't have.

Fear flushes through me as I walk into the hospital's accident and emergency department. I was expecting it to be much busier than it is, but it means I don't have to wait to speak to the receptionist. I explain that I'm eleven weeks pregnant and have been bleeding.

Next, I go through my symptoms in more detail with a triage nurse, who tells me I was right to come in and get checked over.

'It's better to be safe than sorry,' she reassures me.

I'm taken to the Antenatal Assessment Unit and it seems as though within minutes I'm being examined by a male doctor with a bald head and amiable brown eyes.

He explains that bleeding during early pregnancy can be caused by many things – changes to the cervix, a developing embryo embedding itself in the wall of the womb, a cervical polyp, an infection in the urinary tract. He then arranges for me to have an ultrasound scan and I tell him that I'm actually booked in to have one at eighteen weeks.

'Then look on the bright side,' he says. 'You'll get to see your baby a bit earlier.'

I take a deep breath and pray that it won't be the first and last time I see my baby.

An hour later, I'm told that I'm not having a miscarriage and that my baby has a healthy heartbeat. My own heart leaps with relief.

'Things are looking good,' the sonographer says, pointing to the tiny blob on the screen that is my baby. 'We can rule out an ectopic pregnancy and the cervix appears to be fine. So, try not to worry. About twenty per cent of women experience some bleeding during the early stages of pregnancy and in many cases the cause is never determined. We'll keep an eye on things during your routine appointments.'

I'm given a photo of a blown-up screenshot from the scan. It shows my baby tucked into a c-shape with the head towards the stomach and the arms and legs jutting outwards. I can even see the umbilical cord going from the abdomen to the placenta.

What I'm looking at warms my heart and reinforces my determination to keep my baby regardless of the problems and danger it will cause. Under no circumstances will I sacrifice my child.

I thank the sonographer and the doctor and tell them how relieved I am to be given the all-clear. I know that I'm very lucky because things could have turned out so different. And if they had, I would now be blaming myself.

As I head back out through the A & E department, I feel a smile creep onto my face because at last I have something to be pleased about.

However, the sense of euphoria doesn't last long. As I approach the exit, someone taps me on the shoulder. I stop and turn, and the sight of the man who's standing there wipes the smile from my face and causes the blood to stiffen in my veins.

'Hello there, Emma,' Jack Fraser says. 'I've been worried about you.'

CHAPTER FIFTY-TWO

The voices around me fade and it feels like the floor is shifting beneath my feet.

'What are you doing here, Jack?' I just about manage to say.

'I followed you,' he replies, as though it shouldn't come as a surprise.

He's dressed more casually than usual in a padded bomber jacket and tight jeans. But that doesn't make him appear any less threatening.

'I'll walk with you back to the flat,' he says. 'On the way, you can tell me if your baby is okay.'

I try to respond, but the words get stuck in my throat. My nerves are rattled and there's a sudden tightness across my chest that is almost painful.

A grin plays on his face. 'Don't bother trying to tell me that I've got this wrong, Emma. When we're outside, I'll explain how I know. And we can discuss what happens next.'

I feel light-headed suddenly and I can hear the blood beating in my ears.

Fraser takes my arm and I'm in a semi-trance as he leads me out through the exit.

Questions start to stab at my brain like sharp needles. How long has he known my secret? Does Tommy know? If so, then why hasn't he confronted me? And what is going to happen to me now? Should I run and scream and call for help?

Once outside, I take a deep breath to steady my nerves, but it's a struggle to keep the panic in.

Fraser steers me in the direction of the South Bank before letting go of my arm.

I walk beside him at a slow pace along Lambeth Palace Road, my stomach fizzing with anxiety. I don't know what to say to him or how many lies I'm going to have to tell. I'm too shocked to speak or even make sense of anything. This shouldn't be happening. I've been so careful to make sure that no one finds out I'm pregnant. So how and when did I slip up?

I was certain that I wasn't followed when I visited the doctor. But perhaps I was? After all, I sensed I was being tailed today and dismissed the thought when I couldn't see anyone behind me. But Fraser obviously was.

'Shall I start the conversation or do you want to?' he says suddenly.

We both stop and look at each other, and I fail to read anything in his expression other than curiosity.

After an awkward beat, he says, 'I can see you're in shock, Emma, so why don't I get the ball rolling? First let me put your mind at rest by making it clear that Tommy doesn't know. And I've only just found out myself purely by chance, so you've done well to keep a lid on it. And I'm guessing you've done that because it's not Tommy's baby. If you were nearly five months pregnant, I reckon you'd have a much bigger belly by now.'

I feel a rush of relief that my husband doesn't know, but is it misplaced? I can't be sure that Fraser is telling the truth.

He holds my gaze, waiting for me to respond, and when I don't, he gestures for me to carry on walking.

'There's a coffee shop up ahead,' he says. 'We can make a pit stop there and talk it through.'

I nod and start moving, and after a few steps, I find my voice.

'Tell me why you were following me and what it is you think you know,' I say.

Without breaking stride, he replies, 'Tommy called me earlier this morning and asked me to come and check that you were all right after what happened yesterday. He told me not to tell Liam. I wasn't planning to do anything else this morning, so I got a cab from home. It was pulling up outside your flats when I saw you rushing out. You looked flustered so I decided to follow you and I was surprised when you headed to the hospital. I saw you at reception and watched you walk away with one of the nurses. I went up to the desk and told the receptionist that my sister had just come in ahead of me while I parked my car. I gave your name and she said you'd been taken to the Antenatal Assessment Unit. I waited a little while before going there and told one of the nurses that I was looking for my sister. She said you were having a scan but that I shouldn't be overly anxious because a lot of women bleed early on in their pregnancy. And believe me,' he chuckles, 'that wasn't what I was expecting to hear.'

My heart dances in my chest as I think how unlucky I've been. If I had left the flat a few minutes earlier, Fraser wouldn't have seen me. Or if I'd left later, I could have told him I was fine and sent him on his way. But now I've got some explaining to do because it's clearly beyond the point where I can get away with telling him that it isn't true.

We don't speak again until we're facing each other across a table in the otherwise deserted coffee shop.

'Are you going to tell Tommy?' I ask.

'That depends on whether you've lost the baby,' he replies. 'If you have, then I won't need to and it can remain our secret.'

He doesn't spell out the alternative and I won't lie about losing my baby when it so very nearly happened.

'The scan showed that everything is okay,' I tell him. 'I've bled, but it hasn't caused any harm.'

'And how far gone are you?' I note that there's not a trace of emotion in his voice.

'Eleven weeks now.'

This time he does react and his eyes grow wide. 'Jesus, Ems. Who's the fucking father?'

I swallow as tears spring in my eyes, blurring my vision.

'I don't know,' I lie. 'It was a one-night stand. I went to a party with a couple of pals and got drunk. I then made the mistake of allowing some bloke to charm me into bed. I can't even remember his name and I don't want to.'

He inclines his head thoughtfully. 'So why didn't you get an abortion as soon as you found out you were pregnant?'

'I was going to, but then I couldn't go through with it.' My jaw stiffens and I start to feel tears pushing against my eyelids. 'The truth is, Jack, that I thought that Tommy would end up getting a long sentence, and I'd be able to break away from him, have the baby and start over without him ever knowing. But that's not how it's turned out and I'm now in a real mess.'

'You can say that again. He's going to get wind of it sooner or later even if I don't tell him.'

'I realise that, but I can't see a way out,' I tell him. 'And I'm scared of what he'll make you and Liam do to me and my family.'

'You have only yourself to blame, Emma,' he says, stating the obvious. 'You should have known that Tommy won't let you go. You're the only thing on this earth that he really cares about and knowing that you'll be there when he gets out is what's keeping him from going off the rails.'

'But what he's making me do is sick,' I reply. 'He just doesn't want me to have a life of my own. If it was genuine love, he would let me go. But he can't because he thinks he owns me. He's jealous, possessive and controlling.'

Fraser shakes his head. 'But he doesn't see it that way, Emma. And if he knew I was even listening to you say it, he'd hit the bloody roof.'

His eyes hold my gaze steadily as we sip our drinks. He's just about to say something else when his phone beeps with a message. He takes it from his jacket pocket and reads it.

'It's from Liam,' he says. 'I wasn't planning on seeing him until later this afternoon, but he now wants me to meet him at Ruby's house. So, I need to go home to get the car.'

I draw in a long breath and lean towards him across the table.

'What happens now, Jack?' I ask him hurriedly. 'Are you going to report back to Liam, who will no doubt take great pleasure in breaking the news to Tommy?'

He rubs his chin thoughtfully and sighs.

'You've placed me in a difficult position, Emma,' he eventually says. 'You must know that I've always liked you. And believe it or not, I sympathise with your plight. I've even stuck up for you when Tommy and Liam have slagged you off. But the fact is I work for the Driscolls and they expect me to be totally honest with them. If I'm not, and they find out, I'll pay a heavy price.'

'So, what does that mean?' I ask, suddenly terrified.

He responds after a couple of seconds. 'It means I'm going to give you more time to think about it. You have my word that I won't let the cat out of the bag without telling you first. But you need to face up to the harsh reality of your situation. Unless you get rid of the baby, you're going to find yourself right in the path of one hell of a shitstorm.'

CHAPTER FIFTY-THREE

With those last damning words from Fraser, I head straight back to the flat by myself, leaving him outside the coffee shop looking to flag down a taxi.

After closing the front door behind me, I catch a glimpse of myself in the hall mirror and it adds to my misery. My face is slack and bloated, and red veins lace the whites of my eyes. I've never known myself to look so hideous, and all this stress can't be good for the baby.

I try to cling to the one piece of good news I've received – that my baby hasn't lost its fight for survival. I tell myself it's what I need to focus on as I absorb the implications of being found out.

Fraser's words strike me as nothing less than a stark ultimatum – have an abortion or he'll have no choice but to inform my husband and his brother.

But I do have a choice, and the hard truth is that it's between protecting my baby or protecting myself and my family.

It's not as though I'm only up against my psycho husband – a man who can't carry out his threats himself because he's locked up in prison. There's also his mad brother, his powerful, well-connected gang and the bent coppers on his payroll.

It's me versus a ruthless criminal empire that is both feared and respected in equal measure. I'm faced with a deadly dilemma that can only end badly whatever path I choose to take.

An hour later, I'm still trying to unscramble my thoughts. I've had a shower to wash away the blood on my thigh and to try to energise myself. I've even applied some make-up and forced down two slices of toast. But I still don't feel any better or any less fearful. I'm too wired to do anything other than mope around. I can't even ease the tension with a couple of drinks.

When my mobile rings for the first time today, a question leaps into my mind. Has Fraser gone back on his word and is Tommy calling to tell me that he knows what I've done?

My body stiffens as I pick up the phone, but I'm relieved to see that the call is from Amanda.

'Hello,' I say, trying to sound chirpy. 'How are you?'

'The honest answer, Emma, is that I'm confused and annoyed,' she replies. 'I've just read in the paper that Ruby died yesterday and yet you haven't bothered to tell us. What's going on?'

I feel my jaw drop and want to kick myself. I can't believe I didn't get around to letting Amanda know what happened.

'I'm really sorry, Amanda,' I say. 'I was so wrapped up in everything that I simply forgot. It was a bad day.'

'So why didn't you ring me this morning?' she asks. 'I've just talked to Mum and it was news to her as well.'

'I've been busy. Honest. And there's been so much to think about.'

She sighs heavily down the line and I take that to mean she doesn't believe me. 'They're saying in the paper that it was a heart attack,' she says.

'That's right.'

'And have you spoken to Tommy?'

'I have and he's upset, naturally.'

'I'm not at all surprised. I expect him and his brother thought she would outlive the both of them.'

'She hadn't been too well for a while apparently,' I explain. 'I didn't know, but Tommy told me he was worried about her.'

'Well, I'm worried about you, Ems. This is more shit for you to have to deal with.'

'I know, but I'll cope.'

'Mum has told me you're coming over this weekend. Have you decided when?'

'I'm not sure I'll be able to now. There are things I have to do.'

'Such as?'

I hesitate and Amanda immediately picks up on it.

'What's wrong? What are you not telling us?'

I open my mouth, but a lump rises in my throat stopping me from responding, and making Amanda even more suspicious.

'I'm not stupid, Emma,' she sighs. 'Mum and I both know that you've been keeping something from us. It's been so bloody obvious and I think it's time you came clean.'

I shake my head even though she can't see me. 'No, I'm really fine. Just a bit—'

'Stop right there, Emma. I love you and if you've got a problem then it's my problem too. So, I'm coming over to see you and we can talk about it.'

'But there's no need to,' I insist. 'I've got nothing to say that—'

'You can tell me in person,' Amanda says. 'If you're not being truthful, I'll know.'

I feel my heart slump because when my sister is determined to do something, it's almost impossible to talk her out of it.

'I'm going to hang up now and I intend to switch my phone off, so don't bother calling me back,' she tells me. 'I'll be with you in an hour or so and I'll be bringing a bottle of wine.'

I know Amanda means well and that she's only looking out for me, but the last thing I need right now is to be interrogated by her. I fear I'll be tempted to say more than I should, and that will only make a complicated situation far worse.

There's a part of me that is desperate to share my problems, to get a fresh perspective, to find out if there's a way out of the hole that I've dug for myself that doesn't have disastrous consequences.

But if I do open up, how much dare I reveal? Do I tell her about Tommy's rules and the threats he's made to harm our family if I don't abide by them? Do I mention the photo of Amanda and her two daughters walking out of their house in Kennington, the one that was taken to show how much I had to lose if I crossed him? Do I confess about my pregnancy and tell her that I killed the father of my child? And do I disclose that the man named Max who visited our mother might well return in the future in order to hurt her? Or that my yoga instructor was beaten up on Tommy's orders?

It's so tempting to share it all with my sister, but I know deep down that it wouldn't be fair. And I wonder if it would serve any purpose other than to give her sleepless nights. I got myself into this mess and it's up to me to find a way out of it. And I have to do it in a way that doesn't put my family at risk.

CHAPTER FIFTY-FOUR

Amanda turns up at the flat just after three o'clock, with a bottle of wine as promised. I've tried to psych myself up for the visit, but my insides feel like cold, quivering jelly.

Her smile beams at me when I open the door and a sharp stab of guilt twists my stomach. I don't want to have to lie to my sister, but if I tell her the truth, then she's going to wish she hadn't come here.

'Hey, Emma,' she says brightly. 'It's time for you to share your problems with your big sister. Together I'm sure that we can make them go away.'

I don't reply because I feel my throat seize up, so I pull her into a hug instead.

'I don't need to leave until about six,' Amanda says as she reaches behind her to close the door. 'Jacob is out tonight at a work do, so I've got the kids. But it gives us plenty of time to talk and for you to tell me what's been troubling you.'

'Well, it won't take three hours for me to convince you that you really didn't need to come,' I say.

Her eyebrows slide upwards. 'We'll see about that. Now let's head to the bar and arm ourselves with a couple of glasses.'

She slips off her coat and hangs it up in the hall. Underneath she's wearing a vermilion sweater and black jeans.

My pulse is hammering against my temple and my face is growing hot. I still haven't worked out how I'm going to handle this, what I'm going to tell her, and how I'm going to make her believe me. I'm finding it so hard to focus and to see through the fog that's clouding my mind.

In the living room I pour a glass of wine for her and a lemonade for me. I then sit down on one of the armchairs facing her and blurt out the first thing that comes to mind, 'Look, let me apologise again for neglecting to tell you about Ruby. I should have called you. But I was at the hospital when she died and the rest of the day was just a blur.' That at least is the truth, even if I omit to explain it was a blur because the police arrived. . . again.

Amanda sips at her wine before replying. 'I can appreciate that now, but it came as a shock when I read it in the paper and I just couldn't believe that you hadn't bothered to tell me or Mum. It made us both wonder what might be going on and what else you're not telling us.'

I start to speak, but she raises her free hand to stop me.

'Just let me get this off my chest first,' she continues. 'Mum and I have already told you that we don't understand why you're not hurrying to divorce that bastard husband

302

of yours. You've said you're considering your options, but that doesn't wash with us. We know you don't love him and that he's a dangerous control freak who treats you badly. So, we're now convinced that he's putting pressure on you to stay married to him and that's the reason you're not embracing the freedom you've been granted. You should be happy and optimistic, more like your old self. But, instead, you seem to be just as miserable as you were when he was free and controlling your life.'

Her words trigger an emotional response in me that I struggle to hold in. She's absolutely right of course, and I know that she's not going to believe me if I deny it.

'Please don't suffer in silence, Emma,' she goes on. 'I'm here for you and always will be. And I won't rest until I know what it is you're going through.'

My heart slams to a halt, my resolve crumbles, and I suddenly feel the need to tell my sister about the baby. Keeping it from her has been eating me up inside and ravaged me with guilt. There's no one who deserves to know more than she does. She's always been there for me. My rock. My inspiration. My closest friend as well as my sister. As I stare at her, my eyes misting, I realise that the time has come to share at least part of my burden. It's not as if I can keep it secret for much longer.

'I'm pregnant, Amanda, and it's not Tommy's baby.' The words burst out of me and it's like a heavy weight has been lifted off me. 'He doesn't know and if and when he finds out I'm going to be in big trouble.'

A shocked expression freezes on Amanda's face and her

303

eyes grow wide in their sockets. 'My God, Emma. When the hell did this happen?'

'Eleven weeks ago now. That's why it's not obvious yet.'

'And who is the father?'

'A man I met at a party I went to with some friends before the trial started. I had too much to drink and we had unprotected sex. I haven't seen him since and I don't even know his name. I want nothing to do with him. I messed up, and that's why I'm having such a bad time of it.'

I decide not to tell her about the fate of Ruben Swift. She doesn't need to know about that at this time.

'Before you ask, I have considered having an abortion,' I continue. 'But I've decided not to. However, I did have to go to the hospital this morning because I bled. I had a scan and thankfully it's all okay.'

Amanda sits there working her jaw in circles, as though deep in thought. Then the muscles around her eyes tighten and she says, 'So, were we right to believe that Tommy doesn't want to let you divorce him even though he'll be spending five years in prison? And that's why you're in such a state?'

I can feel the tears gather in my eyes as I give a slow nod. 'He's desperate for me to wait for him and he's begged me to stay faithful,' I tell her. 'If I decide not to, or if he finds out that I'm pregnant, then I worry what he'll do to me.'

'Has he already made threats?' she asks.

'No,' I lie.

'Well, if he does, then you'll have to go to the police. Let them deal with it.'

I shake my head. 'Firstly, I'll never be able to prove it, and secondly, there's nothing the police can do to stop him hurting me if he wants to. He just has to say the word and his brother or one of his henchmen will make it happen.'

I see the emotions rush across my sister's face – shock, worry, confusion, anger – and I feel the persistent tug of guilt again. But at the same time, I'm glad that some of the weight has been lifted from my shoulders. At least now there's someone I can talk to, confide in, someone I can share some of my concerns with.

I just hope I haven't made another huge mistake.

Amanda stands up, places her glass on the coffee table and walks towards me with her arms out.

'Come here,' she says, her voice thick with emotion. 'Let me give you a cuddle.'

And that's when I can't hold it in any longer and break down in a wave of tears.

CHAPTER FIFTY-FIVE

My sister doesn't judge me and she makes it clear that she supports my decision not to have an abortion.

'It's something I would never be able to do either,' she tells me.

She offers me comfort, but not a solution to my problem.

'Are you absolutely certain that your fears about Tommy are justified?' she asks me. 'If you tell him that you want a divorce because you no longer love him, then he might surprise you by agreeing to it.'

'He won't, sis,' I reply instantly. 'Trust me on that.'

'You should be upfront with him. If he's got even an ounce of decency, surely he'll cave in and accept that he has to let you go.'

I feel the need to prove to her that I know what I'm talking about, so I give into impulse and go and get the list of rules he gave to me.

'Take a look at this,' I say. 'Tommy put it together and it was handed to me the day the trial ended.'

Amanda reads the words out loud and as she does, her forehead creases and her eyes grow to the size of saucers. *'You must remain loyal to me and not apply for a divorce. You must not go out after 9 p.m. unless in emergencies or on a pre-authorised visit. You must not go to any nightclubs or parties. You must not get a job – there's no need to anyway. You must stay living in the flat. You must not leave the country for any reason. You must do what my mum and brother tell you to do. You must send my brother copies of your bank statement each month.'* She looks at me then and shakes her head. 'This is shocking, Emma. He surely can't expect you to go along with it.'

'But he does. He's made that clear.'

'Then I hope you told him to get stuffed.'

'Not yet.'

'Why? I don't understand. He needs to know how you feel.'

Blood rushes from my face and dread builds in my stomach. Amanda holds eye contact for several long seconds, waiting for a response, and I'm trying to form one in my mind when her face registers alarm.

'My God, you weren't being honest when you said that he hasn't threatened you,' she says. 'He has, hasn't he?'

I should have known that one revelation would lead to another as soon as I opened up to her. Now it must be obvious from my reaction and body language that I lied.

I see no point carrying on with the lie, so I nod. 'He told me I'll face serious consequences if I refuse to abide by the rules. I don't know exactly what he means by that, but I have to believe him. Tommy doesn't make idle threats, and although he's in prison, he still has a lot of clout on the outside. There are plenty of nasty people only too willing to carry out his orders, including his brother.'

'Does Liam know about this list?'

'He was the one who handed it to me. And Ruby was there as well. They both stressed that they would keep me in line to make sure that I don't disappoint Tommy. Ruby might be gone, but Liam isn't and the man doesn't like me. And he'll do whatever his brother instructs him to, which includes hurting me.'

Amanda sits there on the sofa, brimming with indignation, her lips pressed together. I can see her mind working, questions forming, and I decide that I've gone as far as I dare. I'm not going to tell her about the threats made against her and her daughters or about the man who turned up unexpectedly at our mother's house with gifts that he pretended were from me.

'Look, you'll have to go to the police, Emma,' she says and her eyes wield a fierce determination. 'They can put an end to this. And you need to do it before he finds out you're pregnant.'

'I can't. Not yet. I know it seems like it's the only option open to me, but I've already told you why I don't think it will make a difference.'

She holds up the list. 'All you have to do is show them this. It's incriminating evidence.'

'But he'll just say that he knows nothing about it. His lawyers will then accuse me of writing it myself. And while that's going on, there'll be nothing to stop him from arranging for me to be badly beaten so that I'll have a miscarriage and lose the baby that's not his. And then he could bide his time and do something else in the future to further punish me.'

Amanda frowns and the corners of her mouth turn down. 'Ems, be straight with me. Has Tommy threatened to hurt your family? Me, the girls, Mum?'

I give my head a vigorous shake, because I still can't bring myself to tell her the truth. 'No, he hasn't. And I really don't think he would hurt anyone but me. He wants to stay close to me and I can't imagine he would do something that would push me away.'

The lie comes easily, but it leaves a bad taste in my mouth and I can tell that Amanda isn't convinced. Before she goes, I extract a promise from her that she won't share what we've talked about with anyone else. At least not yet.

'And that includes Jacob and Mum,' I say. 'Please bear with me and keep it to yourself for now. I need to give it more thought and work out the best way forward. I've still got some time before I start to show, but if it all explodes into the open now, then Christ only knows what will happen.'

CHAPTER FIFTY-SIX

After Amanda has gone, I'm left with a deep feeling of hopelessness. It's far too early to go to bed and the TV fails to hold my attention for longer than a few minutes. My mind won't be stilled and fresh questions are spiralling through it.

Will my sister break her promise and tell her husband what she now knows? Will she panic and alert the police? Or will Jack Fraser decide that it's more than his job is worth to keep my secret from his boss?

I make myself a hot peppermint tea which goes some way towards quelling the sick feeling that has settled in my stomach. I tell myself that I have to keep my head above the rising tide of fear for as long as possible.

I make a point of calling my mother to check that she hasn't had any more surprise visits and to apologise for not telling her about Ruby's sudden death.

When she says that no one has been to see her, I'm so very relieved.

'There's no need to apologise over Ruby,' she adds. 'I can appreciate how shocking it must have been for everyone. I know she wasn't a very nice person, but I think it's very sad. Do you know when the funeral will be?'

'Not yet. Liam's making those arrangements.'

'Well, I'd like to send some flowers.'

I tell her that Amanda popped over for a sisterly chat, but I don't reveal what we talked about.

'I'm going to lunch with them tomorrow,' she says. 'Will you be coming along too?'

'I don't think so, Mum. There are some things I have to do. Maybe I'll see you in the week.'

After hanging up, I send my sister a text thanking her for coming to see me and imploring her not to tell Mum that I'm expecting. She replies within minutes and assures me that she won't breathe a word.

I then go online to see if there's any news about the Ruben Swift case. The police have had my coat and shoes for twenty-four hours and I'm sure that if they had found any incriminating blood or DNA traces I would have heard by now.

One thing I'm dreading is an announcement that detectives have charged someone with his murder. If that happens, I will have to hand myself in and confess to killing him. I couldn't possibly allow an innocent person to take the blame.

Fortunately, nothing new is being reported, but I'm fully aware that it doesn't mean there haven't been any significant developments.

My phone belts out its tune at eight thirty and I know it will be Tommy before I answer it. My skin prickles uncomfortably because I fear that Fraser has gone back on his promise and revealed my secret to him.

But, in the event, his opening words make it clear that Fraser hasn't grassed me up.

'How are you, sweetheart?' he asks warmly. 'I was going to call earlier, but I didn't get the chance. I'm back in the cell and had to wait for a friendly officer to bring me a phone.'

'I'm all right,' I tell him. 'My sister spent the afternoon here with me. It was nice. I told her about your mum and she told me to pass on her condolences.'

'That's kind of her. Just so you know, Liam has arranged for the funeral to take place on Thursday. There was a slot available and Mum had planned ahead so it was quick to organise. She's being buried with my dad as per her wishes.'

'Will you be able to go?'

'Probably not, but I've been told they might let me go to the grave under escort after the actual service to pay my respects. I want you to be there, though. So don't make any other plans.'

'I won't.'

'I'll fill you in on the details when you come and see me on Monday.'

I feel my stomach tighten. With all the panic of going to the hospital and then Fraser finding out the truth I'd completely forgotten that a prison visit had been arranged.

'Jack will pick you up and bring you here,' he continues.

312

'He told me that you and him went for a coffee this morning.'

Being reminded of this meeting and what was discussed is enough to start my heart racing.

'We did. He said you sent him over to check on me.'

'Only to make sure that you were all right. I've been worried about you. And by the way, I've given Liam a bollocking over the way he spoke to you. He won't be doing that again.'

'Thank you.'

'And I gather you had another visit from the detectives investigating the Ruben Swift murder.'

'Who told you that?' I ask him.

'Liam. He got it from one of our guys in the Yard. They've got you on CCTV apparently.' He sounds suspicious and I have to struggle to keep my voice steady.

'I happened to be out walking that evening,' I explain, willing the anxiety out of my voice. 'And they took away the coat and shoes I was wearing at the time.'

'What the fuck for?'

'They said they wanted to eliminate me from their inquiries by making sure that I didn't have any of the man's blood on me.'

'You should have called our lawyer before letting them do that!' he rages at me. 'You're my wife so I wouldn't put it past the bastards to stitch you up. Call Mosley and tell him I want his firm on the case. He'll talk to them, find out what they're up to and make sure they don't take any liberties.'

Kevin Mosley is not only Tommy's criminal defence lawyer, he's also the family lawyer; it hadn't even occurred to me to enlist his help or seek his advice. I wonder now if that was a mistake.

'I'll get in touch with him,' I say. 'But I know I've got nothing to worry about since I wasn't the person who carried out the killing.'

'And it wasn't me who put that gun in my car's glove compartment,' he replies sharply. 'But the fuckers still did me for it.'

The conversation ends on that note because Tommy needs to make a couple more calls while he has the phone. He tells me that he loves me and that he can't wait to see me on Monday.

'I'm looking forward to seeing you too, Tommy,' I tell him automatically, even though I don't mean it.

CHAPTER FIFTY-SEVEN

I spend the rest of the weekend cocooned in the flat, my mind filled with darkness.

On Sunday, I don't even bother to get dressed. I move between the sofa and the bed, wrapped in my dressing gown, doing whatever I can to stamp down my fears and emotions. But at least I don't bleed any more and that's something to be grateful for.

Tommy phones in the afternoon, but he seems distracted, so it's thankfully a short conversation. He reminds me to call the lawyer and let him know if I hear again from the police.

'The officers are carrying out a routine search of all the cells on the wing,' he tells me. 'It means I'll have to ditch the mobile for the rest of the day. But I'll see you tomorrow.'

Amanda calls me next to ask if I'm okay and whether I've decided what I'm going to do. She sounds worried and speaks conspiratorially, but she's adamant that she hasn't told anyone about my situation.

My mother comes to the phone and I tell her that Ruby's funeral is on Thursday. She says she'll arrange to send some flowers. I thank her before I hang up, hoping that she didn't pick up on how stressed I am.

My mind keeps leaping back to one of the things that Amanda said to me about my husband. *Are you absolutely certain that your fears about Tommy are justified? If you tell him that you want a divorce because you no longer love him, then he might surprise you by agreeing to it.*

The trouble is she doesn't know him like I do. I've never made her fully aware of how I was treated and the lengths he's prepared to go to in order to control me. How he tried to make me feel that I wasn't my own person, that without him I couldn't function.

She did know that he was desperate to start a family, but I didn't tell her that he found out I was taking the pill without his knowledge. Or that I've always suspected he might possibly have been responsible for his first wife's murder after she cheated on him and then framed her new boyfriend before arranging for him to be killed in prison.

There is so much I've kept from Amanda, partly out of embarrassment and partly out of fear of putting her at risk as well. If she knew the truth, she'd realise just how dire my situation is.

I get very little sleep on Sunday night and so on Monday morning, tiredness is tugging at my bones.

I shower and dress in a hurry because Fraser is picking me up at nine thirty to take me to the prison. Naturally, I

316

don't want to go and the thought of another face-to-face meeting with my husband fills me with trepidation. I can almost feel my blood pressure rising.

At nine o'clock, I phone Kevin Mosley. He tells me he's been expecting my call because Tommy managed to get word to him earlier.

'From now on, don't speak to those detectives without me or one of my colleagues present,' he instructs.

He then asks me to tell him what they have said so far to me and the reasons they gave when they took my coat, shoes and rucksack.

'I'll get onto them right away and let them know that I'm representing you from now on,' he says. 'But I have to ask now if it's at all possible that you can be linked in any way to the crime scene?'

'I wasn't there, so I don't see how,' I lie. 'I just happened to be out walking in that area when Ruben Swift was killed. Plus, I never knew the man and I have not the faintest idea why he was interested in me.'

'Well, rest assured that I won't let them harass you, Mrs Driscoll. And as soon as I find out what they've done with your belongings, I'll get back to you.'

I thank him and hang up. There's no time for me to dwell on the conversation because it's time to go downstairs and wait for Fraser to arrive.

He's on time as always and as soon as I'm in the car, he asks me if I've given any more thought on having my baby aborted.

'I haven't stopped thinking about it,' I reply. 'But I still don't want to do it.'

He raises his brow. 'Then I pity you when Tommy finds out, Emma.'

'Please don't tell him yet, Jack. I need more time,' I plead.

'I thought you might say that. I'm sure it can wait until after Ruby's funeral. Him and Liam have got enough on their plates with that. Does anyone else know?'

I shake my head. 'Of course not.'

'Well, at least there's no chance he'll get wind of it before then.' He takes his eyes off the road to glance at me. 'I feel for you, Emma. I really do. But the problem won't go away if you do nothing. Tommy loves you dearly, but we both know that he'll never entertain the idea of bringing up some other bloke's kid.'

I feel the weight of his words press down on me and I lapse into silence for the rest of the half-hour journey across South West London to meet the very man who would most likely kill me and my baby if he knew the truth.

CHAPTER FIFTY-EIGHT

My nerves build as we approach the imposing Victorian structure that is Wandsworth Prison. I hate coming here and dread the thought of having to make regular visits for years to come. I'd hoped that once the trial was over and the sentence given that would be it.

I know that many wives are prepared to stick by their husbands however long they're serving behind bars, but they still love the men they married. Unlike me, they're not victims of coercion and blackmail.

Fraser parks the car in a nearby street where he'll wait for me.

'Try to appreciate how hard it is for him, Emma,' he tells me gently. 'I know what it's like to be locked up and what he's going through. His mind is in a bad place and he doesn't mean half the things he says.'

I shake my head at him. 'I'm afraid I'll have to treat that last comment with the contempt it deserves, Jack.

Tommy Driscoll always means every word that comes out of his gob.'

My throat thickens as I enter the prison and I'm soon being subjected to the usual security checks. My personal belongings, including my mobile phone, are taken from me and placed in a locker. I then have to provide the visiting order and photo ID before I'm allowed through to the visitor hall.

I'm among about two dozen family members and friends and most of them are wearing glum expressions.

When I see Tommy, he's dressed in a baggy grey track-suit and the first thing that strikes me is that he looks like death warmed up. His eyes are glazed and rheumy and there's an intricate map of blood vessels on his pale cheeks.

Limited contact is allowed, and I'm thankful for that, but even a hug and a kiss turns my stomach.

Then we sit down and face each other across a table. I smile and hope that he doesn't see how uncomfortable I am. I feel a chill wash over me and goose bumps rise on my arms.

'It's really great to see you, Ems,' he says, and his voice is thin and reedy. 'I miss you so much.'

I can tell he means it and that he wants me to express a similar sentiment. But I can't bring myself to do it.

'I'm sorry you've had such a hard time of it, Tommy,' I respond. 'The stabbing, then your mum. It can't be easy.'

He reaches across the table and places his hands on top of mine. 'I don't want you to worry about me, Ems. I can cope, even in here. But I know you're struggling without me. I can see it in your face. You look tired and stressed, and if I'm not mistaken, you've put on some weight around the middle.'

My heart misses a beat and I instinctively shift myself closer to the table to shield my stomach from him.

'For fuck's sake, don't let yourself go,' he says. 'I don't want you ending up like some of the mingers who come in here. They're an embarrassment to their fellas because they think they don't have to try so hard. Some of them don't even bother wearing make-up and they look like proper down-and-outs.'

It's clear he hasn't changed. He's still the same vile, condescending control freak. It reaffirms my belief that he'll show me no mercy if I seek a divorce or confess to what I've done.

'Has Liam been in touch with you?' he asks me.

I shake my head. 'I haven't spoken to him since Friday at the hospital.'

'Well, I've told him not to give you any more grief. So, he's probably sulking. I'll have a longer talk with him after the funeral. His head is all over the place right now.'

'Where is the funeral going to be?'

'West Norwood Cemetery. Make your way to Mum's and the cars will leave from there at two o'clock. Liam is organising a wake at the house afterwards.'

'You definitely can't attend?'

'No. They won't let me.'

'That's a shame.'

He shrugs. 'It's about what I expected.'

He then asks me if I've spoken to Mosley.

'We had a conversation this morning,' I reply. 'He's going to talk to the police to find out what's going on.'

'And have you heard from them again?'

'Not since they came to the flat.'

'What about Detective Brannigan? Has he been in touch again?'

'No, but then he's got no reason to contact me, Tommy. There's nothing I can or want to tell him, so he knows it will be a waste of time.'

After that, the conversation becomes banal and stilted. Tommy asks me lots of questions about how I'm filling the time. I tell him I've been watching television, going for walks, doing some painting and meeting up with my sister and mum.

It all seems to be going well until I make the mistake of glancing at my watch. I thought I could manage to do it without him catching on, but I didn't.

'What's the problem?' he snaps. 'Have you got somewhere better to be? Am I keeping you?'

'N-no, not at all,' I stutter. 'I was just—'

'Don't bother with a feeble fucking excuse,' he interrupts and at the same time tightens his grip on my hands. 'You can't wait to get away!'

'That's not it, Tommy. Honest.'

His voice is raised now and the people at the other tables are looking at us. He's also attracted the attention of one of the prison officers who's standing with his back to the nearest wall.

'Calm down, Tommy, please,' I implore him, and then manage to improvise. 'I'm sorry if I upset you, but you're wrong. I looked at my watch because I was hoping that we had a lot more time before I have to go.'

The fire I've seen so many times in his eyes is extinguished in an instant at this and his expression softens. 'Okay, fair enough,' he says contritely. 'I'm sorry.'

He releases the pressure on my hands and blows out a breath.

'Please don't hold it against me, Ems,' he adds, his voice sinking almost to a whisper. 'I look forward to seeing you so much and it worries me that you don't feel the same way.'

'You don't have to apologise, Tommy,' I respond, though I don't contradict him. 'It was a misunderstanding. Nothing more.'

'Well, it won't happen again. I promise. I want you to look forward to these visits. They're what I live for and we have to make them work because this is the only real contact we'll have until I get out of here and we can be together again.' The remark leaves me with a feeling of dread in the pit of my stomach.

Minutes later, the session comes to an end. We hug and kiss again and I'm sure I spot him blinking away tears as I force myself not to run out of there as fast as I can.

Fraser takes me straight back to the flat in the Range Rover. On the way, he asks me how it went and I tell him about Tommy's outburst.

'He's paranoid when it comes to you, Emma,' he says once I finish. 'I suspect he knows that you find those visits stressful and he won't be happy until he convinces himself that they mean as much to you as they do to him.'

'I just wish to God he would come to his senses and realise that this just isn't going to work. This way we're both serving a sentence and I don't know why he can't see that I no longer love him, the more he threatens me, the more I hate him.'

Fraser shakes his head. 'It's because he believes that you do still love him and that your sister and mum are putting pressure on you to cut ties. He thinks that if he can hold onto you now, then you'll find the strength to ignore them and stay the course.'

'And what if I won't or can't?'

Fraser waits a few moments before responding and when he does his voice is unnervingly calm. 'My guess is that if he can't have you in his life, then he'll make sure that you're not able to have a life of your own.'

CHAPTER FIFTY-NINE

Monday evening draws in around me and the silence in the flat seems to almost have a texture to it. I go to bed early in the hope that I'll sleep away my worries because my resolve is beginning to spiral into the insanity that's engulfing me.

But sleep is slow in coming as usual and for much of the night I lay in the dark with despair gnawing at my mind and body. I keep telling myself that this can't go on for much longer. I have to somehow bring my nightmare to an end. But the question I can't answer is how, and that's why I feel so empty and weak. One man is already dead because of decisions I've taken and other lives are now at risk.

As the hours pass, my heart becomes a lead weight in my chest and fear floods through me like acid. Jack Fraser has told me that he won't reveal my secret to Tommy until after Ruby's funeral, but that's only a few days from now.

The only way to stop him is by terminating my pregnancy, but I know that if I have to kill my baby, then I will have to kill myself. I would have nothing left to live for.

I'm out of bed by seven on Tuesday morning and by eight I'm showered and dressed. I face another day with nothing to do except tie myself in knots.

By nine, my stomach can't take any more tea and I decide to go for a walk. It's cold and grey outside, but the sun has begun to claw its way through the clouds.

As I start walking, I become aware of a heavy tang of exhaust fumes in the air. It's a familiar sign that the city has emerged from its slumber and the engines of commerce are firing up. Millions of people are either heading for work or they're already beavering away in offices, stores, hospitals and coffee shops. Others are driving cabs, buses and emergency service vehicles. It makes me yearn to be a part of it, to do something with myself, something that will give my life a purpose. Right now, it's as though I exist solely to keep my husband happy. He doesn't want me to work or socialise, or do anything that might pose a threat to the hold he has over me.

Looking out across the Thames, the city is as beautiful and vibrant as ever. But I can't appreciate it because terrible thoughts continue to pulse through my mind.

I walk past Shakespeare's Globe Theatre, envious of the tourists who are gathered outside, taking pictures and chatting animatedly among themselves. I'm reminded of those early days in our marriage when Tommy and I used to stroll along the Embankment, stopping for drinks or just soaking up the atmosphere. It all seems so long ago now, the time before my husband's true self emerged and I discovered that he was a hard, uncompromising man with no soft edges.

I just wish I could shed all the bad memories I have of our marriage like an old skin. But I can't. They'll be with me as long as I live, a constant reminder of how I let myself drift into a world where I didn't belong.

I walk for over two hours and my phone doesn't ring until I arrive back home.

It's the lawyer, Kevin Mosley, and he starts by telling me he's had a long conversation with Detective Inspector Berry, who's leading the investigation into Ruben Swift's murder.

'You won't be surprised to learn that the forensic examination of your coat and shoes has provided no evidence linking you to the crime scene in Laxton Street,' he says. 'And as for the CCTV footage, there's no way that can be used against you since you told them you went for a walk that evening.'

'Is that the end of it then?' I ask him, and experience a shot of relief. 'Will they leave me alone now?'

'I'm afraid not, Mrs Driscoll. You see, they're still trying to establish why Ruben Swift was so interested in you and whether he made contact in the weeks before he was killed. To that end, they've been granted permission to access the security camera footage that covers your building's reception area. If Mr Swift did visit at any time – or even hung around outside – then they will no doubt want to talk to you again.'

A tight coil of panic twists in my gut and I start to shake. I decide not to tell him that Swift entered the block on no fewer than three occasions. I know he was captured on the security camera the first time because Edward let me view the clip. It showed Swift delivering the envelope containing the note informing me that I was going to be blackmailed. I remember that his face wasn't visible so it will be hard for the police to make a positive identification. However, he did return at least twice, once to leave me the photograph of the pair of us together at the party and once to drop off the note telling me to meet him at Ben's Café.

I have to assume the camera picked him up those times as well and I can only hope that his face can't be seen. But, either way, I need to be ready to lie about what each of the envelopes contained.

CHAPTER SIXTY

I hear from the police within hours. Detective Inspector Berry rings to tell me that they want to ask me some more questions about Ruben Swift. He says they'd prefer it to take place in the more formal setting of New Scotland Yard and they'll send a car to pick me up.

As we agree a time, I feel the block of dread in my gut. This is something I hadn't expected and I'm worried it makes it more likely that I might soon end up behind bars like Tommy. I'm suddenly unsure who I should fear the most – the police or my husband.

As soon as the call ends, I phone Mosley. The fact that the police have acted so quickly after examining the security footage from the reception area doesn't surprise him.

'I'll meet you at the Yard,' he says. 'And try not to worry, Mrs Driscoll. They're just desperate. If what you've told me is true, and I've no reason to doubt it, then this is just a fishing exercise.'

I don't think he's going to be so confident when he finds out what's on the footage. For my part, I still haven't decided what I'll be telling them was in the envelopes that were delivered by Ruben just days before he was killed. I fear that whatever story I come up with will not be believed anyway.

Much to my dismay, DI Berry sends a squad car to pick me up rather than the unmarked vehicle I'd expected. I'm grateful that it's only a short drive across Westminster bridge to New Scotland Yard, but that also means less time for me to compose myself. I'm accompanied by two uniformed officers, who thankfully don't try to engage me in conversation.

It won't be the first time I've been inside the Met's head-quarters. I was interviewed twice while they were investigating Tommy. But I'm far more nervous now because I'm the one they've got their sights set on.

When we arrive at the Yard, my heart is pounding rapidly and I feel myself shaking, the tremors travelling down my arms.

I walk inside on shaky legs and, to my relief, Kevin Mosley is already there waiting for me. I've never liked the man, but I'm pleased to see him.

'I've had a brief conversation with DI Berry,' he tells me. 'It seems that the footage from the security cameras has led them to believe that you did come into contact with Ruben Swift before he was killed.'

'But I didn't,' I insist, and I'm comforted by the fact that none of the footage will show the pair of us interacting at any point.

'That's what I've told them. I haven't seen the clips for myself, but have you any idea what they might contain?'

'None at all,' I lie.

Mosley assesses me with a steady gaze, but as with most lawyers I've come into contact with, his face doesn't give much away. He has a lean, wolfish look and there's a dark, brooding intensity in his sunken eyes.

After a couple of beats, he says, 'Very well, Mrs Driscoll. Let's go and get this done. And please don't answer any questions that I advise you not to.'

We're taken to an interview room, where DI Berry and DS Warwick are waiting. The air in the room is warm and static and as we take our seats at the table opposite the detectives, I feel my heart shudder in my chest.

DI Berry goes through the formalities of saying for the benefit of the tape who is present. He then thanks me for agreeing to be interviewed.

'Am I correct in assuming that you know the questions we're going to ask you relate to video footage from the security camera that covers the entrance to your flat block?' he says.

I nod and Mosley tells them that he's made me aware of it.

Berry gestures towards a TV monitor on a stand to my left. 'We viewed many hours of footage recorded over the past two months, but I'm going to run only three short clips which show a man we believe to be Mr Swift delivering envelopes to the reception desk in the days before his death. Those envelopes were addressed to you and we know that you actually asked the duty concierge to view the footage because you wanted to know who had delivered the first envelope.'

I raise my brow and act surprised. 'I remember that. But the man didn't look up at the camera so I didn't know who he was.'

Berry starts to respond, but Mosley gets there first.

'Can I just pick up on the point you just made about believing the man to be Ruben Swift,' he says. 'Does that mean you can't be sure it is him?'

'I'll answer that question in a moment, if I may,' Berry says. 'First let me show you the clips.'

The first is the one I've already seen in which Swift rushes into the reception area from the street and plants the envelope on the desk while Edward was in the office on the phone.

'This happened four days before he died – the same day that your husband was stabbed in prison, Mrs Driscoll,' Berry says.

'And you can see for yourself that his face isn't visible,' I say. 'So how was I supposed to know who the hell he was?'

The second clip is then run and this time Swift hands an envelope to Sean, this one containing the photo of me sitting on Swift's lap at the party and the note threatening to make my husband aware of it unless I pay up. But once again Swift is wearing the dark parka with the hood covering his head. He can't possibly be identified from it. Less than a minute after he walks out, I can be seen entering the building and being handed the envelope.

'This drop-off took place two days later, Mrs Driscoll,' Berry says.

'And once again there's no way you can tell that the man is Ruben Swift,' Mosley points out.

Berry turns to me and asks, 'Do you remember the concierge telling you that you had just missed him?'

I nod. 'But I don't remember seeing the guy as I arrived.'

The third clip is much the same and shows Ruben turning up and handing an envelope to Edward. This envelope contained the note telling me to meet Swift at Ben's Café.

'This third and final clip was recorded the day before Mr Swift was killed,' Berry says, as his colleague then switches off the screen. 'So first let me explain why we believe he was the man in question.'

From a folder on the desk, he produces photographs taken of clothes he says belonged to Swift.

'The parka he was wearing matches a coat found in his van, the one that was parked in Laxton Street next to the crime scene. The trainers he was wearing when he was killed also look exactly like those he wore during each visit to your building.'

'But even if we accept that the man was Mr Swift, that still doesn't prove that my client came into contact with him at any point,' Mosley asserts. 'And for the record, she insists that she never did.'

Berry looks at me and I know what's coming next.

'You received three envelopes from the man, Mrs Driscoll,' he says. 'We would like to know what they contained and why you didn't see fit to mention them when we spoke to you previously.'

I respond immediately with as much confidence as I can muster, convinced that the story I've concocted will be impossible to disprove. 'The first envelope contained a short note from someone calling himself "Mr Anonymous",' I tell him. 'He said that my husband owed him five thousand pounds and even though Tommy was in prison he wanted to be paid. He said if I didn't transfer the money to him, then he would continue to pester me until I did. There was a bank account number and sort code. The second and third envelopes contained similar messages.'

'And did you respond to them?' Berry asks.

I shake my head. 'Of course not. I ripped them up and threw them in the bin. I just assumed they were from some crank who thought I'd be dumb enough to pay up.'

'Did you show them to your husband?'

'No. There was no point. He would have told me not to take them seriously.'

'And it didn't occur to you to report it to the police?'

I shrug. 'I would have if it had carried on.'

Berry purses his lips. 'So would the ripped-up notes and envelopes still be in your flat?'

I have to resist a sudden urge to grin. 'I'm afraid not. I emptied the bag into the chute a couple of days ago and the rubbish has already been collected.'

Disappointment clouds the detective's face and he lets out a long sigh.

'Would you be willing to swear, on oath, that what you've told us is the truth, Mrs Driscoll?' he asks me.

'Absolutely,' I answer quickly.

The two detectives exchange a look and I see that as a clear signal that they either believe what I've told them or they know they'll have a real struggle trying to prove that I've lied.

CHAPTER SIXTY-ONE

Before I leave the Yard, DI Berry hands me a carrier bag containing my coat, shoes and rucksack that were subjected to forensic examination. He confirms that no trace evidence linking me to the Laxton Street murder was found on them or at the crime scene.

When we exit onto the street, Mosley offers to drive me home, but I tell him I'll walk as I live just across the bridge.

'Thanks for coming, Kevin,' I say honestly. 'Hopefully I won't have to call you again.'

'If your husband contacts me, do you want me to disclose what happened here today?' he asks.

I shake my head. 'Just tell him you came here with me to find out what was going on and that they produced no evidence. Don't mention the security camera footage. That will only worry him and he's under enough pressure as it is.'

He nods. 'I quite understand. And I will, of course, abide by my duty of confidentiality, Mrs Driscoll.'

He sounds sincere, but I'm not convinced I can trust him. After all, he's been on the Firm's payroll for years and has always been loyal to Tommy.

As I start to turn away, he clears his throat and says, 'Do you mind me asking if what you told them about the contents of those envelopes is true?'

I fix him with a hard stare. 'Every word of it was, Mr Mosley. Unlike my husband, and most of your other clients, I'd be far too scared to lie to the police.'

I don't give him a chance to ask me any more questions. I smile icily, thank him again for coming and walk quickly away.

By now, it's six o'clock and the roads are jammed with cars, buses and cycles. As I walk along Victoria Embankment, the cold air rushes into my lungs. I feel ravaged, raw, and my mind is reeling under a jumble of thoughts. But I still manage to give myself a pat on the back. Against the odds, I succeeded in extricating myself from a difficult situation. By holding my nerve and lying about the contents of the envelopes from Ruben Swift, I avoided being sucked deeper into the murder investigation. I don't doubt that DI Berry remains deeply suspicious, but I can't see how he can prove that I was lying.

It doesn't mean that I still don't have a lot to worry about. I have yet to solve the problem of my pregnancy and how my husband will react when he finds out about it. And I can't be sure that the police won't eventually find out that I killed Ruben Swift. The stress of it all is burning me up.

As I cross the bridge, my breathing quickens until it's wheezing in my chest.

When I get home, my nerves are still fluttering and I instinctively head for the bar to pour myself a vodka. But my inner voice kicks in, reminding me that it is not good for the baby so I make a tea instead.

I take it into the living room, sit on the sofa and switch on the television in the hope that something on it will provide a distraction. But just as the screen comes alive, my mobile rings. I assume it must be Tommy, but I'm wrong. It's Liam. I answer because if I don't, I fear he'll turn up on my doorstep.

'Hello, Liam,' I say. 'Are you ringing to check up on me?'

'As a matter of fact, I'm calling to apologise for the way I spoke to you the other day and to make sure that you're coming to Mum's funeral,' he replies.

His words and the pleasant tone of voice take me by surprise.

'Is this because Tommy had a go at you?' I ask him.

'It's true we've had a brotherly conversation, but I'm saying sorry because I want to, not because he's forced me to. What I said to you was unfair and out of order.'

This is totally out of character for the man and I have to wonder if he actually means it.

'Well, that's gracious of you, Liam,' I say. 'Apology accepted.'

'And I want to tell you that it wouldn't be right if you weren't at the funeral.'

'Of course, I'll come.'

'That's great. I don't expect you to make your own way to Dulwich. Jack has offered to pick you up and then take you home after the wake. Plus, I want you with me in the lead procession car.'

'I appreciate that,' I tell him. But, in all honesty, I would rather have been told to stay away.

'Well, I probably won't see you until Thursday so take care and let me or Jack know if you need anything,' he says.

'I will.'

He ends the call and I just stay sitting there feeling bewildered and slightly uncomfortable. It's such a dramatic change of tune on Liam's part that I can't help wondering if Tommy has browbeaten him into submission. Or perhaps there's more to it and Liam's aim is to lull me into a false sense of security? Does he intend the funeral to be the last time I'll be involved in any Driscoll family affairs? And when it's over he'll stand up to his brother and make it clear that he doesn't want me around?

These questions and more get added to the melting pot of misery that is my mind and they help ensure that I'm deprived of sleep for yet another night.

CHAPTER SIXTY-TWO

My sister phones me on Wednesday morning while I'm still in bed. She tells me it's one of her work days so she'll be at her web design office near Borough Market.

'I want to talk to you, Ems, so can we meet at lunchtime?' she asks.

She sounds anxious and that makes my heart flip. I climb out of bed with the phone clamped to my ear. My brain feels sluggish, syrupy, and weakness and exhaustion flood my body.

'What's wrong?' I ask her. 'Has something happened?'

'Not yet, but we both know that something is going to happen very soon and I can't stop thinking about it. I'm sick with worry for you, Ems.'

'But I've told you I'm going to sort it. I just need some time.'

'That's just it. You don't have time, and I don't want you to be forced into doing something that you'll regret just to avoid upsetting your psycho husband. You need to think again about not going to the police, Ems. You've got to tell them about his threats and those wretched rules he's drawn up for you. And. . .' She pauses before pressing on firmly. 'If you don't, then I will.'

I feel myself recoil at her words. 'No. You can't do that. If you do, he'll—'

'Stop, Ems. You have to stand up to the guy. For your sake, as well as your baby's.'

Blood roars in my ears and I feel my jaw set with tension. 'Okay, you've made your point,' I say. 'But we should talk about it at lunchtime. Is there any chance you can come to the flat? We'll have privacy here.'

'I'd rather we met near the office because I'll only have an hour at most. It's going to be a dry day, so we can get takeaway coffees and go for a walk.'

She suggests meeting outside a café we both know on Borough High Street and we agree on one o'clock. It gives me time to get ready and decide what I'm going to say to her.

Do I reveal the true extent of my husband's threats? Do I tell her that he arranged for someone to take a photograph of her and her daughters and sent a man to our mother's home as a warning to me?

And if I do tell her all that, won't it just scare her so much that she'll believe that seeking help from the law is the only option open to us?

My gut is fighting wave after wave of nausea as I shower and dress. There just seems no end to the agony that's being heaped upon me. My husband refuses to let me go even though he's in prison. I've killed my unborn baby's father. I'm a suspect in a murder investigation. I've been told that unless I have an abortion my husband will learn about the baby. And now my own sister is piling on the pressure.

The problem is, I can see her point about time running out. And once it does, my world is going to tip on its axis.

It's a grey, sluggish day, but not as cold as it has been. It only takes me ten minutes to walk to Borough High Street and Amanda is waiting outside the café when I get there. She's holding two large takeaway coffees.

'I'm sorry if I've freaked you out, Ems,' she says as she hands one to me. 'But it's really stressing me out.'

My sister looks tired, her eyes dull and ringed with fatigue.

'I just wish I hadn't got you involved,' I tell her. 'It wasn't fair.'

'Don't be daft. I'm your sister and the last thing I want is for you to suffer in silence.'

As we start walking, I ask her if she's told Jacob and she replies that she hasn't.

'But I can't keep it from him much longer, Emma. It isn't right.'

We cross the road and head towards the Jubilee Walkway down by the river.

'I'm going to Ruby's funeral tomorrow,' I say. 'Can you tell Mum that I'll take some flowers on her behalf so that she doesn't have to worry about sending them.'

'Will Tommy be let out to attend?'

'No. He'll only be allowed to visit the grave at some point afterwards.'

Amanda changes tack, asking me if Tommy and Liam have begun to suspect anything.

I shake my head. 'I don't think so, but there is something I haven't told you. You're right when you say that time is not on my side. . .'

She stops walking and looks at me. 'Go on.'

'Jack Fraser knows I'm expecting,' I tell her. 'He says that if I don't terminate the pregnancy, he'll have no choice but to tell Tommy. He's holding back until after the funeral.'

'Holy fuck, Ems! This is all the more reason to go to the police now,' she implores.

I start walking again and reiterate what I said about how I don't think the police will be able to protect me. But even as I speak, I realise that it's not enough to convince her, because she knows that the alternative is to abort my baby and allow myself to be enslaved by my husband for years to come. What she doesn't know is that if I abandon Tommy and give birth, he might seek to punish me by hurting her, her daughters and our mum.

After walking and talking for twenty more minutes, the pressure on me to come clean is such that I can't hold it in any longer. A combination of guilt, fear and love for my family convinces me that Amanda needs to know the truth.

And so, I let it all spill out – the threats, the photo he had taken of her and her daughters, the man who dropped in on Mum, and the attack on my yoga instructor – and her reaction makes me wish that I hadn't.

'Oh my God, Emma. You lied to me! You swore he hadn't made threats against us and I believed you.'

'I'm so sorry, Mands. I thought I had it under control,' I plead for understanding.

'Well, this changes everything. I can't just do nothing now that I know my family have been threatened! I need to protect them. Let's go to the police today. Now!'

I shake my head, panicked by her reaction. 'And what do you expect them to do – arrest every member of Tommy's gang and jail them? Of course, they won't. The best you could hope for is that they'd move us to safe houses and give us all new identities. Chloe and Grace would have to leave their school and their friends. You and Jacob would have to sell the house and give up your jobs. And even if the police do seek to protect us, which I don't think they will because we'll never be able to prove we're in danger, it wouldn't mean we're safe. You see, Tommy isn't some ordinary bloke. He has contacts, influence, and police officers on his payroll. He would find a way to get to us.'

Amanda stares at me, open-mouthed, as the full scale of the problem facing us sinks in. Tears fill her eyes, teetering on the lashes.

'I've been hoping – praying – that something would happen that would make it go away,' I continue, and I know it sounds pathetic. 'I almost got a way out when Tommy was stabbed. But he survived and he's now more determined than ever to keep me tied to him.'

Amanda starts to cry and the coffee cup falls from her hand onto the pavement.

'So, what do we do, Ems?' she sobs. 'There must be a way out of this where you get to keep the baby and Tommy just accepts that it's over between the two of you.'

I reach out, put my arms around her and pull her close to me. 'I'm sure there is a way. I just haven't worked out what it is yet.'

CHAPTER SIXTY-THREE

Before we go our separate ways, Amanda promises to hold fire on calling the police, at least until after Ruby's funeral. But I'm forced to agree to her making Jacob aware of the situation.

'Just don't let him do anything stupid,' I tell her. 'We'll need to decide as a family the best way forward.'

When I arrive home, I just sit there thinking about it all, my heart in my throat. My eyes feel dry and heavy and the pounding in my head fills my ears.

It seems inevitable to me now that it's all going to come to a head very soon. I therefore have to prepare for it as best I can.

The afternoon rolls on slowly, inexorably, and fear spreads through me like a raging virus.

Tommy calls at seven that evening. He asks me what I've been up to and I tell him I had lunch with my sister.

As we chat – mostly about nothing – there's something

about his voice that jars with me. He sounds different, as though he's trying to keep a lid on his emotions. It's not like him, but I remind myself that it's his mother's funeral in the morning and he has every right to be upset, it's probably that.

He wants to make sure that I'm going and I reassure him that I am. I also tell him that Liam called me with an apology. He says he hadn't been told, but I'm not sure I believe him.

'I hope it all goes well tomorrow and I'm glad you'll be there. I want you to know that my mum didn't really dislike you. She just resented the fact that you replaced her as the most important person in my life.'

After I hang up, I can't shake the uneasy feeling that sits in the pit of my stomach. Something felt off just now, and I can't quite put my finger on it.

Hunger pangs eventually drive me into the kitchen, where I sate them with a bowl of soup and a slice of bread.

Afterwards, I start thinking about what I'll wear for the funeral tomorrow. Only then does it occur to me that I haven't arranged for a wreath or flowers. Still, I don't suppose anyone will care.

I call Amanda at nine to see how she is and discover that she and Jacob have had a blazing row. She tearfully explains that he hit the roof after she put him in the picture. He then told her to tell me that he believes I should have an abortion right away.

'He's very angry, Ems,' she says. 'He doesn't think you should have cheated on Tommy for one thing. And as far as Tommy not letting you go, well, he says you made your bed by marrying the guy, so you should lie in it.'

I'm furious at Jacob for being so unsupportive. It's as though he doesn't care about me or my unborn baby. After I come off the phone, I let out a strangled sob before breaking down.

I eventually pull myself together and get ready for bed. But that's when I'm struck by yet another blow.

As I'm cleaning my teeth, it hits me. Tommy didn't tell me he loved me before hanging up. It seems odd, given that he's been making a point of expressing it at every opportunity. I find it curiously unsettling and wonder if it signals a change in his attitude towards me. Could it be that he's found out the truth and he's deciding how he's going to punish me? The thought plagues me throughout the night and once again I get barely any sleep.

CHAPTER SIXTY-FOUR

Thursday morning arrives and in a few hours Fraser will be here to take me to Dulwich. I have to prepare for the funeral of the woman who, despite what her son said, hated me.

I feel I have to go even though I'm dreading it. I'm just not ready to deal with the consequences of not showing my face there.

It's not hard to decide what I'm going to wear. In my large walk-in wardrobe, there are outfits for every occasion. I choose a black dress with a matching lightweight jacket. Over it, I put on a black single-breasted trench coat that I've had for almost a year and never worn.

In the mirror, I look presentable, but no amount of make-up can disguise the anguish that's etched into my features. My eyes are cold and desolate, and there are heavy bags beneath them. I suppose there's one consolation – at least the other mourners will be given the impression that I'm mourning for my mother-in-law.

* * *

Fraser picks me up on time at one and drives me to Ruby's house in Dulwich. On the way, he's unusually quiet and refuses to be drawn into a conversation about my situation.

When I try to push him, he shakes his head and says sharply, 'Now is not the time to talk about that stuff, Emma. Let's just get through the day and worry about it afterwards.'

I stifle my initial instinct to respond and withdraw into myself. But I can't stop the panic that's rising inside me. Fraser's odd behaviour makes me wonder if he's feeling awkward because he's already gone back on his word and revealed my secret to Tommy. If so, then perhaps that was why my husband failed to express his love for me last night.

Shit! Could it mean that it's all about to unravel? That Liam is going to confront me before or after the funeral?

The thought of it fills me with dread, and the urge to tell Fraser to stop the car so that I can jump out is strong. But I convince myself that it would be a mistake because he probably wouldn't do it and then where would I be?

CHAPTER SIXTY-FIVE

Only about a dozen people are at the house in Dulwich when we get there, including a small team of caterers who are preparing the wake.

Liam is waiting to greet me and I'm surprised when he takes me in his arms and thanks me for coming. The gesture makes me go cold, and I'm sure it's for everyone else's benefit and not a genuine show of affection.

'I spoke to Tommy not long ago,' he says. 'He told me he won't be able to speak to you today but to let you know that he is thinking of you.'

I don't need to respond because he quickly moves on to introducing me to several of the other guests. I note they aren't Liam's shady business associates or employees. They're all Ruby's closest friends and nearest neighbours, and I'm surprised that so many have turned up to bid her farewell since she rarely had a good word to say about them. Still, it means I don't feel as intimidated as I initially feared. Only one of them mentions Tommy and that's just to say that it's such a shame that he can't be here for his mother's funeral.

The hearse and two shiny black limos arrive just before two. Ruby's coffin is surrounded by wreaths and, on one side, flowers spell out the word MUM.

I'm waved into the lead limo and sit alongside Liam and an elderly woman named Julia who was Ruby's best friend. Her other friends are seated in the second car because Ruby has no other living relatives.

Fraser and a couple of men who look like bodyguards follow in the Range Rover.

It takes only about fifteen minutes to get to the cemetery and the conversation in our car is limited to how nice the weather is and what a lovely person Ruby was.

I don't utter a word because I'm finding it hard enough to breathe. My throat is dry and constricted and all I can think about is what is going to happen when the funeral is over and the Driscoll brothers switch their attention back to me.

I already know that it's going to be a graveside service because it was discussed several times during Sunday lunches at Ruby's house. And the coffin will be placed on top of the one containing her husband in a double-depth family grave.

About twenty mourners are already there waiting for us to arrive. Their faces are lined with emotion and I don't recognise any of them. They fall silent as the coffin is carried between the weathered headstones towards the plot.

The funeral director reads the eulogy, but I don't listen to the words because just as it starts, I suddenly catch Liam staring at me with what I perceive to be a look of utter loathing. It makes me shudder and I'm reminded of what he said about me being partly responsible for his mother's heart attack because of the stress I caused her.

He turns away quickly when he sees me watching him, but after that I'm even more uncomfortable and find it impossible to concentrate.

Fortunately, it's a short service and, before I know it, I'm back in the limo and returning to the house. Liam is acting friendly towards me again, but I can't forget the way he looked at me across his mother's grave. It was as though he had dropped his guard, allowing his true feelings to show.

I just sit there breathing in shallow gulps while trying not to let the fear that's building up inside show on my face.

The wake turns out to be a subdued affair, perhaps unsurprisingly. There's plenty of food and drink, but I steer clear of the booze and stick to Diet Coke. I move around as much as I can in a bid to avoid talking to people and I keep checking my watch.

After about ninety minutes, I approach Liam and tell him that I intend to go home. But he doesn't want me to leave just yet and urges me to stay for a bit longer.

'People are already drifting away, Emma,' he says. 'I expect everyone will be gone within the hour and then Jack can take you home so you won't have to call a taxi.'

I agree to hang on, but I quickly come to regret it because for some reason I suddenly come over dizzy and my eyes start to droop. It feels like I'm drunk, but I know I'm not, so I wonder if it could be something I've eaten here.

I start making my way towards the toilets, but before I get there, Fraser appears and takes hold of my arm.

'You look like you need to sit down, Emma,' he says. 'Let me look after you.'

He steers me away from the toilets and along a corridor towards the downstairs spare bedroom. By the time we get there, I'm struggling to stay on my feet and if it wasn't for Fraser propping me up, I'd fall to the floor.

I'm aware of entering the room and I can hear Fraser telling me to lie down on the bed. But then my body seems to almost fold in on itself and I feel myself falling into the deep, dark pit of unconsciousness.

CHAPTER SIXTY-SIX

In my dream, I'm cradling a baby. It's a girl, but I don't know what her name is. I do know she's only a few weeks old at most and ever so pretty, with china doll features. Her eyes are blue and her lips are pink, and just looking at her gives me a warm glow inside.

When she starts to cry for what seems like no particular reason, I stand up and walk around the room while rocking her in my arms. After a while, she stops and goes back to sleep, and I feel immensely pleased with myself.

When the dream ends, I become aware of myself lying in the pitch black, but the pain in my head tells me that I'm awake. And yet I don't know where I am.

As I try to move, I discover that I'm crouched in a ball in a cold, confined space. The vibrating floor beneath me and the growl of an engine register. It's a car. I'm trapped in the boot of a car.

A gut-churning wave of terror overwhelms me and I

instinctively start to cry out and bang my clenched fists against the boot lid.

But it doesn't achieve anything. The car keeps moving and nobody responds.

I gulp in air, trying to fill my lungs, as I attempt to understand what's going on.

Questions scream inside my head. *How did I get here? Where am I going? Who is doing this to me?*

Then a memory swims to the surface and it chills my blood. And in that moment, I know for certain that I won't survive the night.

I recall the last thing that happened to me before I passed out. I was feeling dizzy and disoriented at Ruby's wake. Jack Fraser took my arm and led me into the spare bedroom, told me to lie on the bed.

But why did I suddenly feel like I was drunk when I wasn't? The obvious answer now is that I was drugged. And I have to assume that it was done to stop me leaving the house.

Liam and Fraser. They must have done it to me. It would explain their odd behaviour. The fact that Liam had changed his tune and told me I should attend the funeral. It wasn't because he wanted me there. It was to lure me into a trap.

But did he have Tommy's blessing? Did my husband tell them to kidnap me? I can't think of any other explanation for why I'm trapped in the boot of a car.

I shout louder and continue to punch at the boot. Then I slam my shoe against one of the light fittings, but it doesn't break.

I stop shouting then because I'm not even sure I can be heard. Tears of fear and frustration crawl down my cheeks and my breath becomes a series of violent gasps.

I lay still for what turns out to be about twenty more minutes and during that time I cradle my midriff and pray for my baby.

I feel the car stop and start and hear the sounds made by other vehicles sharing the roads. Finally, it comes to a juddering halt and the engine is switched off. I hear a door open and shut and then another.

And then I hear voices before the boot lid springs open and I find myself staring up at the faces of the two men who've abducted me.

Liam Driscoll and Jack Fraser.

Without speaking, they haul me unceremoniously out of the boot.

The cold evening air chills my body immediately because I'm not wearing my coat, only my dress and light jacket.

'Where am I?' I yell at them feebly, my voice trembling. 'Why are you doing this to me?'

There's no street lighting around us, but I can still see them clearly because the moon is sitting clear and heavy in a cloudless sky.

'We're doing it because your husband told us to,' Liam says, and I can sense the weight of hostility in his voice. 'And we know that you'll go on to betray the rest of us if we let you.'

Liam seizes the back of my hair with one hand and my right arm with his other.

Fraser then steps in front of me and waves a revolver in my face. I note that it has a silencer attached. 'We're deep in the countryside, Emma,' he says to me. 'So, if you scream nobody will hear you.'

I see then that their car, which is not one that I'm familiar with, is parked on a narrow unsurfaced lane with woods on both sides.

My mouth goes dry and I find I can't swallow, let alone scream.

'Get moving,' Liam says and pushes me roughly towards the trees on one side of the lane.

I try to break free, but he tugs harder at my hair and the pain is excruciating.

'Don't bother trying to get away,' he tells me in a voice dripping with menace. 'This is the end of the road for you. Just a few yards on, we'll come to your final resting place.'

I feel a crushing sensation in my chest as a raw terror rushes through my body. I know now that there's nothing I can do to save myself and my unborn child.

The blood storms through my veins as I stagger forward across long grass and clumps of bracken.

Fraser is walking in front and I curse myself for being so stupid as to trust him. He's Tommy's main man; he was never going to keep my secret.

After about twenty yards, he stops and turns around. It's a cue for Liam to let go of my hair and arms. He shoves me forward and I struggle to keep my balance.

I then see that the three of us are standing in a small clearing surrounded by a range of bushes and trees. At the centre of it is a large hole that looks as though it was dug fairly recently.

The sight of it sends a wave of panic through my head because it's in the shape of a grave.

CHAPTER SIXTY-SEVEN

I shift my gaze away from the grave towards Liam and Fraser, who are standing about eight feet away from me.

Fraser is still holding the gun and his face is intense, jaw locked. Liam seems more relaxed, almost as though he's enjoying himself.

'I didn't want you to leave the wake before the other guests had gone, so I slipped something in your drink to knock you out,' Liam says. 'As soon as we were the only ones left in the house, Jack and me lifted you into the boot and we went for a drive.'

'I don't understand, Liam,' I reply. 'What's this about?'

'Don't pretend you don't know, Emma. This moment has been a long time coming and I only wish my mum could be here to savour it. She knew from the start that Tommy made a mistake marrying you. You never did fit in and it was clear to me and Mum that you never really loved him.'

'But I did. . . once.'

His eyes narrow to slits. 'Then why did you betray him by planting the gun in his car and tipping off the police?'

The air shudders in my throat as I take a breath. I can't believe what I've just heard. This is all about him believing I was the one who framed Tommy. It's got nothing to do with me being pregnant.

'I've spent the last four months trying to convince my brother that it was you who did it, but he wouldn't believe me because I couldn't prove it,' he goes on.

'But I didn't do it,' I insist. 'I've told you that so many times.'

'But you lied to us. And not only about that. We've also had it confirmed that you're now working with the police to try to bring me down. That's why you've stayed in touch with Brannigan.'

I frown. 'No, Liam. It's not true.'

'Yes, it is, and Tommy knows it now, thanks to Jack here. A few days ago, one of his contacts in the Met confirmed it all. Jack confided in Tommy and my brother told me to get rid of you. Which is why you're here.'

My frown deepens and I wonder for a second if I am dreaming, after all, because none of this makes sense.

'What you did was unforgivable, Emma,' Liam continues. 'Tommy is a good husband and he was prepared to take care of you, but you've well and truly fucked him over.'

I let my breath escape in a slow whistle and turn to Fraser.

'Why are you doing this?' I ask him. 'I had nothing to do with planting that gun and I'm not working with the police, you know it.'

He doesn't respond and his face remains impassive.

'Just get it fucking over with, Jack,' Liam tells him. 'I don't want to be here a second longer than I have to.'

I watch in silent, stunned horror as Fraser raises the revolver and points it at me.

Just as I'm about to beg him not to pull the trigger, he does something that is totally unexpected.

He moves his body so he's facing Liam and aims the gun as his boss instead.

CHAPTER SIXTY-EIGHT

Disbelief shapes Liam's features and his eyes come out on stalks.

'What the fuck do to you think you're doing?' he shouts.

'Exactly what your brother instructed me to do,' Fraser replies calmly. 'It's not Emma he wants dead. It's you.'

'Are you out of your fucking mind?'

Fraser gives a small shake of the head. 'Soon after Tommy was arrested, I suspected that you had something to do with it. I knew you were fed up playing second fiddle to Tommy and you wanted a shot at running the business. And it was obvious to me that you weren't trying to get to the bottom of it. Eventually, a close contact in the Met pointed the finger at you and confirmed that you did plant the gun and tip them off. So, I told Tommy. I also let him know that I believed it was only a matter of time before you made Emma disappear.'

'You're a traitorous bastard!' Liam yells at him, rage contorting his features. 'You won't get away with it!'

'I already have, Liam. I told Tommy that the only way to keep his wife safe was to take you out of the picture. And he didn't need much persuading after learning that it was you who'd betrayed him. So together we hatched a plan to get you here by making you think that it was Emma who was going to die.'

Liam shakes his head. 'This is fucking crazy. If you get rid of me, who's going to run the business while he's inside?'

Fraser grins. 'I am. You see, Tommy has always regarded me as more of a brother to him than you. He trusts me and that's why he's put me in charge. The word has already gone out and the lawyers are working on the handover, including the transfer of certain assets. Plus, he knows that, unlike you, I don't hate his wife.'

My heart is pounding so hard that I fear it might burst out of my chest. I don't move. I can't. I'm rooted to the spot and cold sweat is forming under my clothes.

Liam decides that there's only one course of action open to him and he goes for it.

He throws himself forward and tries to reach Fraser before the trigger is pulled. But he doesn't make it, and I watch as the bullet smashes into his forehead.

CHAPTER SIXTY-NINE

Fraser fires two more bullets into Liam's body for good measure. By now, I'm shockproof so I don't even flinch. I just can't believe that it isn't me lying dead on the ground.

'You're safe now, Emma,' Fraser says as he pushes the gun into his coat pocket. 'I'm not going to harm you and I'm sorry it had to be played out like this. But Tommy wanted him buried on this spot and it was the only way to get him here. Pauline is buried close by, and since her body has never been found, he reckons Liam's won't be either.'

I feel a rush of blood to my head. I thought I was shock-proof but I'm not any more.

'Are you serious?' I say.

He nods. 'Pauline didn't just disappear. Tommy killed her because she was unfaithful to him. And then he set up the boyfriend to take the fall.'

'And did Tommy arrange for the guy to be killed in prison?'

Fraser nods. 'Of course. No way was he going to let him go on living.'

It's actually something I suspected when I first learned about Pauline, but it's still too much to take in, so I don't respond, just stare at him, my stomach doing flips.

'You need to know that Tommy won't find out about the baby, Emma, because he's not going to be around for long,' Fraser goes on. 'When I told Liam that I was taking over, I didn't just mean while Tommy's in prison. I'm now the new boss. The Driscoll dynasty is over and you're soon going to be a widow.'

A chill grips my heart. 'You're going to kill him?'

When he responds, his voice is totally devoid of emotion. 'Someone will. It can't be avoided. It's the way it has to be. You see, I'm not prepared to take orders from your husband while he's banged up. Tommy has had his day and it makes sense for me to start over. I helped build the business, after all. Plus, it's the best result for you, Emma. You'll be free to get on with your life and have your baby. You'll be well looked after. I'll see to that. You can keep the flat and your regular income and I'll make sure that more money comes your way.'

I swallow hard. 'But why are you doing this, Jack?'

His features harden and he speaks in a firm voice, with conviction. 'Because I hated the way Tommy treated you and I can understand why you fell out of love with him. And those fucking rules he came up with were mental. He expected too much from you. But he wasn't your only problem. Liam confided in me that he was going to get rid

366

of you at some point down the line. He didn't want to have to be responsible for you for five years.'

'But how do you know you can trust me?' I ask him. 'That I won't go to the police?'

I've already decided that there's no way I'll grass him up. Anyone who is prepared to keep me and my family safe deserves my loyalty.

'You've got no reason to,' he tells me. 'I've done you a favour and when Tommy is gone, he'll no longer make your life a misery. And you're also going to help me put this bloke in the grave and cover him up. So, you'll be in this up to your neck as much as I am.'

He removes Liam's phone and wallet from his pockets and then together we drag his body across the clearing and roll it into the grave. It's an unpleasant experience and I could never have imagined that I would ever bury a dead body. But then I didn't think I'd ever kill anyone either.

Fraser then piles earth and bracken on top of him using a shovel that had been lying on the ground behind a tree.

'Your coat is on the back seat of the car, along with your handbag,' he says. 'I want you to lie down and cover your face for the first few miles. That way, you'll never know where this place is.'

That makes sense and I have no problem with it. I hardly want to come back here again and the less I know, the better.

On the way back into London, Fraser tells me to stick to the story that he took me home after the wake and Liam stayed at his mother's house. That was the last we saw of him.

'And just so you know, when we set out earlier, the route we took avoided traffic cameras in the immediate area,' he says. 'We'll do the same now.'

'When do you think that the police will start looking for him?' I ask.

'I'm not even sure they will. After Tommy turns up dead, they'll assume they were both knocked off as part of a gang war.'

Fraser takes us back to Ruby's house where he tells me to get into the Range Rover. He then gets in behind the wheel and says, 'I'll be coming back here tomorrow to make sure that everything is in order and that will be when I discover that Liam is missing and raise the alarm.'

As we drive away I look back at Ruby's house, the Driscoll seat, and feel an overwhelming sense of relief that it's the last time I will ever have to lay eyes on it.

When Fraser drops me off at the flat, he repeats what he said earlier – that I can now get on with my life. This is not how I imagined things turning out but I can't help but feel grateful to Fraser. I even give him a hug.

'I meant everything I told you, Emma,' he says. 'You'll be looked after. We won't be seeing much of each other from now on, but if you need anything or you're worried about something, then call me.'

'I will. But I still don't understand why you're helping me.'

He shrugs. 'It's because I know what Tommy has put you through, Emma. I was adopted at the age of seven by a couple who, to begin with, appeared happy and content. But then my adoptive father changed over the years and became cruel and abusive towards his wife. He made her and my life a misery. Just before my eighteenth birthday, he beat her up so badly that she needed to go to hospital. A week later, I pounced on him while he was walking home from work and slit his throat. No one ever found out who killed him – not even my mum.'

When I close the front door behind me, I don't know whether to laugh or cry. I've been given my life back, but the shock to my system has been seismic. I was kidnapped, witnessed the murder of my brother-in-law and then told that my husband is going to be killed. It's a lot to absorb and react to.

But I'm determined to try to focus on the positive. Provided Fraser is true to his word, I can look forward to the future again. I can give birth to my baby and I won't be chained to my controlling husband while he serves his time in prison.

It does mean that I will have to live with the guilt of allowing Tommy to be murdered. But I don't think that will be difficult now that I know for certain he took the life of his first wife.

EPILOGUE

Six months later

This time it isn't a dream. I'm cradling my newborn baby in my arms as I wait for my mother and sister to come to meet her in the hospital for the first time.

I couldn't be happier. She's such a gorgeous little mite and I'm so pleased that I wasn't forced to terminate the pregnancy.

I've named her Laura and it's a relief that when I look at her face, all I see are parts of me and there's nothing to remind me of her dead father.

It's been a strange six months. Two days after Ruby's funeral, Tommy was stabbed to death in his cell and to this day no one has been charged with his murder. The news of his death was welcomed by Amanda and Jacob as it means they no longer have to fear for their family.

Jack Fraser has kept his promise and taken care of me.

He paid for and organised Tommy's funeral and transferred a large amount of money into my bank. By all accounts, he's also doing a cracking job running the business.

Furthermore, I'm no longer a person of interest in respect of the investigation into the death of Ruben Swift. The case is still open, but the word is that the police believe he was killed by someone he owed money to.

As for Liam Driscoll, well, nobody seems to care that he's still missing. The police aren't looking for him and they suspect he was murdered and that his body was buried somewhere.

So, all in all, things have worked out pretty well for me after so much pain and suffering. I've been extremely lucky. And so has my darling daughter.

THE END

ACKNOWLEDGEMENTS

I'd like to say a special thank you to Molly Walker-Sharp, my editor at Avon, HarperCollins. We collaborated closely on this book and her help and advice were invaluable. She's an absolute star. My thanks also to Radhika Sonagra and Jade Craddock who both did so much to help us improve on the first draft. The rest of the team at Avon deserve a mention too – they're such a great bunch of true professionals. I'd also like to mention my agent Leslie Gardner at Artellus. She continues to provide guidance and encouragement, and I want her to know that I'm extremely grateful.